# PRIZE SURPRISE SWEEPSTAKES!

his month's prize:

# FABULOUS
# SHARP VIEWCAM!

Th... as a special surprise, we're giving away a Sharp ViewCam**, the big-screen camcorder that has revolutionized home videos!

This is the camcorder everyone's talking about! Sharp's new ViewCam has a big 3" full-color viewing screen with 180° swivel action that lets you control everything you record—and watch it at the same time! Features include a remote control (so you can get into the picture yourself), 8 power zoom, full-range auto focus, battery pack, recharger and more!

The next page contains two Entry Coupons (as does every book you received this shipment). Complete and return *all* the entry coupons; **the more times you enter, the better your chances of winning!**

Then keep your fingers crossed, because you'll find out by November 15, 1995 if you're the winner!

Remember: The more times you enter, the better your chances of winning!*

*NO PURCHASE OR OBLIGATION TO CONTINUE BEING A SUBSCRIBER NECESSARY TO ENTER. SEE THE BACK PAGE FOR ALTERNATE MEANS OF ENTRY, AND RULES.

**THE PROPRIETORS OF THE TRADEMARK ARE NOT ASSOCIATED WITH THIS PROMOTION.

PVC KAL

**PRIZE SURPRISE**
SWEEPSTAKES

## OFFICIAL ENTRY COUPON

This entry must be received by: OCTOBER 30, 1995
This month's winner will be notified by: NOVEMBER 15, 1995

**YES,** I want to win the Sharp ViewCam! Please enter me in the drawing and let me know if I've won!

Name_____

Address _____ Apt. _____

| City | State/Prov. | Zip/Postal Code |

Account #_____

Return entry with invoice in reply envelope.

© 1995 HARLEQUIN ENTERPRISES LTD.                    CVC KAL

## Leslie pressed her hand against Simon's chest, as if to push away

"Don't," he whispered. "Stay. I won't let anyone hurt you."

She gave a shaky laugh. "What about you? Will you hurt me, Simon?"

"No promises. But I haven't been in the house except by invitation."

Abruptly she moved away. To his surprise, her eyes flashed angrily as she paced the room. "I'm not going to let anyone drive me out. Obviously my tormentor knows how to avoid the police, so I'm going to have to take my own precautions."

"Move out. You can stay with me."

"I need to be here," she said stubbornly.

"Leslie, come here," Simon said softly.

Her eyes met his, saw the gentleness there. Unable to help herself, she stepped forward into his arms.

Dear Reader,

What is it about mysterious men that always makes our pulses race? Whether it's the feeling of risk or the excitement of the unknown, dangerous men have always been a part of our fantasies, and now they're a part of Harlequin Intrigue. Throughout 1995, we'll kick off each month with a DANGEROUS MAN. This month, meet Simon Korvallis in *Killing Her Softly* by Tina Vasilos.

Tina Vasilos has written romantic suspense for many years. She has traveled widely around the world, and she uses the trips to research her novels. Tina and her husband live in Clearbrook, British Columbia.

With our DANGEROUS MEN promotion, Harlequin Intrigue promises to keep you on the edge of your seat...and the edge of desire.

Sincerely,

Debra Matteucci
Senior Editor and Editorial Coodinator
Harlequin Books
300 East 42nd Street, Sixth Floor
New York, New York 10017

# Killing Her Softly

## Tina Vasilos

# Harlequin Books

TORONTO • NEW YORK • LONDON
AMSTERDAM • PARIS • SYDNEY • HAMBURG
STOCKHOLM • ATHENS • TOKYO • MILAN
MADRID • WARSAW • BUDAPEST • AUCKLAND

ISBN 0-373-22341-2

KILLING HER SOFTLY

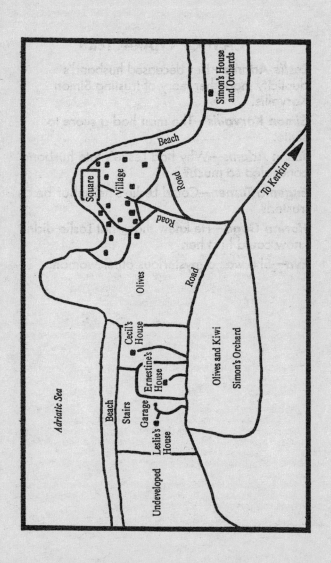

# CAST OF CHARACTERS

**Leslie Adams**—Her deceased husband's duplicity made her leery of trusting Simon Korvallis.

**Simon Korvallis**—The man had a score to settle.

**Jason Adams**—Why had Leslie's late husband concealed so much?

**Eugenia Turner**—Could Leslie's neighbor be trusted?

**Harlan Gage**—He knew that what Leslie didn't know could hurt her.

**Eva**—She was a mysterious other woman.

# Chapter One

"I suppose you've come to finish the job, have you?"

The man's voice jerked Leslie out of her comfortable somnolence. She lifted her head, squinting against the glare of the setting sun. "Excuse me?"

"Character assassination."

Leslie blinked at the angry man standing before her. The handsome, angry man, she noted irrelevantly. She straightened in her chair, suddenly aware that the chatter of the Greek voices around her had stilled, as if the patrons of the small seaside taverna were holding their breath. "I beg your pardon?" she said distinctly. "I've never seen you before in my life."

"Your husband has, Mrs. Adams."

"Has he?" she said, suppressing the twinge of guilt she felt. Any strong feelings between her and Jason had died years ago; she found it difficult to grieve for the loss of him. Yet wasn't she here on Corfu because of unfinished business? Jason's business.

She had a feeling that that business had just surfaced in the form of the man glaring down at her. "Well, Jason's dead, isn't he?" she added.

"Is he?"

An odd chill ran through her. She opened her mouth to speak, then snapped it closed again as the deep voice continued, the words clipped and intense, faintly British-accented.

"They never found a body, did they? Only the sailboard, washed up on the beach. Knowing what a devious man Jason was, I wouldn't put it past him to fake his own death."

Leslie felt her face turn pale. Involuntarily, she shivered. "The police closed the case," she said in what she hoped was a dismissive tone. "Accidental drowning. They said only fools and tourists sailboard in April, especially with the cold spring this year."

*This is not a tropical island.* She could still hear the police captain's pedantic voice rumbling in her ears. The first thing she'd done after landing at Corfu airport yesterday was go to the police station. The report was brief, incomprehensible to her, but the captain had translated the dry facts into passable English.

Death by misadventure. A fall into the cold spring sea, hypothermia in spite of the wet suit witnesses said Jason had been wearing. Perhaps even a heart attack—Jason hadn't been a young man. As for the body, it would probably never be recovered. The strong undertow could have washed it across to Italy or up the coast of the troubled country once known as Yugoslavia. The Adriatic was a treacherous sea.

The captain had offered his condolences, but as far as the police were concerned it was over, another unfortunate case of a man underestimating a ruthless sea.

"I hear you're living in the old Adams house," the stranger said, sitting down without asking her permission.

Curious about his outrageous statements, she said nothing. Not that he would have listened if she issued a protest; the stubborn set of his jaw told her he did what he pleased.

"News travels fast," Leslie said dryly, picking up her wineglass and sipping from it. Her fingers shook only a little.

He gestured toward the people around them, who'd returned to their meals. "In a place this size it does. A beautiful stranger in town, who just happens to have been married to Jason Adams, once a local celebrity. Why did you come, Mrs. Adams? There's nothing for you here."

"There's the house," she reminded him, glancing up to thank the waiter as he set plates of lamb chops, french fries, and salad in front of her.

"Good evening, Simon," the waiter said to the man sitting across from her. "Can I get you anything?"

"A coffee, please. Strong, with sugar." He tilted back his chair and crossed his ankle over the opposite knee.

"Make yourself at home," Leslie muttered, picking up her knife and fork. She cut a piece of meat and ate it, savoring the rich flavor.

The coffee came and he sipped it thoughtfully, his dark eyes narrowed as he studied her. Defiantly she stared back at him. His face was lean and tanned, compelling rather than conventionally handsome. Unruly black hair in need of a trim gleamed in the dim light. His expression was cool, almost austere in its remoteness.

Leslie felt an odd flutter in her midsection, and sweat broke out on her palms. Desperately hoping the warmth creeping under her skin didn't reach her face, she let her gaze slide down his body. His chest was broad, and his waist and hips were narrow. It was the cleanly muscled body of a man accustomed to work. Warmth stirred within her, latent desire arousing and stretching.

Drawing a deep, fortifying breath, she checked her wandering thoughts, reminding herself that she was a thirty-one-year-old woman who had long outgrown adolescent hormones, and was glad of it. "How long did you know Jason?" she asked.

"Since I was a child. He and my father had business dealings once."

Leslie nodded, understanding at last. "And it ended badly."

He stared at her, dropping the raised chair legs to the floor with a thump. "Why do you say that?"

"Your attitude. You're bitter about something. Jason went to Canada at least twelve years ago. Since you mention your father, I presume there was trouble between them." She leaned forward earnestly. "I assure you it had nothing to do with me."

"Didn't it? Then why have you come here? And, more to the point, how long are you planning to stay?"

She frowned, her temper beginning to simmer. "What possible business is that of yours? What did that waiter call you—Simon?"

"Simon Korvallis," he said, extending his hand.

She shook his hand, feeling the heat of his skin and the callused roughness of his palm. His grip was firm without crushing her fingers. "You are—?" he asked.

"You know who I am," she said, snatching back her hand.

"I mean, your first name."

"It's Leslie. Jason never mentioned you."

"He never mentioned you, either," he said. Obviously he'd seen Jason in the past year, or at some time during their marriage. Leslie didn't even feel surprised that Jason might have come back here without telling her. When had he ever kept her informed about his activities?

"How long did you know Jason?" Korvallis asked.

"Almost twelve years. We were married for most of that time. Until we divorced last year."

"You were divorced?" His brows lifted. "And he left you the house?"

Leslie paused, then decided that the ambiguity surrounding her position in the house was none of his business. "His lawyer said I could use it." For how long, she didn't know, nor did she have any idea of the ultimate disposition of the house, since the estate hadn't been settled.

"Twelve years," Korvallis said softly. "You must have been awfully young when you married him."

"I was," she said wistfully. She'd married him with youthful impulsiveness and optimism, and lived to regret it. "I was nineteen when we met. Jason was forty-one at the time."

He didn't even blink. "Any children?"

"No."

"So it's just you to claim the house."

A odd note in his voice flicked at her nerves. "I didn't even know about the house until a month ago. I didn't know Jason grew up on Corfu."

This time his brows lifted, one higher than the other, giving him a sardonic look. "Didn't you and your husband communicate, Mrs. Adam?"

"Not often," she admitted flatly. "I told you we divorced."

"But of course you must have known that your husband was married before, didn't you?"

She gaped at him, the food she'd eaten turning to lead in her stomach. "He was what?"

"Married. Forgive me, I see you didn't know." He gestured with one hand. "But don't worry, he wasn't a bigamist. His first wife died a long time ago."

"Did they live here?" Her face felt tight, her mouth dry. She could feel a nerve jumping in her jaw and slowly unclenched her teeth.

"Some of the time, yes. Although in the last years before she died, she lived in Athens and in England. I guess she'd had enough of him by then. Jason was a strange man."

She couldn't argue with that statement; she'd have added *secretive* and *manipulative*.

"He has no relatives, so I guess if anybody's entitled to the house, you are. What are you going to do with it?"

She knitted together her frayed emotions. This had gone on long enough. "Why do you want to know, Mr. Korvallis?" she said sharply.

He looked unfazed, calmly drinking the last of his coffee and setting down the thimble-size cup. "A number of reasons, Mrs. Adams," he said at last. "None of which you would like."

"Wouldn't I? Then don't bother to tell me." She lifted her hand to summon the waiter. She'd eaten only half the food, but her churning stomach warned her of disastrous consequences if she forced more of it down. Standing, she took the bill from the waiter's hand.

Korvallis also stood up. He reached across and grasped Leslie's elbow. "Mrs. Adams, there are people in this village who would like to see an end to the legacy of Jason Adams. What happened may be old news by Canadian standards, but Greeks have long memories. And we don't forgive easily. In fact, I could contest that will on moral grounds."

"There—" *Wasn't a will,* she almost blurted but stopped herself just in time.

"Not that I want that mausoleum of a house." He frowned speculatively. "On the other hand, if you want to sell it, I might be willing to help you find a buyer."

"Who are you?" she gasped, struggling to free her arm. To her relief, he let go at once. "What do you want?"

"I'm not sure I want anything," he said, his expression bleak. "Except, perhaps, justice."

SIMON RESEATED HIMSELF and watched as Leslie paid the bill and walked away. Her hips swayed gently beneath the denim skirt she wore. She crossed the circle of light cast by a street lamp. His gaze moved up to her hair, a glossy swath that reached to the middle of her back. Thick and wavy, so blond that it was almost white, it shimmered like moonbeams on water.

Her hair was a beacon that drew eyes toward her, the last visible part of her as she stepped beyond the light. Either she didn't notice the attention or she ignored it as she disappeared into the shadows farther up the path.

Under other circumstances, and if they were both different people, he might have been attracted to her. She was a good-looking woman. Her features were a little too strong for classic beauty, but her skin had the glow of good health. The gray eyes, large and shaded by surprisingly dark lashes, shone with character and maturity. The dark ring around the iris gave them a silver luminance that made them seem too transparent to contain secrets. Yet he sensed secrets. And an old, deeply rooted pain.

She wasn't mourning her husband's death, that he knew for sure, feeling a perverse satisfaction. Hard on the heels of this thought came the realization that, against his better judgment, he *was* attracted to her.

Not wise at all.

He hadn't reached the age of thirty-six without having had his share of female companionship. In fact, there had been one woman with whom he'd been fairly serious for about a year, until she decided he was too involved in his career to make a good husband. His life was different now. Still, Leslie Adams had awakened something in him he'd thought had died long ago.

Maybe it was a romantic notion, that for every man there was a special woman, but deep down inside him he had to admit he half believed that. He'd had his parents as an example of two people who were truly one.

Was Leslie the one for him?

He shook his head, gazing moodily into his coffee cup. She couldn't be, not after having been Jason's wife. Jason, who'd earned his contempt. Jason, who'd almost ruined his reputation.

Was it over? Or was Jason still alive, waiting and watching?

Maybe he should have gone back to London after the Melanie fiasco, to avoid the gossip. But while his years of real estate development in England had brought him financial security, they hadn't brought him contentment. The orchards right here in Platania had done that, and the small business he'd built up.

He'd survived, and the talk had died down. He could only pray that Leslie's presence didn't revive it.

LESLIE'S FOOTSTEPS slowed as she neared the top of the hill on which the house stood. Her breath rasped in her throat. Months of too much work and too little exercise were catching up to her. She couldn't even make it up the path without stopping to rest, and in the afternoon she'd seen gnarled old ladies tramp up it without even breathing hard. There were a lot of old people in the village; the constant walking up and down the hills must have been the reason for their longevity.

Those people—why did they stare at her? She'd noticed it from the moment she stepped off the bus at noon. Was it only curiosity? She didn't think so. The stares were too intense, making her self-conscious and uneasy.

Of course, she might be imagining half of it, coming to a small village where she felt unsure of herself, not knowing the language or the customs.

She sat down on a stone wall next to the path, her shoulders hunched. Jason had lied to her, if what that man, Simon Korvallis, said was true. It shouldn't have come as much of a surprise, but deep inside her it still hurt.

She knew she shouldn't feel this mixture of anger and disillusionment, not when she hadn't been entirely honest with Jason herself. She'd been working in a doughnut shop and putting herself through college when she met him. After their first conversation, Jason had made a point of coming in more and more frequently. When he asked her out to dinner, she'd accepted. She'd enjoyed herself; the age difference hadn't seemed important.

A month later, he'd asked her to marry him. She hadn't been sure what she felt was love, but he'd been charming and persuasive and she'd sensed he was lonely. Having grown up in a succession of dreary foster homes, kept sane only by her keen intelligence and determined spirit, she knew what loneliness was. She'd consented to marry him.

At first their marriage had been a success. In fact, they had gotten along better than most couples she knew. And they'd traveled across Canada that first summer, seeing the country and getting to know each other.

At least Leslie had thought they were. It had only been later that she became aware of the gaps in Jason's life, the huge areas she knew nothing about.

A previous marriage? She'd never questioned him, and Jason had never mentioned any family. He'd lied, at least by omission. He'd had a wife; she wondered what other important facts he'd kept from her.

Perhaps he had children, children who could be near her age. No, Korvallis said Jason had no family left. Which might explain the circumstances that had brought her to Corfu.

The letter she'd received a month ago from a law firm in Athens had come as a complete surprise. A partner in the firm, Mr. Papadopoulos, had expressed his condolences on her loss and informed her that Jason had asked that she be notified in the event of his death. Since there was no one else, her participation might be required to settle his estate. They would contact her again.

It was all very odd—practically a summons from the grave.

It hadn't taken her long to make up her mind what to do. Summers were traditionally slow in the investment business. She'd decided to take a long-overdue holiday, her first in the five years she'd worked as a loan officer for an investment bank. She would attend to Jason's business in person. If it took longer, she would ask for an extension of her holiday time, an unpaid leave of absence if necessary.

Despite the distance that had grown between her and Jason in recent years, there was the sweet memory of the early years when they had been happy together; she figured she owed it to Jason to see to his affairs.

Leslie got up from the low wall, turning abruptly as a disembodied voice floated up from the shrubbery next to the path. "Lovely evening, isn't it? Have you seen a small brown dog?"

Before she could summon words to her suddenly dry mouth, a man stepped out into the open. "I'm sorry," he said with a courtly bow. "I didn't mean to startle you. My dog seems to have run off."

He came forward, a small, slight man with a scholarly face topped by a thatch of white hair. He pulled a small plastic bag of dog biscuits from the pocket of a thread-bare Harris tweed jacket, tossing a handful on the path and calling, "Come, Scruffy. Where are you hiding?"

Glancing up the slope, he frowned worriedly. "I hope that woman hasn't got him. No telling what she would do."

"What woman?" Leslie asked, confused.

"That woman next door to you. She's always harassing my poor Scruffy. No, I didn't name him. His previous owners, who horribly mistreated him, did. And that dreadful bird of hers is always terrorizing him with its screams."

Leslie hadn't heard any screams, nor had she met her neighbor, although she'd glimpsed the house through an overgrown hedge.

Stuffing the bag back into his pocket, he extended his hand. "Forgive my bad manners. I'm Cecil Weatherby. And you are—?"

"Leslie Adams." She hastily gathered her wits and shook his hand.

He frowned. "You were Jason's wife. How interesting." He examined her face, his deep-set eyes intent, his expression unreadable. Just when she was feeling uncomfortable enough to step back, he nodded. "If I were a portrait painter, I'd paint you. In a Victorian dress." His fingers drew patterns in the air. "With a cameo at the throat and your hair swept up. Such a virginal neck."

Leslie wavered between amusement and indignation. Virginal? She'd been married for ten years.

"My condolences on your husband's death," he said. His tone was curiously flat and emotionless, at odds with the words, leaving her more puzzled than before.

"Thank you," she replied, not knowing what else to say. The orange light from the street lamp cast his face in shadow, but she guessed that the man was in his seventies. Older than Jason, then.

"Did you know Jason?" she asked.

"Yes." He did not elaborate, adding after a brief pause, "I'm sure we'll see each other again. Perhaps you could come for dinner. You might be interested in seeing my paintings."

At her startled look, he smiled faintly. "Yes, my dear, I am an artist. I'm surprised Jason never mentioned me, since he sometimes helped me market my work."

He lifted his hand in farewell. "Have a good evening." Like a wraith, he seemed to dematerialize as the dense shrubs closed around him. She heard his voice drifting on the night air. "Here, Scruffy. Where are you? Come and get your treat."

A LOW-WATTAGE BULB over the front door welcomed her with a pale yellow light that barely made a dent in the darkness. She stopped in her tracks, the heady fragrance of jasmine closing around her.

Who had turned the light on? She was sure it hadn't been on earlier. She shrugged. Perhaps it was fitted with an electric eye that turned it on automatically at dusk.

Her initial reaction to the house this afternoon had been disappointment. In her mind, she'd imagined a cube-shaped whitewashed Greek island house.

Reality was a rectangular two-story building with dark green shutters and ugly ocher walls. The house had a closed, deserted look about it, as if it held secrets. Only the tangled subtropical garden in which it sat softened the harsh lines.

Suppressing her uneasiness, she'd opened the front door with the key she'd picked up in Corfu town. And instantly forgot the exterior shortcomings.

The spacious rooms had shimmered with noon light, ornate ceilings hinting of gentility long past. Sunbeams caught dust motes and turned them into sparkling fairy dust. She'd been enchanted.

Now she wasn't so sure. It was too dark, too quiet, as if the night were holding its breath. The scent of jasmine was strong and cloying and carried an undertone of sweet, rotting vegetation. A funeral smell.

She paused before opening the door. Included with the letter from the law firm had been a note from Jason, in a separate envelope. It had been short and not very enlightening.

If you're reading this, I'm no longer alive. I wasn't much of a husband to you, and that is my only regret. My attorney will be in touch when the estate is settled

That was all. No explanation. And only the most perfunctory apology for his deceptions and omissions.

The message had accomplished one thing—it had brought her to Platania. Two days ago, after landing in

Athens, she'd gone to the law office. That she was not expected had become immediately evident.

"Jason's affairs are very complicated," she'd been told. "His will is incomplete. Our Mr. Papadopoulos is looking after it. Meanwhile, you may as well go to Platania. There's no problem with you staying at the house, since you seem to have power of attorney over all of this."

The lawyer's look implied that he meant "this mess" but was too polite to say so. Leslie had thanked him, baffled by the whole situation. The answers must be in Platania, she had decided late that night. And the next morning she'd caught a plane to Corfu.

Now, instead of answers, she had even more questions.

A rustle in the shrubbery brought her head snapping around. The old man again? Or someone else? Key ring in hand, she tensed, acutely conscious of her isolation.

She gave a shaky laugh as an enormous cat strolled across the flagstones. He sat down, gazing at her with clear amber eyes that seemed to hold both curiosity and wisdom. Leslie smiled. "Well, hello. Do you live here?"

The cat regarded her silently, then licked a paw and began to wash his face. He was a far cry from the lanky stray cats she'd seen slinking around the village square earlier. His coat was thick and sleek, a dark steel gray, with the dense texture of velour. Dropping his paw, he pricked his ears. As dignified as a grand duke, he rose, turned and melted into the shadows.

Leslie blinked, half expecting to see some echo of his presence, like the smile of the Cheshire cat. Laughing ruefully, she shook herself. She had no time for fancies.

Putting the key in the lock she turned it, again surprised to note its well-oiled condition. All in all, the house was in good shape. But then, Jason must have lived here on occasion, even during their marriage, which would explain some of his long absences. Business trips, he'd called them.

The furnishings, draped in dustcovers, were ghostly white shapes in the gloom. On the wall opposite the door, Leslie could see the amber porch light dimly reflected in a baroque mirror.

She groped along the wall for the light switch, wishing she'd noted its location earlier, in daylight. Moving forward a step, to the left of the open door, she felt the raised edge of the brass switch plate.

A blue flash blinded her, and pain sizzled up her arm. "Ouch!" She jerked back her hand, the keys dropping from her nerveless fingers.

Muttering under her breath, she rubbed her tingling arm. She hadn't had a shock like that in years. Too strong to be static electricity. She would have to have an electrician out in the morning. She'd heard that the voltage here was twice that in Canada—nothing to fool around with.

A soft meow told her the cat was back. She bent to pick up her keys, brushing against the velvet fur. In the darkness outside, a bird or animal shrieked, making gooseflesh break out on her skin.

The scream was followed by a crash. The foyer mirror opposite the door shattered into jagged pieces.

# Chapter Two

"It's a bullet, Mrs. Adams."

Leslie stared at the distorted gray pellet in the policeman's hand. Going to the open door, she hugged her arms around her waist, suddenly chilled, despite the hot sunlight pouring into the hall.

Someone had shot at her. No doubt she'd made a perfect target, spotlighted by the outside light. Bending to pick up her keys had probably saved her life.

"Mrs. Adams?"

She turned to face the policeman. He had an earnest, youthful face. Did they hire cops right out of high school here? He hardly looked old enough to shave, but at least he spoke English.

"Mrs. Adams," he said patiently, now that he had her attention. "You say this happened last night, sometime after ten o'clock? Why didn't you call us then?"

"I thought the mirror had fallen and broken. I couldn't turn on the light, because the switch gave me a shock. I figured I'd clean up the glass this morning, but when I came down, I saw the hole in the wall and the frame still intact."

Frowning, he strode over to the light switch. He pushed it with the eraser end of the pencil he held. The ornate chandelier over their heads burst into prisms of light. Sticking the pencil in his pocket, he flipped the switch off. "Seems to be okay. Maybe it was a short circuit."

"Probably," Leslie agreed. She'd already decided to get an electrician to check the wiring. Last night she'd used a flashlight to get ready for bed, not wanting to risk the lights. She hadn't wanted to burn the place down on her first day, especially when she wasn't sure what was going to be done with it.

The policeman gazed around the spacious hall, and up the stairs that led to the upper floor. In spite of his youth and apparent nonchalance, she had a feeling he missed nothing. She sat down on the cool marble stair tread. The gray cat poked his head around the corner and came in, sniffing at her hand before climbing into her lap. He settled down to purr, his body vibrating under her palm.

"Nice cat," the policeman said. "Where did you find him?"

"He found me," Leslie said. "Last night."

The policeman pulled out a notebook and retrieved his pencil from his pocket. "Did you see anyone last night?"

"I met one of my neighbors on the path. An old man named Cecil Weatherby. He was looking for his dog, Constable—? I'm sorry, I didn't catch your name."

"Just call me Jimmy." He grinned. "You're from Canada, aren't you? I grew up there. Came here when I was eighteen, when my parents moved back. I didn't like it at first, but I do now."

That accounted for his English, his familiar accent. "Cecil's all right," Jim continued. "He's British, but he'd visited Platania for years during holidays, had his house built. When he retired, he decided to stay. You don't have to worry about him. He'll invite you to dinner. He always does that with newcomers."

Jimmy had already written down her account of what
had happened and noted her passport number. Pulling the
little bag in which he'd placed the bullet out of his pocket,
he bounced it in his palm. "We'll check this out. It's a
small bullet. Could be from a pellet gun. It was probably
just kids shooting at birds."

"In the dark?" Leslie asked.

Jimmy shrugged. "With kids, you never know. And it
hadn't been dark that long. Your garden is just the sort of
place they'd hang out."

"Have you had a problem with kids coming around
here? Perhaps vandalism?"

"Actually, no," Jimmy admitted. "And, as you probably know, the house is looked after. A property management company in Corfu town—we call it Kérkira—
sends somebody down to check on it at least once a week.

"I know. I got the key from them. Didn't Jason live
here?"

"Now and then he'd come. They took care of it when
he was away. Last time he was here, he stayed four or five
months, until he died. He didn't write to you?"

Leslie shook her head. "No, but we weren't enemies."

The young man's face grew painfully red, and he shuf-
fled his feet. "I'm glad to hear that. People say—"

Leslie frowned when he broke off. "What do people
say?"

Clearly ill at ease, Jimmy took a deep breath. "Since no
body was found, there's been gossip that maybe he isn't
dead. His business wasn't going well at the end—" He
shrugged. "You know how people talk."

"When we were married, his business was successful,"
Leslie said. As far as she knew. "We lived in a nice house,
which he had before I met him. He seemed to have plenty
of money."

"Maybe things went downhill later. That's what I'm getting at. If he's alive, maybe he doesn't want you here. Maybe he's angry because of the divorce."

Leslie sighed. "I don't think so."

Jimmy looked relieved. "That's it, then. The gossip's probably all wrong, anyway. And I'm sure this was an accident. Let me know if you have any more problems."

"I will," she promised, getting up and standing in the doorway as he turned his Land Rover and drove off.

Nerves jumping under her skin, she sank back down on the stairs. She hugged the gray cat, taking comfort from the soft warmth of the furry creature.

In the past twelve hours, two people had voiced the theory that Jason might still be alive. She couldn't deny that the thought had crossed her own mind, in spite of the police report and the brief note from Jason included with the lawyer's letter.

Why had word of his death taken so long to reach her, coming more than a month after the fact? She'd asked the lawyer. They hadn't known of her existence until they located Jason's personal papers, which had been misfiled in the office.

The whole thing gave her an unsettled feeling, as if Jason were reaching from the grave to put her under some obligation to him. After all this time.

Their divorce had been amicable, insomuch as such transactions could be. She would have sworn that Jason was as relieved as she at the dissolution of their marriage, a marriage that had limped along during its last years, with Jason away half the time.

And now she found herself in his house.

A shadow slanted into the hall, and she jumped to her feet. It was stupid not to have closed the door. Then she laughed ruefully. This is a small village in Greece, not downtown Toronto. Still, nobody had killed her mirror there.

"Hello? Anyone home?" The deep voice washed over her, and she closed her eyes. This was all she needed, that annoying man from last night.

To her chagrin, the cat squirmed out of her arms and leaped to the floor, stropping himself on the visitor's ankles in effusive welcome.

Simon bent and stroked the thick fur. "Hi, cat. You remember me, do you?"

"You know this cat?" Leslie asked. "What's his name?"

"No name. Just 'cat.' He used to hang around the docks when the fishing boats came in. Still does, sometimes. But last year he decided he would preside over the garden here."

A man who liked cats couldn't be all bad. Some of Leslie's leftover resentment faded.

"Has there been a problem, Mrs. Adams? I saw Jimmy coming down the hill."

Would it matter if she told him? Jimmy hadn't said to keep it quiet. Besides, she wanted to see his reaction. He hadn't made any secret of his animosity toward her. What if he'd followed her last night, and tried to scare her?

"Someone shot at me." She gave a short laugh. "Unless they were aiming at the mirror they hit." She gestured toward the shards of glass on the floor, without taking her eyes from his face.

"What?" Unless he was a superb actor, his shock was real. In fact, she could have sworn his face paled. "When was this, last night? Why didn't you call the cops sooner? This house is pretty isolated. Or doesn't the phone work?"

"It works. As I told Jimmy, I thought last night the mirror had simply fallen. I couldn't use the lights. You wouldn't know a good electrician, would you?"

He glanced at the chandelier, which was casting rainbows around the hall, even though it was off. "The lights work, don't they? I know an electrician went over all the wiring less than a year ago, when Jason came back. Everything checked out."

"Well, the switch gave me a shock last night." With some trepidation, she reached out her hand toward it, hesitated, then, biting her lip, flipped the switch. She yanked back her hand, feeling like an idiot when nothing happened, other than the chandelier lighting up. No flash. No shock.

She turned it off, making sure her contact with the switch was brief.

"Could have been static," Simon said. "The air's dry here. When it's about to storm, that happens sometimes."

"But it hasn't stormed."

"Still." He shrugged, looking at her for a moment. He dropped his gaze to the floor, seeming to find something fascinating about the pale, veined squares of marble at his feet. He looked for all the world like a schoolboy summoned to the principal's office.

"Uh, Mrs. Adams— May I call you Leslie? Seems more friendly, somehow."

She wasn't sure she wanted to be friends with a man of his arrogance, especially after the way he'd acted last night. But curiosity again won. "Okay."

"Leslie, that's why I came. I was out of line last night. I want to apologize for what I said. After I thought about it, I knew that if you'd had anything to do with Jason's schemes, you would never have had the nerve to show up here. So I'm sorry."

To her, it sounded as if the words were dragged from him. Nevertheless, she decided to give him the benefit of the doubt. After all, it wasn't as if she'd be seeing much of him after this.

"All right," she said. "It was an understandable mistake." She rubbed her hands together briskly. "Now, tell me something. You live here in Platania, don't you?"

Frowning slightly, he nodded. "Yes, except one day a week when I'm in Kérkira, taking care of business."

What kind of business? The question popped into her head. But she didn't voice it aloud. "What can you tell me about Jason's death?"

He looked startled. She saw his throat convulse as he swallowed. "Why didn't you ask Jimmy?"

"Because I already talked to the police. I want to know what people are saying and what you think."

She sat down on the bottom stair tread and patted the space beside her. "I haven't shopped yet, or I'd offer you a drink."

"That's all right." Picking up the cat, he sat down next to her. She sensed the tension in him, as if he thought it might be better to leave while he could. His knuckles were pale against the cat's dense coat.

In the silence, the cat purred like a well-tuned sports car. Simon's scent wrapped itself around her, subtle, pleasant, a mixture of herbal soap and warm man, with an undertone of sun-dried cotton.

"What happened to Jason?" she said quietly.

He started, as if he'd been so far away in his thoughts that he'd forgotten her presence. "He drowned. They didn't find the body. But it's a very treacherous coast, with strong currents. It's not the first time something like this has happened."

"What was he doing sailboarding in April?"

"Reliving his youth, perhaps?" Simon's tone was just short of sarcastic. "Or maybe because the waves are better in winter and spring."

"I never knew he sailboarded," Leslie said. "But then, I've lately discovered I didn't know much about Jason at all."

"He sailboarded for years, even before the sport became popular here. He liked the sea."

"And it killed him," Leslie said.

"His parents drowned, as well, in a ferry sinking. And maybe his daughter. Some say there's a curse on the family."

Leslie turned her head to stare at him. "A curse?"

"Yeah. They say his family will all die on water."

"Superstition, I suppose."

Simon shrugged. "Maybe. But superstitions are funny. If you believe them, they sometimes come true."

"So he had a daughter," she said in a resigned tone. In the past twelve hours, she'd discovered more about Jason's past than she had in ten years of marriage. Nothing could surprise her anymore.

"Yeah. She was twenty-five when she died."

"What happened to her?"

For a long moment, he said nothing, his body so rigid the cat broke off his purring and meowed inquiringly. When he spoke, the words beat into her brain like blows from a hammer.

"I killed her."

THAT WAS FOOLISH and cruel, Simon told himself. For some reason, he'd been driven to shock Leslie, to ruffle the composure she had maintained even after his revelation that Jason had had a daughter.

He certainly got a reaction. She paled, and edged away from him, standing up and hugging her arms around her waist. "You killed her," she said slowly, deliberately, looking at him as if she expected him to pull out an ax and start hacking her into small pieces.

"You would have found out soon enough anyway. Plenty of people here say I did kill her." He stroked the cat, his movements gentle and easy. "Just between me and you, I don't think she's dead."

Some of the color seeped back into her cheeks. "What happened to her?"

"The official version is that she drowned. I think she left, went back to England or something. It would have given her a perverse satisfaction, knowing I was left to face the questions the police asked. But there wasn't enough evidence to make the charges stick, no matter how much Jason ranted."

"Jason?" She looked sick and, for an instant, he felt sorry for her.

"Yes, Jason. He came to me, accused me of sexually harassing his daughter. When she supposedly drowned, there were those who believed she committed suicide because of me, and others who said I murdered her to keep her from bringing charges in court. In their minds, I killed her, either directly or by driving her to it."

A tense white line formed around Leslie's mouth. The only thing was, he couldn't tell whether she was feeling fear and disgust with him, or merely sympathy for the unfortunate young woman.

"Her body was never found," he continued.

The tendons on the backs of her hands stood out as she gripped her elbows. "Just like Jason's."

"And Jason's parents. As they say, the sea took them and didn't give them up."

Leslie sank down on a wicker chair that stood near the open door. "What about Jason's wife?"

"I'm not sure. Some kind of accident, I think, but I was in England then, and she hadn't lived here for a long time."

"Was Jason with her when it happened?" Leslie didn't like what she was hearing. She didn't like it at all. It seemed that everyone around Jason had died in an unnatural manner.

"I don't know," Simon said. "Why?"

She hesitated, her stomach feeling cold and hollow. "Curiosity, I guess," she finally said, knowing her answer sounded lame. Her mind went back to the shot last night. Was Jason dead, or had he brought her here to kill her, for whatever insane reason? Except that he hadn't brought her. She'd done that all by herself, driven by memories and curiosity.

"How did you get mixed up with a man like Jason in the first place?" Simon's words were a welcome interruption to her disturbing train of thought.

What she would have replied died on her lips as a scream made the hair at her nape stand on end. It was followed by a cackling that echoed through the house. The cat launched himself from Simon's lap, skidded across the polished marble floor and vanished out the open door.

"What was that?" Leslie gasped.

The maniacal laughter came again. To her astonishment Simon chuckled and stood up. He walked past her into the living room. "Here, Pretty Baby," he called softly. "Come here." She heard an indistinct crooning sound, followed by, "How did you get out? Don't you know a cat will get you?"

Leslie frowned, Cecil Weatherby's words jumping into her mind. A bird—the neighbor's, perhaps? She was about to join Simon when an odd figure came through the open doorway. A stout woman of indeterminate age brushed past her as if she were invisible, trailing a fringed scarf and clouds of Je Reviens.

"Oh, Simon!" the woman trilled. "You've caught him."

Leslie entered the room in time to see her visitor gently pluck a bird that resembled a crow from Simon's grasp. Obviously he'd flown in through the window she'd opened earlier. "Bad Baby," the woman scolded, shaking her finger next to the creature's yellow beak.

"Pretty Baby," the bird squawked, tilting its head to one side. It stared straight at Leslie, and let out a piercing wolf whistle.

"He's got good taste, hasn't he?" Simon said conversationally.

The bird whistled again, its bright eyes studying Leslie. "Pretty Baby."

The impudence of the thing. In spite of the shock that remained as an icy knot in her chest, Leslie couldn't help smiling. This had to be the bird Cecil Weatherby said terrorized his dog.

The woman shifted the mynah to a perch on her shoulder, where it promptly tangled its claws in the fringes of her scarf. She extended her hand. "You must be Leslie Adams. I'm Eugenia Turner."

Giving Leslie's hand a firm, businesslike shake, she tilted her head in much the same manner as her bird had. In fact, at once the bird on her shoulder mimicked the pose. Leslie fought to keep a straight face. "I'm happy to meet you. How did you know my name?"

"Jason mentioned you," Eugenia said. "Not that he ever talked to me much. Dour sort, wasn't he? He didn't like Baby at all. Used to get all upset if he came over here."

"Aren't you worried that he'll get lost?" Leslie asked as the bird gave another high-pitched laugh.

"Hush," Eugenia said admonishingly to the bird. To Leslie, she said, "His flight feathers have been trimmed, so he can't get far."

Leslie stretched out a tentative hand. The bird regarded her solemnly for a moment, then hopped onto her finger, claws gripping like cool, brittle twigs. Muttering in his throat, he preened his glossy black feathers. "Pretty Baby. Pretty Baby."

"Come and have tea with me," Eugenia said. "Tomorrow. At four. We'll talk." Taking back the bird, she headed for the door, her high-heeled mules clicking on the marble floor. The scent of her perfume lingered after her departure, like an aura infusing the room.

"And where is it that I'm to join her for tea?" Leslie asked a little breathlessly.

Simon straightened from his appraisal of the empty fireplace. "That's easy. Go around to the far side of the garage and you'll see a break in the hedge. That's the shortcut. If you want the more formal entrance, just go down the street toward the village. It's the first driveway on the left. She's your nearest neighbor."

"Has she lived here long?"

"Years. She was born near here, but her husband was British. It was natural for her to retire here, since she had the house."

"Then she'll be able to tell me where I can get a car. I want to do some sight-seeing." Snooping, she reminded herself. There were too many questions about Jason's death. "There seems to be nothing to rent. I asked yesterday in—what do you call it?— Kérkira?"

"I think Jason had a car. You could use that. It should be in the garage."

She cast him a sidelong look, debating the wisdom of letting him stick around longer than necessary. "Awfully helpful, aren't you, all of a sudden?" she said bluntly. "Especially after last night, when you were ready to run me out of town."

A faint flush colored his elegant cheekbones. "I said I was sorry. It was more of a reflex than anything personal."

She studied him for a moment longer. Whatever he was after, she'd figure it out sooner or later. Meantime... "Okay," she said briskly. "Let's find the keys."

"They'll be in the kitchen. That's where Jason kept all the keys, next to the door." He led the way down the hall.

"You know your way around this place, don't you?" Leslie said. "Isn't that kind of odd, considering you and Jason weren't exactly friends?"

"My father was a contractor. When I was a kid, I helped him do repairs around this house. It hasn't changed much."

"Oh. Does your father still do that kind of work?"

She saw his shoulders stiffen. All the earlier tension rushed back. "My father's dead. And your husband was at least partly to blame. Here's the keys," he added brusquely.

Jason seemed to have a lot to answer for, Leslie thought dismally as they went out into the heavy heat of midmorning. One man's death, another's character assassination, to use Simon's own term. Bodies of relatives strewn all over the seabed.

What kind of life had he led here? It was beginning to appear that on Corfu Jason had been a vastly different man from the one she'd known, a man up to his ears in controversy.

Their marriage had been uneventful. Jason had been preoccupied with his import-export business, which he had never discussed. When he was home, he'd eat dinner, read the paper, then go to bed precisely at eleven.

Only in the last years of their marriage had things changed. Jason's behavior had become erratic. Mysterious phone calls late at night. Ever more frequent trips away, from which he'd returned days later, looking as if he'd been in a war.

Once he'd gone out at midnight, in response to a call, and returned in the morning with a black eye. He'd said he'd had a flat tire on a country road and stumbled into a ditch in the dark while changing it. When she asked him what kind of people he was mixed up with, his mouth had tightened and he'd said it didn't concern her.

But it did concern her; she'd had phone calls after he moved out of their house, the house they'd later sold. The callers had never spoken but had left the line open just long enough to make her nervous. Not exactly a threat, but somehow a kind of intimidation.

Which was why she was here now. She needed to find out exactly why and how Jason had died. Maybe his death was an accident; but maybe it wasn't.

Jingling the two key rings in her hand, she followed Simon down a path composed of flat, square stones in shades that ranged from tan and gray to the more exotic pink and mauve. He took the keys from her hand, inserted the largest one into an ornately carved lock and threw open the garage door.

Cautiously she peered inside. The air inside was cool, the dirt floor giving off a musty smell. The building contained the usual clutter, rusting garden utensils, and a workbench with assorted tools hanging above it.

A sailboard stood against a small, dusty white car. The edges were battered, one end gone, with a huge gouge like a shark bite.

This must be the craft that had killed Jason. Regret and an unexpected grief tightened Leslie's chest and, for a moment, tears burned in her eyes. Such a flimsy thing to trust your life to on the sea. Why had he done it? Had he indeed been trying to recapture a lost youth?

She let out a little shriek as something small and furry ran over her foot. The cat rushed out of the bushes and streaked after it. "What was that?"

"Only a mouse, city girl," Simon said, giving her that rare smile she'd seen only in his dealings with Eugenia and her mynah. The smile transformed his face, crinkling his eyes at the corners and softening the habitual austerity. He looked almost friendly, and she wondered if she had been too quick in jumping to uncharitable conclusions about him.

Perhaps it would be wise to cultivate his friendship; he might prove helpful to her. Even if his relationship with Jason had been less than amicable, he must know things she would have difficulty discovering on her own.

She stepped into the garage, gingerly putting one foot ahead of the other. "Do you think the car will start?"

"I'll give it a try." He handed the door keys to her, reaching for the ring with the car keys. His eyes narrowed, and he took her hand in his. "You're shaking," he said, not unkindly. "I'm sorry. I should have thought you'd be upset when you saw the sailboard. The police brought it back. I forgot it was here. They never found the sail, must have blown out to sea.''

At his touch, her control shattered. She blinked away fresh tears. Why was she crying? For the good times, perhaps, long ago, when she'd been young and thought she loved Jason? Or was it grief at the waste of a life? ''He should have known better,'' she whispered.

''Yes, he should have,'' Simon said.

He gently stroked her hand, his fingers warm, comforting. Touched by his kindness, she regained her composure. Her opinion of him rose another, less reluctant notch.

''If you're going to stay here awhile, Leslie, you'll have to put up with mice and such,'' he said, a trace of amusement in his voice. ''I wouldn't be surprised if there are mice in the basement, as well.''

The basement? A shiver of dread stirred within her. She'd looked down the stairs yesterday afternoon but, put off by the damp-smelling darkness below, she'd slammed the door shut and postponed further exploration. But her cowardice nagged her now; sooner or later she would have to enter the cellar, if only to inspect the water system or look for Jason's missing belongings. Without thinking, she placed her free hand on Simon's chest and dropped her forehead against his shirt, inhaling the scent of sun-dried cotton, soap and clean male skin. ''I'll set a trap. And call you to empty it if I catch something.''

His stroking hand stilled. She heard the sharp intake of his breath at the same moment her words echoed in her head. *I'll call you.*

''Would you really?'' he asked softly. ''Would you really call me, Leslie?''

Her face burning, she stared at the ground, at the battered canvas sneakers he wore. The top of one had the frayed beginning of a hole over the big toe. She didn't know what was worse, to stand there feeling his heartbeat strong against her palm, or to move away and let him see how easily he could destroy her equilibrium.

Pulling herself together, she took a step back. To her relief, he let her go at once. "I'll check the basement later." Her voice only wobbled a little. "When the electrician comes. Which reminds me, could you recommend someone?"

"I'll call him for you when we get back in the house." He lifted one black brow. "The car keys?"

"Oh." She stood aside as he got into the little car and cranked the engine, which came to life with a cough and a wheeze, then ran more smoothly. Blue exhaust, reeking of stale gasoline, enveloped her in a choking cloud, driving her out of the cool building and into the blazing sunlight. She stood there, gasping for breath and holding her nose.

Simon backed out the car, adjusting the choke to a slow idle. Opening the door, he got out, moving around to the passenger side to check the insurance document mounted in the corner of the windshield. "You're in luck," he said. "It seems to be valid. Would you like me to drive it down to the village for you to have the gas-station mechanic drain out the old gasoline and do a service on it?"

"I'll come with you," Leslie said quickly. After all, how long had she known this man? A gut feeling told her he could be trusted with her property. Whether she could trust the stability of her emotions around him, or believe his version of Jason's life, was another story. "I need to go to the grocery store anyway. I'll get my purse."

"Sure," he said easily. Whistling something that sounded like Mozart, he leaned back against the car, crossing his legs at the ankles.

Leslie walked back to the house through the green-filtered sunlight on the path. The kitchen door stood open, just as they'd left it.

On the counter, next to the sink, stood a vase of blood-red roses that hadn't been there twenty minutes earlier.

# Chapter Three

Spooky. That was what it was. Who would bring her roses? Not to mention sneaking into the house to leave them. A florist would have left them on the back step.

No, maybe not. She pulled at her earlobe. The open door could have seemed like an invitation. Who knew what people did here? Maybe they were so at home with each other, they just walked into people's houses without knocking.

After all, Eugenia had, earlier. But she had been chasing her bird.

Frowning deeply, Leslie ran upstairs to get her purse. The house seemed undisturbed, though her nose twitched when she reached her room. Was that roses she smelled up here? She wasn't sure, and the scent could be drifting through the open French doors from the overgrown garden.

This room was the master bedroom, with a large bathroom next door. She had removed the dustcovers and made up the bed with linens from another closet in the hall yesterday afternoon. Good thing she'd done that in daylight; otherwise she'd have been poking around in the dark last night when the apparent short circuit made her nervous about the lights.

She closed the French doors and let the roller shutters cover them against the sun, which would turn the rooms into saunas by midday. Downstairs, she locked the front door, walked through the house and did the same at the back, casting one black look at the roses as she went by.

"What's wrong?" Simon said as soon as she emerged from the path onto the graveled apron in front of the garage. He'd shut off the car engine and relocked the garage door.

"What makes you think anything's wrong?" Leslie asked, smoothing out her frown.

"That look you get when you hear bad news. Like about Jason."

Surprised by his perceptiveness, she shrugged lightly. "I don't know if it means anything, but someone left a bouquet of red roses in the kitchen. While we were out here."

Simon ran his hand over the back of his neck. "Probably Cecil. He's got plenty of roses in his garden."

Her unease lifted. "That's probably it, then. But he shouldn't have walked in. He could have left them outside."

"They would have wilted," Simon said, pulling open the car door and untwisting the seat belt for her when she got inside. "You'll find the sun's a lot hotter here than you're used to." He tapped one finger on the top of her head. "Wear a hat if you're going to be out."

"I'll get one," she promised, not sure whether to be annoyed or flattered by his advice. She wasn't a child; she didn't need a keeper.

"THE CAR will be ready in an hour," Simon told her after he talked to the mechanic at the small service station. "I trust you know how to drive with a gearshift?"

"Not every car in Canada has an automatic transmission," Leslie said. "I drive an old Peugeot there. I'm used to a stick shift."

Simon nodded. "Fine. I'll leave you, then." He pulled a business card from his shirt pocket, straightened the corners and handed it to her. "Call me if you need anything. Anytime."

Surprised, she looked at him. His expression told her nothing. "Why?" she asked. "Last night—"

"Last night I made a mistake," he said, interrupting her. "See you later, Leslie."

He walked away, his long, lithe strides taking him quickly out of her sight around a corner. Leslie chewed on her bottom lip. What kind of man was he, friendly one moment, prickly the next? She looked down at the card in her hand. Simon Korvallis, Premium Agricultural Services. It didn't tell her much, except his phone number and an address in Kérkira. That must be where he spent one day a week, taking care of business, as he'd put it last night.

She tucked the card into her purse, glancing back at the mechanic who had his head buried under the hood of the car. "I'll be back," she said, not sure he'd understand.

He grinned impudently, his teeth very white in a strong face darkened by sun and liberal streaks of engine grease. "One hour, miss," he said in heavily accented English. "Maybe one and a half."

She had shopping to do, but first she wanted to ask Simon something she'd forgotten to ask the police yesterday. If she hurried, she could catch him. He'd been heading for the square.

Out of the shelter of the garage, the sun beat on her head. Sweat trickled down her temples, making stray hairs stick to her skin. She brushed back the strands, lifting her heavy ponytail from her nape. The narrow street between the pastel houses seemed to condense the sun's glare into a white heat. She squinted against the intense light interspersed with deep shadow, glad she'd remembered her sunglasses.

Within moments she emerged on the flagstoned square, where lime trees cast meager pools of shade. She saw Simon at the far side. Holding up the edge of her flared skirt, she sprinted across the open space, ignoring the stares of villagers sitting at the coffee shops.

"Simon," she called as he entered an alley between two shops. "Wait."

Stopping, he turned, shaking his head as she ran up to him. "You shouldn't rush in this heat, especially when you're not used to it."

Breathless, she brushed the damp hair from her forehead. "Simon, were there any witnesses to Jason's accident?"

His eyes narrowed, casting his face into forbidding lines. For a moment, she was taken aback. Did the question bother him? "Didn't the police tell you?" he asked slowly.

"No." She paused. "Or at least I don't think so. I didn't ask specifically."

"Well, there might have been a witness. No one is too sure. Before the sailboard capsized, there was a powerboat cruising in the area."

"Then why didn't the boat pick him up, if he was in trouble?"

"They might not have realized. Jason was pretty far out to sea. The boat was closer to shore. The wind was very strong and gusty that day. The board was found in a cove south of the house. He probably had a broken universal."

Leslie frowned. "What's a universal?"

"It's the part that holds the sail to the board. The boards don't sink, but if he lost the sail and then somehow got separated from the board, he wouldn't have lasted long in the cold, choppy water."

"Didn't the police find out who was in the boat?"

"I don't think so. The coast south of here is rocky and isolated, especially in the colder season. Only a shepherd with a flock on the hills above the cove saw it. He reported it after he heard about the accident."

Leslie clenched her hands into fists and stuck them into the pockets of her skirt. "In other words, Jason took a risk and lost."

"Going by past history," Simon said, "Jason took a lot of risks."

"Are you sure about that?" Leslie asked skeptically. "In Canada he was conservative to the point of boredom."

"Was that why your marriage failed, Leslie? Out of boredom?"

She scowled at him in annoyance. "It's none of your business," she retorted. "But I'll tell you anyway. It failed because near the end Jason was never there. That's why all the things you're telling me about him are a surprise. It's as if he was two people, one in Canada and another here. And I didn't even know about here."

"I'm sorry, Leslie." He laid his hand on her shoulder, then jerked it back as if he feared she'd be offended. Which struck her as odd, since he'd held her in his arms at the house. Still, this was a public place.

"There's not much you can do about it." Her annoyance faded into despondency and self-recrimination. How could she have been so blind? Why had she been so complacent, so unquestioning, that she'd never suspected Jason of having a double life? "I'm going to find out more about this whole thing. Why did Jason die? Who was in the boat? I want some answers."

"If there are any answers," Simon said darkly. "Boat or no boat, Jason's gone. As far as the people here and the police are concerned, the case is closed. Be careful, Leslie. Remember what happened last night."

She stared at him. Despite the heat, a chill crept up her spine. "What do you mean? Jimmy thinks it was an accident. Kids."

"Jimmy is a good cop, but he hasn't been here very long. He's probably right, but you can't be too careful. And if the person in the boat saw Jason and left him in the sea, what can you do?" He shrugged. "Stay at the house, enjoy your holiday, but let the dead stay buried."

A warning, or just friendly advice? His words haunted her as she bought bread and milk and vegetables, nagging like a toothache. And the worst of it was the thought that Jason wasn't buried, no matter how dead he was.

BY THE TIME she drove home, Leslie could hardly keep her eyes open. Jet lag? Or the dense heat that wilted the leaves in her garden and pressed down on the parched earth like a massive weight? It suddenly struck her why Mediterranean countries so religiously observed the practice of siesta.

Her movements slow and languid, she carried the groceries into the house and put them away. The roses stood on the counter, filling the oppressive air with a heavy fragrance. She glared at them, then picked up the vase and carried them into the living room.

Sunlight freckled the dim room, a pattern of tiny rectangles coming through the small holes in the roller shutters. Halfway across the worn wooden floor, Leslie stopped. She swept her glance around, abruptly realizing why the room looked different. The sheets were gone from the furniture, and the tables were polished, no longer covered with a layer of gritty dust.

Leslie set the vase down, splashing the water. She clasped her shaking hands together. Who else had a key to the house? She had locked the doors, and they'd been locked when she came back. Unless—

She ran into the hall and checked the front door. Closed and locked, with a modern dead bolt. Opening the door, she stared out at the forecourt.

Heat waves hovered above the flagstones, dazzling her eyes. The garden beyond shimmered with a strange, surreal light, a green jungle. Leslie shook her head, trying to clear the wooliness of fatigue from her brain. She felt as if she were swimming in a dream, that nothing was quite real, not the lush garden, nor the dark house with its mysterious, invisible visitors.

Back in the kitchen, she drank a couple of glasses of the faintly brackish water. Reminding herself to buy bottled water next time she went down to the shops, she ate a slice of bread and one of the succulent peaches she'd bought.

Then she staggered up to her room, fell on the bed and slept.

WHEN SHE WOKE, the angle of the light told her it was late in the afternoon. For a long moment, she lay on the bed, her mind groggy, buzzing in counterpoint to the sawing of cicadas outside.

The discomfort of lying on her twisted skirt drove her up. She set her feet on the floor, pulling her sweat-damp T-shirt over her head. A movement by the window brought her head spinning around. She laughed ruefully when she saw it was only the long, lace curtain stirring in the breeze.

She'd opened the French doors but left the shutters closed. Walking across the room, she rolled them up. The sun had moved around the house, its eye no longer baleful although the heat still bore down, unabated even late in the day.

She went downstairs after her shower and drank more water from the jug she'd set in the ancient, wheezing refrigerator. Cold, it tasted fine, if a little rough.

Looking out the window, she saw that the little Renault still stood where she'd left it, its windows rolled down. She walked outside. Shade dappled the patio outside the kitchen door, making the temperature bearable.

The gray cat, which she hadn't seen since morning, slept on the driver's seat. Leslie rattled her keys. "Come on, cat. Move. I want to turn the car so I can wash it."

The sun sank lower. Leslie splashed her bare feet in the puddles forming around the car as she washed, momentarily forgetting her problems. The cat stayed out of range of the hose, his expression telling her he couldn't understand her pleasure in playing with water. After a while, he grow bored and wandered off.

She turned off the hose and wiped down the car with old towels she'd found in the linen closet. Frowning, she paused as she polished the windshield. That was another odd thing: the cupboard was full of towels, sheets, pillowcases, even several age-yellowed tablecloths. Some were new, and others were worn almost threadbare. Hadn't Jason ever thrown anything away?

Yet where were his clothes? If Simon hadn't told her Jason had stayed here, she would have thought he'd never come near the place. There was no trace of him at all.

Of course, she'd only glanced briefly into the other bedrooms upstairs, but the old-fashioned wardrobes contained nothing but cobwebs, and the beds were stripped, the bare mattresses protected with muslin dust-covers.

At the end of the upstairs hall, she'd discovered a steep flight of stairs leading to the attic. Glancing up at the heat waves still shimmering over the russet-tiled roof, she figured it must be like an oven up there. Tomorrow morning, when it was cooler, she'd have a look.

She finished the car and hung the towels over the clothesline that stretched from the back step to a tree. The sun's rays tangled in the treetops, sending fragments of light dancing around her. She rolled up the hose, hanging it on its rack.

"Good afternoon, Mrs. Adams."

She snapped her head up. "Oh, hello, Mr. Weatherby."

He stood diffidently behind her, a small brown dog of dubious breeding tugging at the leash he held. "Please," he said, "call me Cecil. If I may call you Leslie?"

"Of course." She straightened, groaning as her thigh muscles cramped. Blowing back a strand of hair that had worked loose from her ponytail, she tugged down the legs of her shorts. "I see you found your dog."

He glanced down with a fond smile. "Yes, he was waiting on the step when I got back to my house. Simon isn't here?"

"No, he's not. Any reason why he should be?"

Cecil shifted from one foot to the other, his eyes downcast. The little dog strained at the leash. "No, I suppose not. I just noticed him here this morning."

"Oh?" Leslie said coolly. "I didn't know your house was that close."

"We share a common boundary." He gestured toward the sea. "Along the side over there. There's a path, although it's hard to find unless you know where to look."

Leslie nodded. The secretary at the property-management office where she'd picked up the key had shown her a plot plan and pointed out the dimensions of the lot. The property Jason's house stood on was L-shaped. At the short end of the L, the shrubbery was most overgrown and dense. Reluctant to brave the jungle, Leslie hadn't explored that corner of the garden.

"By the way, thank you for the roses," she said. "They were lovely."

A strange look crossed Cecil's face. "Roses? I didn't bring you any roses."

"You didn't? Simon said they probably came from you." A little frisson of alarm shifted within her. "I wonder who did bring them."

The old man shrugged. "I wouldn't know. But plenty of people have roses in their gardens. June is the season for them. Anyone could have brought them to welcome you."

Leslie was skeptical, although she kept her thoughts to herself. The villagers hadn't given her much of a welcome, although yesterday she'd been treated with guarded cordiality. Still, it was unlikely anyone would have hiked up here to bring her a housewarming gift.

Cecil was silent, his eyes wandering about the garden, as if he were searching for something. Or someone. The little dog sniffed at Leslie's ankles, his nose cold and wet.

"What do you know about Jason's death?" Leslie asked, following him across the patio. She had to start somewhere, if she wanted answers.

Cecil stopped abruptly, the dog coming up short on the leash and letting out a startled yelp. For a moment, his flat eyes locked with Leslie's, and then they skittered away. "The police questioned me, as they did everyone who'd had any contact with Jason.

He paused, but before she could say anything, he added, all in a rush, "Would you have supper with me one evening? If you're not too busy, of course."

Why, he was lonely, Leslie realized in surprise. She would have expected that a man who had lived so much of his life in one place would have many friends. But perhaps he didn't.

"I would love to have supper with you," she said. She couldn't deny that he made her a little uneasy, not to mention that she suspected he knew more than he was letting on. The way he'd neatly sidestepped her question about Jason's death. He knew something. Of that she was certain.

She would go to his house and wait for an opening to ask more questions. "Would tomorrow evening be all right? No, tomorrow I'm having tea with Eugenia. You know Eugenia, don't you?"

He scowled and muttered something she could have sworn was a nasty word. "What's wrong?" she asked.

He set his mouth in a prim line. "Nothing. Watch out for that bird of hers."

"I've met her bird. How about if I come the next night?"

The old man beamed. "Perfect. Shall we say at eight?"

At her nod, he inclined his head politely. "Good evening, then, Leslie. I'll look forward to it." He put down the dog and began to walk away.

Scruffy yelped a high-pitched bark. The gray cat glided out of the bushes. The dog pulled at the leash, growling. To Leslie's surprise, the cat, until now the most benign of creatures, sank into a defensive crouch. His tail lashed the ground. He hissed at the little dog, who barked hysterically.

"Scruffy, that's enough." Cecil gathered the leash around his hand and picked up the dog. The cat, having won the skirmish, rose and stalked to the step, where he began to wash his paws, tail still twitching.

"Goodbye, Leslie," Cecil said again.

"Goodbye," Leslie said.

Her frown remained as he slowly walked down the driveway and disappeared around its curve.

Like a genie from a bottle, Eugenia popped around the side of the house. She wore a ragged sweat suit and her hair was in disarray. "Was old Cecil here? I thought I heard his little beast yapping."

"Yes, he was here," Leslie said calmly. "He invited me for supper."

Eugenia looked faintly horrified. "You're not going, are you? He'll probably poison you."

Unsure whether to take this remark seriously, Leslie decided to ignore it. "I think he's lonely. I've accepted his invitation."

"Well, mark my words, he'll start thinking of you as a relative—his have all died, or he's alienated them—and you'll never get rid of him. Don't say I didn't warn you."

Leslie couldn't help her smile, and she no longer cared if Eugenia noticed. With her secure ego, Eugenia could take it. "I won't. I want to talk to him. He must have known Jason. And I'd like to see his paintings."

Eugenia's voice dropped to a whisper. "They're weird. That's what they are. Weird. I don't know where he gets his ideas, but they're frightening."

"In what way?"

"Oh, all dark colors and strange shapes. You can see things in them." Eugenia shuddered. "One of them has eyes that watch everything you do."

"Does he sell these paintings?"

"Oh, yes. They fetch good prices, too. I can't imagine why, but then, tastes aren't what they used to be." Eugenia put her hand on Leslie's arm. "Be careful. I can see you have a kind heart, but don't let him take advantage of you."

"Why, did Cecil take advantage of you?"

Eugenia looked embarrassed, her eyes dropping to the puddle next to the back step. "Not exactly. He hasn't spoken to me since I told him what I thought of his paintings, over twenty years ago."

"Twenty years ago? That's a long time."

"Yes, but I'm entitled to my opinion. And he had the nerve to complain about my singing, when everyone knows I'm a true artist. He calls opera incomprehensible caterwauling, so I think he owes me an apology, if there are apologies to be made."

Leslie was beginning to get the picture. Neither was likely to back down and, after twenty years, the situation was probably hopeless.

"He's too old." Eugenia sniffed disdainfully. "And too stubborn by far, that man." She patted Leslie's arm again. "Don't forget our tea tomorrow."

THERE WAS STILL plenty of light after her hasty supper of canned soup and toast to have a look at the beach. Leslie picked her way down an overgrown path through the dense jungle of the garden. She winced as blackberry thorns scratched her bare ankles. It was dark and gloomy under the trees, the path swallowed up at times by the rampant undergrowth. Only the setting sun assured her she was going in the right direction.

She emerged from the trees at the edge of the promontory on which the house stood. A steep stairway, stone steps bounded by a wooden rail, led down to the beach, at least a hundred feet below. The gray cat, who had followed her, licked at the scrapes on her ankles, his tongue warm and as rough as a rasp.

Pushing him aside, she grasped the rail, testing the sea-weathered wood. It appeared sturdy enough, festooned with morning glory vines.

She climbed down carefully, the vines grabbing at her hands and tangling her feet where they grew across the stone treads cut into the hillside. The plants needed to be cut back, if she was going to use the stairs regularly. She would have to hire someone to do it, or buy a machete. Once they were cleaned up, she could run down to swim every morning. No use wasting her own private beach—however temporary it might be.

Soft, fine sand sifted into her shoes as she stepped from the last stone step onto the beach. The sea murmured and hissed, its gentle melody soothing her.

Taking off her shoes and carrying them in her hand, Leslie walked up the deserted beach. Delicately avoiding the shifting water, the cat kept pace with her. The stretch of sand extended a couple of hundred yards before ending in a rocky headland that hid the village from her. The beach seemed completely private, although the young woman at Corfu Property Management had explained that other houses also had access to it.

The sun sat on the horizon, a bronze ball turning the water to molten gold. Pink-and-mauve clouds, like wispy silk scarves, muted its light. Leslie turned back. Night fell quickly once the sun set, and she didn't fancy climbing those stairs in the dark.

A flash of light sent her gaze up the precipitous hillside. No windows were visible through the dense shrubbery. She shrugged. Probably the sun reflecting off broken glass.

She began to climb, avoiding the handrail, with its tangle of vegetation harboring who-knew-what insects. Her calves ached from the unaccustomed exertion, and she paused, catching her breath. In the bushes above her, she heard a faint rustling sound. The shrubs at the top of the cliff swayed and Leslie frowned. There wasn't enough of a breeze to cause that much motion.

The cat suddenly yowled and flung himself against her leg. Her breath hissed out as his distended claws left raw scratches on her skin. She grabbed at the rail.

It gave way under her hand. She uttered a startled cry and clawed at the vines, managing to snag one with her fingers. Scrabbling for purchase as her feet skidded out from under her, she felt a muscle wrench painfully in her side. She twisted to regain her balance, then sat down abruptly. Pain shot up her tailbone, but she was safe.

A rumble came to her ears, and a pebble bounced past her. Launching himself at the stairway, the cat leaped upward, his tail like a bottlebrush.

More pebbles rained down, a fist-size rock narrowly missing Leslie's head. She looked up, then flung herself two steps down, into a niche between the rail and a huge boulder. An avalanche of rocks and uprooted shrubs poured down, sand exploding upward as it hit the beach.

For a moment, Leslie lay there. Then she pushed herself to her feet, sneezing violently. She stared up the hill terror clawing at her chest.

Only a few broken branches showed where the landslide had passed. And the haze of settling dust.

Leslie stared at the broken rail right above her head, the one she'd grabbed to break her fall. Her throat constricted around a stifled scream.

The rail wasn't rotted. A fresh white edge ending in jagged splinters showed where it had been sawed almost all the way through. The slightest weight against it would have caused it to break away.

She sank down on the step, her blood congealing in her veins.

Someone had tried to kill her.

And she was suddenly convinced that this was the second attempt.

# Chapter Four

Her legs shaking, Leslie climbed to the top of the steps, making sure she placed each foot carefully to avoid using the handrail. The sky had darkened to deep indigo, displaying a single star and a sliver of moon, but she was blind to its beauty.

The tree-shrouded path leading back to the house lay before her, almost invisible in the gloom. Leslie hesitated, biting her lip. What was waiting for her in the dense shadows? The hair on her nape prickled. Was that the rustle of a large body passing through the shrubbery?

The sound died, and the crickets began their nightly serenade, reassuring her that there was no one around. Stiffening her spine, she plunged into the undergrowth. She ran toward the house, brambles catching at her clothes. Once a branch whipped across her face and she swerved violently, almost braining herself against a tree trunk. Gulping in relief when she smelled the fragrance of jasmine that told her she was near the house, she slowed to a walk.

She'd turned on the light over the kitchen door before going to the beach. The yellow bulb glowed feebly, moths and gnats kamikazeing against the glass fixture.

"Safe." She ran across the patio, closing her eyes for an instant as a wave of dizziness coursed through her.

Mistake. She crashed headlong into a solid wall, realized at once that it was a man and recoiled, stifling a scream. "Get away from me!"

"What? What's happened?" Simon's voice. Simon himself, spotlighted by the yellow bulb.

She kept her hands raised in a defensive position, not sure whether she should be glad to see him—or run as fast as she could in the opposite direction.

"Someone tried to kill me," she said starkly, still poised for flight.

"Well, it wasn't—" He broke off, shock racing across his face. Shock that appeared genuine. He couldn't be that good an actor. "You did think that—that it might have been me."

She hugged her arms around her waist, trying to still the inner trembling. "Well, what was I supposed to think? The rockslide didn't start by itself. And now I find you up here. How do I know you weren't responsible? You made your feelings clear enough last night."

"I was wrong. I told you. Besides, I just got here." He clasped his fingers around her elbows, steadying her. "You look as if you're about to pass out. And you're bleeding."

She brushed her hand over the scratch on her forehead, gingerly exploring. Her fingers came away smeared with blood, which she wiped on the tail of her T-shirt. The scratch burned, as did numerous abrasions and scrapes on her legs and arms. With an odd detachment she recognized as shock, she noted that her sleeve was torn, hanging halfway down her arm. Simon's voice came to her as if from a great distance; she couldn't concentrate, and her knees felt rubbery.

"Where's your key?"

She didn't respond, only stared at him through wide-open eyes that were beginning to glaze over. Alarmed, he shook her slightly.

"Leslie!" To his relief, she blinked and groped in her shorts pocket for the key. He took it from her and unlocked the door, drawing her with him into the kitchen. Just as he was about to close the door, the gray cat streaked past their feet, disappearing down the hall.

"What's eating him?" he muttered. Hair standing on end, tail bristling, the creature had looked well and truly spooked.

The room was hot. Leslie hadn't closed the shutters, and the sun had been glaring through the west-facing windows for most of the afternoon. He turned the handle and pushed the window open, letting in the jasmine-scented night breeze.

A thud shook the floor, and he jumped, his heart hammering in his chest. Under his hand, Leslie's body jerked. If he hadn't been holding her arm, he thought, she would have jumped a foot into the air.

Another thud, as if a heavy object had fallen somewhere in the basement. He scowled in the direction of the basement door. What was it? Never mind. He'd check it out later. Leslie needed his attention now.

He sat her down on a kitchen chair, propping her against the table. Going to the sink, he wet a cloth and brought it back to wipe her face.

The scratch wasn't deep, but he figured it must sting, from the way she flinched when he ran the cool cloth over it. "Feel better?" he asked.

She nodded, offering him a shaky smile. Her hair was tangled and matted, coming loose from the habitual ponytail. He brushed it back, tendrils clinging to his fingers, wrapping around them the way she was wrapping herself around his heart. He'd fought against it, but even at their first meeting he'd unwillingly admitted that Jason had had excellent taste in his choice of a second wife. Confident, yet vulnerable. Beautiful, but seemingly unaware of that beauty, which was a refreshing trait after the vanity of the women he'd known in London.

He rinsed out the cloth and washed her arms. He saw that she looked a little more alert, less exhausted. "Why do you think the landslide didn't start by itself? They do, you know—goats disturbing the ground, rocks loosened by rain, earth tremors so deep underground you don't feel them. We get a lot of earthquakes, as you must know."

Leslie's head was clearing, her body recovering from the deadly lethargy that was the aftermath of terror. Logic also reasserted itself. If Simon had tried to kill her, why would he be here now, offering first aid?

He had seemed stunned by her bedraggled condition. Of course, he might be good at faking his reactions, but she didn't think so. If he had started the slide, he wouldn't be hanging around. It would be much better if he, or someone else, discovered her body in the morning.

Still, she didn't know him. The little nagging doubt remained; she would stay on her guard.

She forced a tiny smile. "I have to confess I don't know much about earthquakes, or about Greece, except in terms of history."

Simon stared at her in disbelief. "You mean Jason never talked about Greece at all? Why, he grew up here."

"Did he? I thought he was British."

"He was," Simon said. "But his father was stationed in Greece, with the British diplomatic service. They divided their time between Athens and Corfu. This was their summer house for many years."

"They didn't own it from Jason's childhood, then?" Leslie asked, her voice strengthening.

"They didn't own it at all. They rented it for their holidays. And for several years Jason lived here year-round, with his first wife. In fact, his family and mine were on good terms." He paused, then added, "My great-grandfather built the house."

"Oh? Was he a contractor, too, like your father?"

"No, my great-grandfather was a businessman, like me, except that most of my business is running the family orchards. Most of which, incidentally, date back to my great-grandfather's days. He built the house for his wife, but when she died, he couldn't bear to look at it. He sold it to a company who rented the house to various tenants, and leased the land to a commercial winery. I believe even Cecil lived in the house for a while, when he was having his own house built."

Leslie frowned. "What happened to the land? The lawyer showed me the plot plan, but there's only the garden."

"The vines developed a disease, phylloxera, which destroyed them. The land was sold separately. Part of it is planted with olives, the rest is where Cecil's and Eugenia's houses now stand."

"When did Jason eventually buy the house?"

"About five years ago."

Leslie nodded. The scratch on her forehead burned. Her skin felt tight and cold, and her head was beginning to throb. She closed her eyes, the pain in her heart suddenly overriding her physical aches. "So it was during our marriage," she whispered. "He came back here and never even told me."

"He was here when he bought the house, and again about two years ago, as well as before his accident."

"I didn't know." Distressed, she twisted her hands together. She shouldn't let it bother her, she knew, but somehow it still rankled. Jason had lied and betrayed her. Not with other women, perhaps, although how would she have known if he had? But he'd betrayed her trust, and that was just as painful as sexual infidelity.

She lifted her head, her gray eyes transparent as rain. "What happened with the house?"

Simon hesitated, debating with himself. Was he ready to tell her the sordid facts? He could evade the question. An innocuous comment and she would be put off for now.

No, he couldn't do that. It would be better if she heard it from him, before one of the village busybodies decided to fill her in on the less savory aspects of her husband's character.

"My father wanted to buy the house. He planned to give it to my mother. She does work for several charities, and at the time one of them needed a country house to use as a convalescent home. Buying this house would have brought it back into the family and pleased my mother at the same time."

He cleared his throat. "But Jason cheated him out of it. If I'd been here, I might have been able to do something. But I was living in London at the time."

He stopped, guilt coursing through him. Maybe if he'd been here, he would have been able to prevent Jason's perfidy. "How?" Leslie asked.

"Jason got hold of inside information, through strategically placed friends. He heard that a hotel corporation was considering this land to build a resort." Simon prowled around the room, his fists clenched at his sides. "My father knew nothing about the resort proposal, though he had discussed his plans for the house with Jason many times, as he considered him a trusted friend. Then Jason went behind his back and made a higher offer for the house. It was accepted. Within days, the hotel corporation announced that they would buy it for the planned resort. Jason stood to double or triple his money.''

"And your father was left out in the cold," Leslie said. Jason's manipulations might not have been illegal under the circumstances, but they had certainly been immoral.

"Yes. He was devastated. He'd counted on being able to give the house to my mother. And he always did business with only his word and a handshake. He'd thought of Jason as a brother, and now the brother had stabbed him in the back."

Simon gripped his hands on the edge of the sink and stared out the window into the dark night. Leslie's heart ached. She'd known him for only twenty-four hours but the secrets of the past, exhumed brutally by her arrival in Platania, had cut through social convention and forced them both to expose their inner souls.

Leslie could feel his pain as if it were her own. When he spoke, she had to strain to hear him. "My father had a heart attack a month later. The doctor ordered him to take it easy, so I came home from London to help him run his business. My mother spent a lot of time in Athens, doing charity fund-raising. Papa decided to sell his business and join her there. Before he could do it, he had another attack and died.''

"I'm sorry." Leslie knew the words were inadequate, but what else could she say?

"Thanks." He turned toward her, clearing his throat. "I sold the business and kept the orchards. I went back to London only long enough to finish a couple of projects. Then I came here and started my own company, to market fruit and olives throughout the European Community." He shrugged. "It's a living."

"Wait a minute. The house is still in Jason's name. What happened with the resort?"

"An earthquake triggered a rockslide that blocked off the village's main water source. The hotel corporation decided to build elsewhere."

Simon went back to the window. "The irony is that a better spring was discovered later, and it supplies the village with water to this day.

Leslie's thoughts spun back to the evening before. "One thing confuses me. If you had nothing to do with the house deal, why did you accuse me of character assassination?"

His chocolate brown eyes turned black with rage. The overhead light intensified the harsh lines that formed over his nose and along his mouth. He lifted his hands and clenched them into fists so tight the tendons stood out. In an instant he'd changed from a man racked with pain to a man ready to kill.

Leslie drew back, almost falling from the chair. His eyes were hard and cold as an Arctic storm. Simon must have seen her fear. His teeth flashed in a grim smile that made her think of a snarl. "I won't hurt you, Leslie. I realize now you probably never knew."

"Knew what?" she said, eyeing him warily.

He gestured with his hands, extending them toward her as if he wanted to reassure her. But before he touched her, he drew back. "I guess you might as well hear the whole story. It happened later, after my father's death, when my marketing business became successful. A young woman came to my office to apply for a job. She called herself Melanie Clark."

He walked past her and stood at the open window, a dark silhouette. Beyond him, she could see the outline of the trees against the starlit sky, the trees that hid the village from her view. Out on the water, a Kérkira-bound ferry hooted, the forlorn wail carried on the light breeze.

"She had excellent credentials, spoke several languages, knew how to work a computer. I hired her, and the trouble started right away. I don't date people who work with me—I saw how awkward that got when I worked in London. But Melanie kept nagging me to take her out. I finally did, once or twice. After that it got worse. She wouldn't leave me alone.

"I had to fire her. I couldn't work. She was supposed to look after the office when I was out here. But she would lock it up and drive out when I was working in the orchards. Oh, she always had some paper for me to sign or some proposal I was supposed to approve. But they were only excuses. It was her job to take care of these things. And I paid her accordingly. So I gave her notice."

"And instead of trying to kill you, she tried to destroy you," Leslie said. "Hell hath no fury, and all that."

"Yeah. She left quietly enough. Then, the next thing I knew, the police served me with a summons. She said I'd been stalking her and that I beat her when she refused my advances."

Leslie gasped, although she should have expected something like this.

"She even had bruises and a black eye. Don't ask me how she got them. I never laid a hand on her. By that time, I found her completely repulsive. And as if that wasn't enough, she spread a story around that we'd been secretly engaged."

The story he'd told yesterday fell into place with this one. "She was Jason's daughter, wasn't she?" Leslie was surprised to hear the steadiness in her own voice. Inwardly she seethed with a mixture of emotions. Outrage. Sympathy. And that little nagging doubt because she had only his word as to the veracity of the story. A moment ago he had looked more than capable of violence.

"Yes, Melanie was Jason's daughter." His voice was harsh and angry. "Another fact she omitted from her résumé."

"Would it have mattered? Maybe she needed the job and knew about the trouble between Jason and your father. She was afraid you wouldn't consider her."

"Not likely. You didn't know Melanie."

Leslie stifled a rueful smile. It seemed she didn't truly know—or trust—anyone.

"No sooner was I served with a summons to answer charges of sexual harassment and breach of promise," Simon went on, "than Jason charged into the fray. He raged about his innocent daughter and said he was going to sue me for every penny I had. I suddenly saw what was behind it. Money. The local gossip had it that Jason was in debt. Probably true, because he had the house for sale at the time."

Simon clenched his fists at his sides. "It was August, almost two years ago. I went to see Melanie, to try to talk sense into her. She was staying here, at the house. In fact, she might even have stayed here when she worked for me, whenever she came to Platania. I never suspected her connection to Jason."

"You hadn't seen her before? You told me Jason and his first wife lived here for a time."

"When they did, Melanie was away at boarding school in London, and she was a child. No, I didn't know her at all."

"What happened that night?"

He dragged in a long breath. "Jason wasn't around. Melanie met me at the door in a robe, a very sheer robe. Her eyes were wild, and she seemed edgy. She said she didn't like her father's involvement in the situation, and would I settle out of court? I don't know where she got the information, but she seemed to have a good idea of my financial situation and even where I have money invested from my previous job in London. Probably through the computer. It struck me that I'd been set up, likely from the day she walked into my office."

"Did you agree?" Leslie sat on the edge of her chair, her headache forgotten.

"Hell, no. I turned her down flat, said I'd take my chances in court. I walked out, but she followed me. I figured to take a shortcut through Cecil's garden. The next thing I knew, she was running down the stairs toward the beach. It was a hot night, and she was a strong swimmer. I never gave it a thought, and went home. The next morning they found her robe on the beach. They assumed she'd drowned. By noon the story had been embellished to the point that she'd died of unrequited love, or I'd killed her. Either way, I got the full blame."

He stared off into space, his eyes hard and angry. "I never believed she drowned. I think she faked it, and left—her final revenge. She came out the tragic victim and I was left to face the gossip and the accusations."

"What was Jason's reaction to all this?" Leslie asked.

"Jason? He tried one more time to get money from me, but without Melanie's testimony he knew he didn't have a chance in court. He went away for about six or eight months."

"That must have been when we divorced," Leslie said slowly, feeling numb.

Simon paced back toward the table. "He still had the nerve to come back. After your divorce, I guess it must have been. You'd think even a man as thick-skinned as Jason would realize how the villagers resented him. They were angry not only over his cheating my father, but even more because he would have sold the house to build a resort and they didn't know about it. They had a right to know." He spread his hands. "So, Leslie, now you know."

"Yes, now I know," she said bitterly. She didn't doubt for one moment that Jason had been capable of everything that Simon had related. It all fit. His frequent trips away from home. His secretiveness about his business that purportedly traded in antiques. Now she wondered what else he'd traded in on the side. Would she ever know? On the other hand, would it matter if she didn't? She'd already learned more than she wanted to.

"And that's why everyone was looking at me. They were wondering how much like Jason I was."

"It wasn't because of that." Simon stared at her, with all the intensity of an artist about to paint a portrait. When he spoke again, his voice was soft, as if he were talking to himself. "You're really not like her at all. They should have seen it right away."

"Like who?" she said impatiently. "What should they have seen?"

"When you got off the bus, I heard what people said. They thought Melanie had come back."

"Why?"

"She had long blond hair, just like yours."

Leslie clasped her suddenly cold hands together in her lap. "Did she? And I suppose you thought she'd come back to haunt you?"

"Only for a moment. But the villagers watched with great relish. I think they were wondering if I would kill you, too."

"What? Surely they don't think you killed her. Didn't anyone see you walk home that night?"

"According to the police, no. The streets were strangely deserted that night. They hadn't enough evidence to bring charges, but they thought about it. If they'd found a body, and there was any mark on it, I would be living at the convenience and goodwill of the state."

"Oh." She swallowed, tasting the grittiness of dust in her mouth from when the rocks had plunged past her. "So I look like Melanie. Does that mean you thought I might be like her, too, and that's why you spoke the way you did?"

He gave a humorless laugh. "No. Believe me, no. I never mixed you up with Melanie. I knew her better than the villagers did, especially since she thought herself too high-and-mighty to associate with them. You're taller, slimmer, and her eyes were hazel, not misty gray like yours. And she was cute."

"Thanks," Leslie said dryly. Not that she'd ever worried that she wasn't beautiful, but it wasn't very chivalrous of him to point it out so bluntly.

To her surprise, a flush ran up his cheeks. "Leslie, I didn't mean it that way. She was cute in a childish sort of way. You're unique, lovely. With those bones, you'll be gorgeous when you're eighty, after the cute ones like Melanie have fallen apart."

She stemmed the sudden warmth that flooded her heart. Sweet words were all very well, but she had to be practical. "Do you think anyone will ever know for sure what happened to Jason? And to Melanie?"

"No. Because nobody cares. That may sound harsh, but it's the truth. A lot of people here and, I imagine, in other places where Jason did business aren't a bit sorry he's gone." He scowled blackly.

"Before I forget, you haven't seen a strange man around, have you? About my age, a little soft around the middle, brown hair, thinning on top. He's been asking questions about Jason."

Leslie shook her head. "Nobody's been here, that I know of. Unless he was the one who brought the roses."

"I doubt that," said Simon. "He didn't get very far. Several people told him to leave it alone, let the dead rest." He came to stand in front of her, fixing her with a pointed look. "And I'd suggest you do the same. Asking questions won't give you any answers, and you'll just alienate the people who could become your friends."

"That's hardly likely, when I've already got a strike against me," she said coolly. "The assumption that I was part of Jason's schemes."

She hardened herself against the wounded look that came over his face, and added, "Well, you were the first one to do it."

He didn't deny it. Nor did he apologize again. "Don't say I didn't warn you, then."

"I won't." She forced nonchalance into her voice. She should be angry at his presumption to interfere in her life, but instead the intellectual wheels had started rolling. What didn't he want her to know? Sooner or later she'd find out.

She rubbed her hands together briskly. "It's late. Good night, Simon. And thanks for your help."

His keen gaze rested on her a moment too long for comfort. But she managed to keep her eyes locked with his, giving nothing away. He shrugged faintly. "Maybe I'll buy the house from you," he said. "I'd give you a fair price."

Leslie's mouth dropped open. "Buy the house? Why would you want it?"

"Sentiment, perhaps. And it's possible that one of my mother's charities could still use it. If not, with a little promotion I could get rent off it, at least during the summer. And summers are long here."

Leslie snapped her mouth closed, her brow knitting. What was he after now? He couldn't want the house, not after he'd told her what a white elephant it was. Unless that had been the purpose of the story, to bring the price down. Not that she had a clue what a house like this would sell for on Corfu. "The truth is, I'm not sure if the house is mine to sell," she said carefully. "The will hasn't been settled, and the lawyer in charge of it is away."

His smile turned gentle. He tapped her softly on the cheek with one finger. "Are you sure you'll be okay here? You could rent a room in the village."

"I'll be fine." In spite of her fatigue, she lifted her chin. She wasn't going to be driven out of the house that easily. There had to be an explanation for the incidents.

"Okay," he said. "I'll just go through the house and check the windows and doors, and then I'll let you get to bed."

Making a circuit of the house, he found no evidence that anyone had been inside. Leslie followed him through the rooms. "These locks are pretty old," he said. "But it looks like they do the job. That business of the roses bothers me."

"The door was standing open, remember."

"Yeah, but still . . . If I were you, I'd have a locksmith change the locks on the front and back doors."

"I'll see to it in the morning," Leslie said.

"Okay." He unhooked the kitchen key ring. "Just let me check the basement."

He walked into the pantry next to the kitchen and unlocked the heavy wooden door set into the far wall. The door swung smoothly on oiled hinges, as it had yesterday, when Leslie tried it. The stairwell had looked merely uninviting then. Now it was as if an icy wave of musty air rushed up from a dark abyss.

Leslie's heart slammed against her ribs, and she recoiled, cold sweat breaking out on her skin. The cat, who had been supervising their tour of the house, hissed and fell into a defensive crouch, his thick fur bristling.

Leslie stared at him. He felt it, too. That indefinable aura from the basement, almost as if it were warning them to stay away. She edged closer, chiding herself for her runaway imagination. Aura, indeed. It was ridiculous.

"I'll bet no one's been down there since Jason died." Simon took a step toward the stairs.

A shudder ran up Leslie's spine. Without thinking, she grabbed his arm. "No, don't go down there."

## Chapter Five

"What?" Turning his head, Simon stared at her. Leslie looked down at her hand clutching his forearm, and let it slide away, retaining only the impression of soft hairs and hard muscle.

"I'm sorry." She gave a shaky laugh. "I don't know why I did that. Heebie-jeebies, I guess." She stared down the dark stairwell, inhaling the odor of lichen and damp stone. The cold apprehension she'd felt before didn't return. She shook herself, feeling foolish. She'd always been guilty of having an overactive imagination.

"I want to see what made that thud we heard when we came into the house," Simon said, flipping the switch next to him. Light flooded the stairs, banishing the void below them. "There might be a broken window or something and a small animal's gotten in."

They started down. Behind them, the cat meowed plaintively, his demeanor more anxious now than defensive. He didn't follow.

The basement was a cavern formed out of solid stone, Leslie saw as they reached the bottom of the stairs. Only the square corners and straight walls showed that it was man-made, not natural, blasted out of the rocky bluff the house stood on. Wooden partitions divided the huge space into storage rooms and closets.

"Well, you don't have to worry about the foundations collapsing," Simon said wryly. "That stone could withstand any earthquake."

"I see that." Their voices echoed eerily around the room. A rustling sound drew Leslie's attention to a bank of shelves almost hidden in the shadows. Several boxes lay on the stone floor beneath them. One of the sturdy cardboard cartons had split open, spilling greasy machine parts. "That must have been the thud I heard." Leslie frowned. "But what made them fall?"

As if to answer her, a small gray creature scurried away. She jumped back, letting out a little squeal.

"Only a mouse." Simon's mouth curved as he hid a smile. "Nothing to be afraid of."

"A mouse couldn't knock down those boxes."

"Who knows how precariously they were balanced on the shelf? Any little motion could have toppled them."

Moving away from the shelves, he opened a door set into a wooden wall beside him. A light bulb, suspended from a cord in the middle of the ceiling, flared to life. Leslie peered over Simon's shoulder. A great conglomeration of machinery filled the small room, machinery she assumed to be the boiler system that heated bathwater and, in winter, the entire house. He disappeared behind the machinery to check some valve.

The light bulb swayed, making Leslie's shadow waver and loom over her. She glanced around apprehensively, remembering the mindless terror that had assailed her when they opened the basement door.

Beneath her feet, she heard a whispering sound, a hissing sibilance, like voices in the distance. Her skin crawled. Could she be hearing the souls of Melanie, Jason and his parents, lost at sea and forever crying to be freed from their watery prison?

No one's there, she told herself sternly, trying to shake off the fancy. She swallowed to moisten her dry throat, goose bumps breaking out on her skin. Nervously she backed toward the door.

A moment later, she laughed ruefully. The drain in the floor. Water was running under a grate near her feet. The diameter of the hole told her it was probably a storm sewer, or the access point for a sump pump.

Simon emerged from behind the boiler. "Looks fine." He led her out, closing the door behind them. Leslie let out the breath she'd been holding. He eyed her closely. "Are you okay?"

She shivered. "I don't like this place."

"It's the cold and the dampness. You might find it has more appeal some August day when we're having a heat wave."

"Not a chance," she muttered.

Simon grinned. "Let's have a look at the rest of the place while we're here."

They passed what appeared to be more storage rooms. Random drafts ambushed her out of nowhere, making her jumpy. She kept her eyes on Simon's broad back, but even his presence gave her scant comfort. She knew little enough about him. And she'd had enough warnings that she wasn't welcome in the house. What was to stop him from leading her into a secret corner of the cellar and disposing of her?

Get a grip, she rebuked her imagination. But she kept her eyes on the grotesque black shadows that climbed the walls ahead of them. The corners remained secretive, invisible, silent except for the rustling of a few dry leaves that must have drifted in at some point.

Simon paused before a door made of massive oak planks crisscrossed with iron straps. It was closed by an ornate iron handle fitted with a modern dead-bolt cylinder lock. Checking the brand name engraved on the lock, he found the key to open it.

It turned easily, as if it had been oiled yesterday. Simon frowned. "Someone's been taking good care of this."

"Corfu Property Management," Leslie said. "They told me Jason had paid them in January, for the whole year. They had every intention of looking after it unless the lawyer told them otherwise."

Cold air hit them, smelling of old dust and wine, a not-unpleasant yeasty scent. Mixed with it was an indefinable chemical odor. Again Leslie was assailed by a feeling of dread, as if icy fingers were walking up her spine. She wanted to get out of here, out of the dank blackness and into heat and light.

She dismissed the fear, chalking it up to leftover childhood terror of dark closets where monsters lurked. Chiding herself for being a coward, she stood her ground.

Simon groped for a switch, clicking on the inadequate light bulb. Leslie's mouth fell open. Sturdy wooden racks of bottles reached almost to the low ceiling. "Did Jason own all this?"

Stepping forward, Simon took a dusty bottle from the nearest shelf, wiping off the cobwebs with the tail of his T-shirt. He whistled as he read the label. "I'd say it's been in the house for years, probably ever since the winery was operative," he said, carefully returning the bottle to its place in the rack.

A thought struck Leslie, as if her head had collided with one of the oak beams overhead. "If Jason's business wasn't going well, why didn't he sell them? He could have set himself up as a wine merchant. I don't know much about wine, but some of these bottles should be pretty valuable by now, after sitting down here for seventy-five years."

"Some of it's been sitting longer than that," Simon said. "If I remember the old story, the wine cellar existed here before the house was built."

They turned back to the door. "What are those crates?" Leslie asked, pointing to the heavy wooden boxes stacked to the right of the door.

Simon bent close to the nearest box, squinting to read a label in the dim light. "It's blank," he said. "Unless it's been in here so long the printing's faded. In any case, it's probably more wine. They ship it in crates like these."

A dark stain on the floor caught Leslie's attention. She squatted on her heels, running her fingertips over it. Holding them to her nose, she sniffed. The chemical odor she'd noticed before, sharper now. She rubbed her fingers together. "This isn't wine. It looks more like oil."

Simon shrugged. "We'll look again tomorrow. Let's get out of here."

Her feelings exactly. Leslie wiped her hands on a tissue she drew from her pocket and followed him out, waiting while he locked the door.

They were halfway across the cellar when the lights went out.

Leslie let out an involuntary shriek and froze. Was that a new and more sinister rustling she heard from the corners? Nightmare visions rushed through her head, and she swallowed to stifle another scream.

Beside her, she heard a sharp intake of breath. "Damn, why didn't I bring a flashlight?"

"You told me the electricity was fine."

"It was," he said acerbically. "Wait. Listen."

Over their heads, the floorboards creaked, as if feet walked across them. "There can't be anyone up there," Simon whispered, as if he feared they'd be overheard. "Everything was locked."

"Unless someone was in the house all along," Leslie suggested, surprised at her own calm now that her heartbeat had slowed. Or maybe it was the warm strength of his arm around her waist that kept the demons temporarily at bay. "We didn't check the attic."

"No. Have you been up there yet?"

"No. But no one could live up there in the daytime. They'd suffocate. We had a attic like that in Toronto, and it was unbearable in summer. Here it's even hotter."

Simon's arm tightened. "If we go ahead slowly, we should—"

He broke off as the lights flared on, as suddenly as they'd gone off. After a moment of blinking to accustom their eyes to the relative brilliance, they both sprinted for the stairs, pounding up the wooden planks three at a time and emerging breathlessly in the pantry.

There was no one there. And no sign that anyone had been. As if to mock them, the floorboards Simon trod on groaned in complaint.

"Get that electrician to check all the wiring and the fuse box tomorrow," Simon said. He scribbled on the back of an envelope. "That's the locksmith's number. Good night, Leslie."

He unlocked the back door and left. The cat, purring rhythmically, rubbed his sides against Leslie's ankles before he, too, exited the house. She made it a point to lock the door securely, making a mental note to call the locksmith first thing in the morning.

THE ROOM lay dark around her, the night hushed. The crickets had fallen silent. Leslie sat up in bed, her heart pounding. What had awakened her?

She groped in the recesses of memory. A dream. No, not a dream. Some subconscious thought surfacing in her sleep.

The cat lay at her feet. She could feel the warmth of his body. Undisturbed by her restlessness, he slept, giving an occasional snore.

She settled back on the pillows, shivering, and pulled the single sheet over her shoulders, as if a wintry breeze had blown through the room.

The cat.

How had he gotten inside again?

DAWN faintly tinted the sky when she got up. She'd barely slept a wink since she'd awakened in the dead of night. She waited until six before she dialed the number Simon had left with her. Not that she entirely trusted him, but she didn't know anyone else.

Jimmy, the helpful but slightly patronizing cop? No, she couldn't go to him with every fancy, especially since he hadn't gotten back to her about the pellet through her window.

The phone was on its eighth ring. She tapped her foot impatiently. He had to be there. Unless he'd already gone to the orchards to do whatever one did to olives at this time of year.

The ringing was cut off in midnote. She heard a clatter, then a muffled curse. Finally a voice, thick with sleep, grunting something in Greek, or maybe it was English.

"Simon," she said. "Are you there?"

Pause, a pregnant silence. "I'm here," he said at last, his voice hoarse. Another clatter. "It's six in the morning." He didn't sound pleased.

"I know—I'm sorry to wake you. Simon, was the cat out or in when you left last night?"

"How on earth should I know? Don't tell me you phoned at this hour to say you've lost the cat. He took care of himself for years. He'll come back."

"No, you don't understand." She rolled her eyes. "He's here now." She held the receiver close to the cat, and he obligingly meowed, probably because he'd been doing so for the past minute, demanding to be let out. "What I want to know is if he was in or out when you left last night."

There was a brief silence. She could hear the faint ticking of a clock, then a quickly squelched jangle as the alarm rang and he shut it off. "He followed me out, I think." Simon sounded wide-awake now, his voice grim.

A sensation of heat washed through her body, followed by a chill so profound she shuddered. "I thought so. Then how did he get back inside during the night? I locked the door after you—and him." She managed to get the words out through trembling lips.

"It's not necessarily anything to get alarmed about," Simon said reasonably. But under the quiet logic she heard the echo of her own fear. "For all we know, he has his own ways of going in and out."

"Maybe," she conceded.

"You didn't hear any noises in the night, did you?"

"No, except that after I realized someone must have come in to the house in order for the cat to get in, I couldn't sleep a wink. But I didn't hear a thing."

"Okay," Simon said. "Go to Jimmy this morning and tell him everything. I think he'll be in the police station around seven, so you can get that done before the electrician comes. Did you call the locksmith?''

The number. Where had she put it?

As if he'd read her mind, Simon said, "On the kitchen table."

"Just a second. I'll get it." She put down the phone and went into the kitchen. Yes, there it was. She lifted the crystal saltshaker and pulled out a wrinkled paper.

Her eyes widened in horror, and she ran back to the phone, her hand scrabbling for the receiver. It slipped through her sweaty palms and banged against the side of the cabinet on which the phone sat. She could hear Simon yelling something as she picked it up and put it to her ear. "What happened? Did you drop the phone? You nearly broke my eardrum."

"Simon," she said, cutting in. "Someone was in the kitchen."

"What? Are you okay?'' Panic sharpened his voice.

"No. Yes. I'm okay," she said hurriedly. "He's not here now. But he left a note."

"What does it say?"

"It says, 'Locks can't keep me out.'"

Simon burst into a string of curses. Leslie held the receiver away from her ear until he paused for breath. "Leslie, are you there?"

"I'm here."

"Okay. I'm getting up now. I'll call the locksmith. We'll see if locks can keep your intruder out." He hung up.

Leslie pulled the receiver away from her ear and stared at it, exasperated. He was going to drive her crazy. She knew it. Those mercurial moods—he was either scolding her or trying to protect her. And he was definitely not a morning person, although she gathered from the ringing alarm that he forced himself up shortly after six.

She put down the phone and picked up the cat. "Yes, you want to go out, don't you?"

He nuzzled her chin with a cold nose as she opened the back door. She glanced at her watch. Too early to go down to the village. She'd have a look around the garden. Maybe whoever had left the note had also left some footprints.

In the garden, with the house securely locked, she examined the ground outside the living room windows. No sign of footprints, but then, the ground appeared too hard and dry to retain them. She made a studied survey of the ground, but knew it was hopeless. Years of accumulated leaf litter covered any sign that might have been left by a trespasser. But there was no doubt in her mind that someone had been lurking around her house last night—in search of what?

SEVERAL HOURS LATER, in the police station, Leslie was wondering why she'd bothered to take Simon's advice and report the note.

"You say it was wrinkled like this when you found it?" Jimmy asked, regarding the threatening message.

"Yes, just like that," Leslie said.

Frowning, Jimmy turned the ragged sheet of paper over in his hands. "Looks as if it was stuffed in somebody's pocket."

"What are you going to do about it?"

"It was probably the same mischievous teens who shot that pellet through the window. Still, I'll have someone go by the house after dark, check that there's no one in the garden. Once you change the locks, the house will be secure."

Leslie stared at him. "That's all?"

Jimmy steepled his fingers before his nose. "Mrs. Adams, this note is likely a prank. And you have to understand that the roses you got yesterday are probably perfectly innocent. We Greeks like to welcome visitors."

"Not me. They don't want me here, because of Jason."

"Jason is dead. Has anyone been unfriendly to you?"

"No, but they haven't gone out of their way to be friendly, either." Except Simon, she added silently. And maybe he had his own ax to grind.

"They're sizing you up," Jimmy said complacently. "You'll see. In a few days they'll be bringing you food or inviting you for dinner."

"Well, my neighbor Eugenia invited me for tea. This afternoon."

"There you have it." Jimmy stood up. "We'll keep our eyes and ears open. If there is the slightest suspicion that somebody severely resents you, we'll have a word with him. With new locks, anyone who had a key before won't be able to come in. You'll be safe. And, of course, you can call me if you're the least bit afraid."

Dissatisfied but not knowing what else she could do, Leslie thanked him, shaking the hand he offered. At the door, she turned. "By the way, has anyone been around inquiring about Jason?"

Jimmy shook his head. "Not that I know of."

BY LATE AFTERNOON, the electrician had checked the wiring and pronounced it sound. He'd found a scorched wire in the front hall switch, and replaced it. "A small short, probably from a loose connection. It should have tripped the fuse, but these things happen sometimes," he explained in careful English.

"What about the lights going out in the basement?"

He shrugged. "I found nothing wrong. It could have been a general power failure. We get those quite frequently, since the electricity grid that covers the island is old and in need of updating."

Leslie paid him, and the locksmith who had just finished. "I'll have to give a set of keys to Corfu Property Management," the man said, "since they're still the official caretakers of the house."

"How do you know that?" Leslie asked in surprise.

"I do other work for them," the man said. "Here's my card. If you check with them before you leave, they'll probably reimburse you for the expense."

"That's fine," Leslie said, slightly uneasy about not having all the keys in her possession.

Upstairs, giving her face a quick wash before her appointment with Eugenia, she wondered why Simon hadn't come by. But then, he wasn't her keeper. She guessed he figured that by sending the locksmith he'd completed his duty.

EUGENIA'S GARDEN was a riot of flowers, in contrast to Leslie's, which contained mainly shrubs and trees in every shade of green imaginable. Leslie inhaled the heady perfume of the blossoms as she walked up the gravel path.

A raucous wolf whistle made her laugh. "Pretty Baby, Pretty Baby." She scanned the gingerbread-trimmed veranda. There he was, sitting on a swaying jasmine that draped a trellis, his beady eyes impudent. The fragrance from the tiny white blossoms filled the air. The bird fluttered his wings and pecked at his perch. A moment later, an object dropped with a clatter at Leslie's feet.

She picked it up. A gold charm bracelet.

Eugenia came bustling out of the house. "Hello, Leslie. I'm glad you could come." She noticed the bracelet in

Leslie's hand. "So that's where it is. I've been looking for it."

She crossed the veranda, and shook her finger at the mynah bird. "Bad Baby. How did you get out?"

"Out," Baby echoed. He obediently hopped onto her shoulder, falling for the bribe she offered, a slice of orange. She stroked a gentle hand over the bird's ebony feathers. "He's a wild thing at heart, doesn't like his cage, and I think he's found a way to unlatch the door. I'm sure I fastened it."

"I don't mind if he comes over to see me," Leslie said.

"I can't let him get into the habit of flying off all the time. He's bound to get lost." She returned the bird to his cage in the front hall, firmly closing the little door and twisting the intricate latch. "There you go, Baby. You can take a nap."

Baby squawked rudely. "Out."

"Not out." Eugenia laughed. "Sometimes I swear he understands everything I say." She hooked her hand into Leslie's elbow. "Come into the living room and sit down, while I fetch the teapot from the kitchen."

Leslie wandered around the room, looking at the numerous family photographs displayed on cloth-covered tables and hanging on the walls. On the grand piano, an ebony monster gleaming in the corner of the room, stood more photos, of Eugenia accompanied by various people in evening dress. Leslie picked one up, staring at a familiar face she couldn't quite put a name to. She glanced down, saw the autograph.

A pleasure as always, Placido Domingo.

The clatter of cutlery told her Eugenia had come back. "You're a singer," Leslie said, with more than a little awe.

"You're famous."

"Retired now, my dear," Eugenia said, smoothing her blouse over her ample bosom. "But I had some grand times."

Eugenia related amusing stories about her career, and Leslie found herself relaxing. But a subtle tension returned when Eugenia fixed her bright black eyes, eyes that were so like the mynah's, on her. "I hear you've been talking to Jimmy the Cop. No, you don't have to give me that look. Everyone calls him that."

Leslie set down her teacup so abruptly it rattled in the saucer. "I found a threatening note in my house this morning."

Eugenia's eyes widened. "You don't say."

"Yes, but I changed the locks today, so that should solve the problem, according to Jimmy. You've been here a while. You wouldn't know who had keys besides Jason and Corfu Property Management?"

Eugenia shook her head. "No. And I offered to look after the place, you know, just keep an eye on things, whenever Jason was away. But he turned me down—rather smartly, I might add. Said he liked his privacy and didn't want his keys spread around."

"That sounds like Jason," Leslie said gloomily. "Did you know him well?"

"As well as anybody, I suppose. He came and went over the years, but we didn't talk often. Of course, I was away a lot of the time until I retired, after my dear husband died." Eugenia picked up the pot and offered more tea. "So tomorrow you're having dinner with old Weatherby."

Leslie frowned. "I hope he hasn't forgotten."

Eugenia made an inelegant noise. "He won't. He has an eye for a pretty lady. But watch out for him. He has moods. And that nasty little dog of his is going to kill Baby one day. If I don't get it first."

Leslie leaned back in her chair. "Funny thing...he told me his dog is afraid of your bird. What about the cat that lives at my house? He hasn't been a bother, has he?"

"That gray tom? No, he's never a bother. I sometimes let him into my cellar to get rid of mice."

Leslie grimaced wryly. "I wish I could get him down in my basement. I've got mice there, too, but he won't go in there."

"Too dark and gloomy, probably," Eugenia said. "I understand there's a well-stocked wine cellar down there."

"Yes, I've seen it." Leslie hesitated, then plunged on. "You didn't bring me roses yesterday, did you?"

Eugenia frowned. "No, but it could have been one or another of the villagers. To welcome you."

"That's what Jimmy said. So I've got people welcoming me and people telling me to leave."

"Are you planning to stay long?" Eugenia didn't look at her, and her fingers picked at a loose thread in the poppy-patterned skirt she wore.

Was there some hidden meaning behind the question? Leslie couldn't put her finger on it, but somehow a faint tension shimmered in the room. "However long it takes until the lawyer contacts me about the will. I can arrange a further leave of absence from my job if I have to. I need to find out more about Jason's death."

"It was an accident," Eugenia said abruptly. "Leave it at that."

Leslie stared at her, but Eugenia got up and went to the kitchen, returning a moment later with a kettle of hot water that she used to top up the teapot. Leslie finished her tea, lost in thought. Two people had warned her to leave the subject of Jason's death alone. Did that mean what Simon had said it did, that no one was likely to mourn Jason? Or did it mean they knew more than they were telling, something they didn't want her to know?

HER MIND CHURNING, Leslie escaped as soon as she could, cutting into her own yard through the prickly wall of cypresses. She barely noticed the astringent scent of the needles, and carelessly brushed off those that clung to her shirt.

Pushing open the kitchen door, she nearly fell over the cat, which had somehow gotten shut up inside. He gave a pained yowl and stalked off into the garden, tail twitching in annoyance. She sent a silent apology after him as she closed and locked the door.

In the hall, she felt a draft. Going into the living room, she found a window open. She leaned out over the sill. It was too high for a person to climb up, but the shrubbery below would no doubt support the weight of the cat. A measure of relief flowed through her. That must be how the cat had gotten in and out.

The relief ebbed, leaving behind new worry. It didn't explain how the window had gotten open. She was sure she'd closed all the windows before going to Eugenia's.

The wind was rising, and ominous clouds were banked on the horizon, tinted deep purple and scarlet by the lowering sun. At the edge of the garden, the gray-green leaves of an ancient olive made a faint clicking sound, as if a skeleton walked. She shivered. A storm coming? Or just her imagination?

She pulled the window shut, sliding the latch into place. It was a little loose. Maybe it hadn't locked properly and the wind had swung the casement window open.

Thoughtfully she walked upstairs and turned on the taps in the huge claw-footed bathtub, pouring in a generous amount of gardenia-scented bath salts. Running back downstairs while it filled, she loaded a plate with crackers and cheese and picked up the book she'd been reading at odd moments.

Pulling the shower curtain around the bath to preserve the steam, she settled into the hot water with a sigh of contentment. The wind rattled around the eaves, and a loose shutter banged on the far side of the house. Storm coming, for sure. But she was safe. The new locks would keep intruders out, and she'd double-checked the windows.

She munched on crackers and let her mind drift.

Thunder suddenly boomed, making her jump. Rain or, more likely, hail pattered against the window. Leslie closed her eyes. She'd stay only a moment longer. The water had cooled, and by now the cat was probably scratching at the door, demanding to be let in.

Her mind was floating drowsily on the edge of sleep when a hand reached around the curtain and grabbed her ankle.

# Chapter Six

She had only enough time to register that the hand wore a thin black leather glove before she found herself slipping violently beneath the surface of the water. Gardenia-scented bathwater shot up her nose, cutting off her breath. The room turned dark and spun crazily around her.

As she sank toward a black whirlpool of oblivion, some lucid part of her mind told her to fight. The urge to open her mouth and gasp for breath was almost overwhelming. Clamping her lips tightly together, she clung to the last shreds of consciousness.

The slickness of the bath salts saved her life. That, and the fact that the taps were mounted on the long side of the tub, rather than at the opposite end to where she'd been sitting.

Her clawing hands latched on to the tap and she hung on, at the same time flipping her body over and away from her assailant. The hand slid off her foot, a great wave washed over the side of the tub, and she was free.

The lights went out.

Gasping, choking, Leslie rested her head against the plastic hose that fed the shower nozzle. She coughed; it was a strangled retching that hammered at the top of her head. Her throat and the back of her nose felt raw, as if she'd inhaled acrid smoke. She swallowed hard, tasting gardenias, and held her breath.

She heard nothing except her own frantic heartbeat. Was he out there, crouching in the dark, waiting to try again? If he did, she would have no defense.

Fighting against her rising panic, she exhaled and pressed her hand to her chest. Her ragged breathing seemed to fill the dark room.

Cautiously she hooked a toe around the edge of the shower curtain, at the same time dragging the towel, now half-soaked, off the side of the tub. She wrapped it around her body and sat up, using her foot to maneuver the vinyl curtain out of the way.

There was enough light from the hall to show her the room was empty. The door stood ajar, indicating how the intruder had left. She'd closed it when she got into the bath. Not that it would have kept anyone out, since the privacy latch was broken.

She lifted her head, her nostrils flaring as an alien scent hit her senses. The gardenia scent from her bath pervaded the room, but she could smell an underlying odor— after-shave or perfume.

Again, dizziness buzzed in her ears. She shook her head to clear it. Pulling the plug, she stood up, reaching for another towel off the rack. She dried herself hurriedly, and put on the thick robe that an hour ago had seemed too heavy for the warm evening.

Sitting down on the edge of the tub, she clutched the robe closed, shivering as if it were the middle of winter. Her breath hitched in her throat, and she coughed wretchedly.

She got up and turned on the light. Opening the tap, she splashed her face with water and drank from her cupped palm. Her teeth clattered together and she clenched her jaw. A jolt of pain shot up her temple.

Leaning on the edge of the sink, she closed her eyes to shut out the image of her white face and wild, tormented eyes.

Had she fallen asleep and dreamed that black hand reaching for her? She was sure she'd been awake, thinking about letting the cat in.

The cat. Her legs trembled so violently that she could hardly stand. Hanging on to the smooth wooden banister, she crept down the stairs, moving slowly, as if her joints had aged and stiffened.

She flipped on every light switch she passed as she crossed the front hall, peered into the living room and entered the kitchen. There was no one in the house.

The back door was locked. She heard a faint meow, and opened it a crack. The cat slid inside, then stopped, growling faintly. He sniffed the air, then set his nose against the floor and trotted a few steps toward the living room.

Leslie's foot slipped as she went after him. She looked down. There were wet marks on the marble floor, like footprints, although on the glossy surface no tread pattern was visible. Relief washed through her. She hadn't dreamed it. She should have thought to check before she let the cat in. The bathroom floor had been awash with water. Her assailant must have stepped in it.

She went back to the stairs. Yes, there, too, faint wet marks, rapidly evaporating. But not much use, since they were just that, wet patches. The man must have been wearing smooth-soled shoes.

If the intruder was a man. Come to think of it, all she'd seen was a black glove, and that only for a second. It didn't take much strength to pull an unsuspecting person under water. She'd seen a movie once, one of those thrillers shown at two in the morning for insomniacs. If you pulled the legs of a person sitting in a bathtub, water rushed up her nose and she could be unconscious in seconds. And dead in minutes, if no one lifted her out of the water. Foolproof murder. It would look as if she had fallen asleep in the bath and drowned; who would suspect foul play?

Going into the living room, she yanked the curtains closed across the windows. She paced around the room, her movements jerky and agitated. Digging her fingers into the rough terry of her robe, she hugged her arms around her waist. Would she ever feel warm again? Or safe?

As if to mock her, something thudded in the basement, barely audible above a roll of thunder. Well, she wasn't going down there again, not by herself.

The cat trotted at her heels, his steps quick and nervous. Something—the storm, the intruder, or her own tension—had affected him. The fur stood out around his neck like an Elizabethan ruff. She missed his purr; the sound would have been comforting, normal.

Her assailant had left awfully fast. He hadn't checked to make sure she was dead. In fact, he had to have known she was not. Her rasping breathing must have been audible outside the bathroom.

Nor had he made a second attempt to drown her, and he'd quickly doused the lights.

All this pointed to two possibilities. The first was that the entire episode had been staged to scare her, not to kill her. The second was that he'd been afraid he wouldn't succeed once he lost the element of surprise.

In any case, he'd been careful she couldn't identify him. Which meant she must know him, or was apt to run into him in the village.

She frowned. That might or might not narrow down the number of suspects. She had to start with those she knew, repugnant as that might seem. Still, how well did she know any of these people? She had to start thinking as a criminal would.

"Simon." She said it aloud in the empty room. The cat, marginally calmer now, meowed inquiringly. Rain no longer drummed on the windows, and the thunder had subsided to a faraway mutter.

Could Simon be behind all the incidents? He'd had opportunity, although she couldn't see how he'd have gotten in through the locked doors and windows tonight.

Still, someone had. And Simon had motive, she thought, remembering the accusations he'd flung at her the first evening. Of course, he'd backed down on that, but how did she know he was sincere?

On the other hand, he'd cleaned her wounds and checked the house. She remembered the concern in his dark eyes. No, it couldn't be Simon. In any case, he would have succeeded. He was easily strong enough to overpower her.

Unless he hadn't wanted to leave bruises... Forget that. If she continued like this, she'd really be paranoid.

What about Eugenia? She was friendly, and the only person Leslie had met who didn't seem to be hiding anything. Except earlier—what had they been talking about? Oh, yes, Jason's death. Eugenia had reiterated what everyone so far had said, that it was an accident. Had her manner been too vehement?

Perhaps her friendliness was an act to put Leslie off her guard. An opera singer had to be a pretty fair actor.

Leslie rested her forehead against the nearest wall. This was getting her nowhere.

She paced some more, pausing at the empty fireplace. It was laid with wood, gnarled roots she thought might be from olive trees, neatly stacked on a tent of paper and kindling.

Cecil. The idea of the frail old man as a suspect was ludicrous. Why would he want to harm her? He could have ignored her; he didn't have to invite her for dinner. He was lonely and wanted to be a good neighbor.

But he'd acted weird about Jason, too.

Come to think of it, everyone she'd talked to acted weird about Jason and his accident.

She sank down on the sofa, covering her face with her hands. Despair washed over her. Why had she even come here? It had been an insane idea from the beginning. She must have been crazy to think she would find out anything about Jason's death. Or his life.

And why should she even care?

The phone rang.

Dimly she heard the noise jangle through the room, flailing her already raw nerves.

She grabbed the receiver. "Yes?" Glancing at her watch, she noticed with surprise that it was only a little after ten. Early by Corfu standards.

"Leslie?"

She closed her eyes. Simon. Hadn't she been through enough this evening?

"Leslie, are you all right?"

She found her voice. "No, I'm not all right!" she yelled. "I don't know if I'll ever be all right again! This place is making me crazy!"

He didn't say anything for a moment, but she felt his shock at her outburst as if he'd telegraphed it over the wires. "Leslie," he said in a shaken voice, "are you alone?"

"Yes," she whispered, beginning to tremble again. She had to trust him. She had to trust somebody.

"I'm coming right over." She heard a curt click and the buzz of an empty line.

As if drawn by a magnet, she focused on the fireplace. Yesterday, had the fire been laid? She couldn't remember, but somehow the picture in her mind was that of a black, empty space between the bricks.

She pressed her fingers into her forehead, trying to subdue the ache behind her eyes. Never mind. She would ask Simon. He might remember.

It took him less than five minutes. Gravel crunched under his tires as he braked in the driveway. His footsteps scuffed on the flagstones, and then he hammered on the door. "Open up. Leslie, it's me."

Running to the door, she jerked it open. He practically fell into the front hall. He recovered at once, kicked the door closed behind him and grasped her upper arms. His dark gaze searched her face. She felt the heat of his palms and wanted nothing so much as to lean her face against his chest and pretend she was safe.

She couldn't afford to indulge this fantasy. New despair filled as she realized she didn't even know if she could trust Simon.

SHE WAS ALARMINGLY WHITE, Simon thought, obviously scared. But she wasn't in hysterics, and in her eyes, along with the fear, he saw resolution. That grit and toughness he'd sensed in her from their first meeting controlled her panic.

Twisting the dead bolt into place on the door, he steered her into the living room. He wanted to fold her into his arms and hold her, keep her safe from harm. He firmly reined in the impulse. The tension in her body, and the way she quickly freed herself from his hands, told him she would resist any further closeness.

He felt torn, just as he had yesterday. He wanted to protect her, but it wasn't likely that she would let him. And he wasn't sure whether it was just him she was rejecting or if she mistrusted men in general. Not that he blamed her. Living with Jason had probably reinforced in her mind the belief that men were liars who could not be depended on.

And didn't he have his own agenda? He hadn't been honest with her, either. Deep down he would just as soon see her leave the house and Platania, and let him get on with his own search into Jason's past.

Jason owed him. And if he was still alive, Simon was determined to make him pay.

He'd been willing to let it drop, but Leslie had shown up. And the almost simultaneous appearance of Harlan Gage—he'd found out his name from the inn register— pointed to the need to question more closely what Jason had been up to.

Oh, he was certain Leslie knew little or nothing about Jason's activities immediately prior to his "death." He suspected she was an innocent pawn who already regretted coming to Platania.

Well, he hoped she'd leave now. She was already in danger and would be in more soon, unless he missed his guess.

Briefly he entertained the thought that Harlan Gage was behind the harassment. Or maybe Jason himself, in hiding somewhere close by after faking his death. One thing was certain, Gage hadn't gone to the police with his questions. A word with Jimmy had told Simon that much.

"What happened tonight?" he asked, sinking down onto a chair. "You'd better sit, too, before you fall down."

She moved to another chair across the room, letting herself collapse onto the dusty upholstery as if she'd been cut off at the knees. "Someone was in the house," she said, twisting her fingers together.

The cat sniffed at Simon's ankles. He scooped him up, strode over to Leslie and dropped him on her lap. "Here, you'll feel better. Since you won't let me touch you."

Leslie stared at him, piqued by the sardonic note in his voice. But he was right; the soft texture of the cat's fur, lying flat now, comforted her. Especially when the creature began to purr.

She wrinkled her brow. Didn't that indicate that Simon wasn't her assailant? The cat had growled at the footprints. He had welcomed Simon.

She almost groaned aloud. She was really going crazy, using a cat's judgment to decide whether she could trust someone.

"Tell me what happened," he said, his voice so gentle her heart flipped in her chest. He couldn't be the person who was trying to drive her away from this place. Haltingly, she told him everything that had happened since she'd returned from Eugenia's.

"You didn't call Jimmy," Simon said when she'd finished.

"No. I wasn't sure he'd believe me." Her voice rose. "But I saw the black glove. And the wet footprints. And the cat acted strange, too. He knew someone had been here."

"You couldn't see how he got out by following the footprints?"

Leslie shook her head. "No. By the time I noticed them, they were almost dry. There were some in the kitchen and in here and, of course, on the stairs. Besides, it had been raining, so it would've been hard to tell if he'd made them coming or going. There were no tread marks. That's all I could see."

He sat with one ankle resting on the opposite knee. The soles of his gray leather loafers were smooth, but the heels showed a pattern of small circles around the edge. He followed her gaze to his feet. "I know what you're thinking," he said, smiling thinly. "They could have been mine. They also could have been any of several hundred shoes in the village."

He dropped the foot to the floor and leaned forward, clasping his hands loosely between his knees. "Leslie, why did you come here?"

"I had to find out about Jason. When I got the lawyer's letter saying he was dead, I knew he'd lied to me. About a lot of things. And the lawyer indicated I may be Jason's only heir."

"How convenient," Simon said.

"What do you mean?" she asked suspiciously, although she couldn't tell whether his tone was sarcastic or not. "I didn't know about any of this, and I didn't ask for it. For all I know, he owes everybody in the country and the house is mortgaged to the hilt and I'll be stuck with it all."

"That's possible, knowing Jason."

Leslie eyed him sharply. "Is that supposed to make me feel better?"

Simon stood up and walked to the window, twitching back the curtain to look out for an instant. He exhaled sharply. "No, it's supposed to make you feel like going home."

Leslie groaned. "Not you, too. I was hoping you could help me. To be honest, I don't know if I can trust you, but I'm sure I can't trust anyone else."

"No high recommendation, I see." He came over and crouched before her, covering her hands with his own. Under them, the cat flexed and stretched, then slid off Leslie's lap and sat in the middle of the floor. "Leslie, I believe someone is trying to scare you, maybe even kill you. It's not safe. Go back to Athens. I'll see if I can find out what's going on with this house and what Harlan Gage wants. I'll let you know."

"Harlan who?"

"The man I mentioned yesterday. He stayed at the inn a couple of nights ago. He was around again today. By this time he must know about this house and that you're here. And he hasn't been to the police, so I suspect he's probably either an old friend of Jason's, or an old enemy."

Leslie pulled her hands free, liking his touch far too much. She couldn't think when he was so close, his dark chocolate eyes opaque with worry. She got up and paced to the fireplace, laying her arm along the mantel. She had to get away from his potent presence for a moment. Not that she was complaining—he'd managed to distract her from her earlier panic.

Simon regarded her thoughtfully. What was he going to do about her? She was in danger and he didn't know who was behind it. She certainly wasn't going to invite him to move in so that he could keep an eye on her.

"I'd like to check your bathroom, and the other rooms upstairs." At least he could reassure himself that there was no one still in the house.

She nodded, climbing the stairs ahead of him. "I haven't heard anything up here since it happened. I'm sure he's gone."

Simon looked in the bathroom. The air smelled faintly of gardenias. No one lurked behind the shower curtain. The tub was empty, the floor still wet where water had splashed out of it.

He went back into the hall. Leslie stood in the doorway of her room. At the sight of her, his stomach lurched. She had an odd, newly distraught look on her face, and her mouth trembled. "My room—someone's been there."

To his horror, her face crumpled and tears filled her eyes. Leaning against the doorframe, she buried her face in her hands. "Someone searched my room," she said between sobs.

Simon wrapped his arms around her and held her tightly. Her body felt slight and fragile against his. An unexpected tenderness tightened his throat. Even through the terry robe he could feel the delicate bones of her spine. Her breasts pressed against his chest, small, soft mounds.

Sucking in a breath, he realized her hands were no longer clenched in front of her. She clung to his waist with a strength that astonished him, as if she were drowning. As perhaps she was, reliving the episode in the bath.

He balled one hand into a fist. If he caught the person terrorizing her . . .

She stiffened as if she'd just realized where she was. Peeling one arm away from his waist, Leslie pressed her hand against his chest, as if to push away.

"Don't," he whispered. "Stay. I won't let anyone hurt you."

She gave a shaky laugh. "What about you? Will you hurt me, Simon?"

"No promises. But I haven't been in the house except by your invitation."

Abruptly she moved away. To his surprise, her eyes flashed angrily as she paced around the room. "I'm not going to let anyone drive me out. Jimmy said he'll keep an eye on the house, but obviously my tormentor knows how to avoid the police. So I'm going to have to take my own precautions."

"Move out," Simon suggested. "You can stay with me."

"I need to be here," she said stubbornly. "I need to check out all of the house, find out what else Jason was hiding."

"Leslie, come here," Simon said softly.

Her eyes met his, saw the gentleness there. Unable to help herself, she stepped forward into his arms. Against his chest, she allowed herself to relax, rubbing her fingers back and forth on his shirt. Through the thin cotton she could feel the roughness of his chest hair, the hard curve of the underlying muscle, the heat of his skin. She also felt him stiffen, felt the comfort he'd offered change to a darker, more primitive emotion.

Simon took her hand in his. She thought he was about to push her away, but he merely held it. His palm was hard and callused. Absently she rubbed her thumb over the raised scar of some old injury.

"Leslie." His voice was low, a whisper that seemed one with the night.

Leslie looked up into his face, saw the dark heat in his eyes. She knew what he wanted without his asking, and was torn between anticipation and terror.

He lowered his head, and she held her breath as his mouth covered hers. His kiss was seduction itself. His mouth was firm, neither reticent nor predatory. She parted her lips, her hands clutching his shirt. He explored her teeth with his tongue, gently requesting entrance. "Leslie, open your mouth." His breath feathered her skin, the sensitive inner lining of her mouth.

This couldn't go on. Her heartbeat hammering in her ears, Leslie shook her head and unclenched her hands, taking a step back. "No. Don't."

Her skin felt hot, too tight for her body, and her nipples stung as though burned. She was grateful for his hands on her shoulders, afraid her trembling knees would collapse and drop her ignominiously at his feet.

"Why not?" he said, so calmly he might have been discussing the weather.

"Because I don't play games."

His hands tensed. "It's not a game. I wanted to kiss you, and I did."

"We hardly know each other." Her voice was ragged, her breathing rapid and shallow. And she knew she lied.

"You wanted it, too," he added.

Her nostrils flared with temper, an anger ignited by her confusion. "Did I? If I did, it was because I'd had a scare. Don't take advantage of that."

Abruptly he released her, so quickly she lost her balance and almost fell. He steadied her with one hand, then let go as if he'd scorched his fingers. Raking his hair back from his face, he turned away. "Hell!"

Grinding his teeth, he fought for control, not even sure why he was angry. Maybe because she was right. He *had* taken advantage of her momentary weakness.

"It worked, didn't it?" he said tightly. "You forgot you were scared. You don't seem to realize that you're an attractive woman."

He turned abruptly away. "Go downstairs while I check your room."

In her room, he found the sheets lying in a heap beside the bed. Clothes still hung in the wardrobe, but her suitcase was upside down next to it. The dresser drawers all hung open, and the garments they had once held were strewn on the floor. He picked up a lacy bikini. The silk clung to his hand. Was this what she wore under her conservative clothes?

He rebuked the desire that coiled in his stomach. This wasn't the time to indulge it. Or to admit to the need that shook him when he was close to her.

He checked the French doors. Closed and locked. Just to be safe, he looked in all the upstairs rooms, with their empty cupboards and stripped beds. Nothing. Not a trace of an intruder.

Leslie sat huddled on the sofa, her eyes red and swollen. Her fingers twitched nervously, shredding a damp tissue. She looked up at him, a question in her eyes.

"No, there's no one there. And everything's locked."

She nodded. "I'm sorry."

"For what?"

"I—I think I gave you the wrong impression." The words spilled out in a rush.

He walked over to her and drew her to her feet, lifting her chin with his forefinger. "I'm not sorry I kissed you. And I don't play games, either. But I'm not going to deny that I'm attracted to you."

He pulled her against him. Sliding one hand down her back, he pressed her hips close to his. "You've been married. You understand when a man wants you. I want you." The cool green-apple scent of her hair filled his nostrils, his being.

"Yes, Leslie, I want you," he repeated when she remained silent. "And now, what the hell are we going to do about it?"

WHEN LESLIE WOKE the next morning, the episode with
Simon seemed like a dream. She remembered giving him
a look that she'd hoped was quelling but that probably
had conveyed only her uncertainty. She'd pushed him out
the door as quickly as possible, brushing off his offers to
spend the night, or to send a policeman to guard the
house. "The intruder won't come back," she said, hoping she wasn't just trying to reassure herself. "And if he
does, I'll be ready for him."

She'd double-checked the locks on all the doors and
windows, left a light on downstairs and gone up to bed.
As an added precaution, she had wedged a chair under the
doorknob in her bedroom and locked the French doors
leading to the balcony.

To her surprise, she'd slept well, long and dreamlessly.

The rising sun slanted into the room, illuminating one
of the ornate plaster cherubs that graced the corners of the
ceiling. Leslie licked her lips, tasting Simon on them,
which was absurd, since she had thoroughly brushed her
teeth before going to bed. The cherub smirked, the tiny
arrow in the bow he held pointed directly at her.

"Oh, go away," she muttered. She hated the four
plump creatures, with their knowing smiles and their eyes
that seemed to follow every move she made.

The faint scent of wood smoke drifted past her nostrils. She glanced at the door. The chair still stood braced
against it. She buried her face in the pillow, wishing she
could stay in bed instead of facing Simon, who would
undoubtedly show up right after breakfast. When he left
last night, he'd promised to come back to check her cellar again.

What could she say to him? She'd acted like an af-
fronted virgin, while he'd treated the episode with ma-

ture honesty. He didn't play games, he'd said. Which meant he truly was attracted to her.

What was wrong with that? Plenty, she thought savagely. She'd just recently ended a relationship that hadn't left her eager for another. She was doing just fine on her own.

A pair of mourning doves cooed in the huge fig tree outside her window, their gentle *hoo-hoo* mocking her. Knowing she wouldn't sleep any longer, she pushed aside the light blanket and sat up. There wasn't time for Simon's flirtation, no matter how good it felt to be held tightly to that hard, lean, male body. Her eyes softened briefly as she straightened the bed. He had the ability to make her feel like a desirable woman, and that was what made him dangerous.

The smell of smoke was stronger. Turning her head, she looked at the French doors. They were closed, but the lace curtain stirred faintly, and she remembered a small crack in the glass. Someone must be burning brush outside.

Outside?

Fireplace. The image of kindling on the hearth leaped into her head. Had someone started the fire? And if the chimney was blocked, the house could be filled with smoke.

She jumped out of bed and ran to the door.

# Chapter Seven

Leslie kicked aside the chair and flung open the door, remembering too late that she should have checked it first for heat. The hall was clear, smelling only of the musty potpourri used in the linen cupboard opposite her room.

She ran back inside to the French doors and stepped out on the balcony. The crisp morning air enveloped her with the fragrance of jasmine and wood smoke.

Down the slope toward the village, she saw a thin blue wisp rising from a stone chimney visible through the trees. An unseen donkey brayed, a raucous sound like a creaking gate. On the patio, the cat rolled over in the sun, his paws kneading the air like a kitten's.

She laughed. The serenity of the scene filled her with sheer relief and a sense of euphoria she couldn't—didn't want to control.

She laughed out loud, shuffling her feet in a little dance. In daylight, last night's events seemed unreal, as if they'd happened to someone else.

The storm the night before had taken the edge off the heat. Leslie filled a bowl with cornflakes and milk and took it out to the patio to eat. The little table was pockmarked with rust and the cane seats of the chairs were unraveling, but the fresh air and the exotic scent of the garden made up for these deficiencies.

The cat lay in sprawling slumber next to the back step. When Leslie walked past him, he got up, stretched, shook himself to settle his coat and meowed inquiringly. She set a saucer of milk before him and, after a suspicious sniff, he began to lap it up.

Footsteps crunched on the gravel as Simon, dressed in work boots, a yellow T-shirt and ancient jeans bleached almost white, strode around the corner.

"Last night you drove. Today you walked. How far away do you live?" Leslie said by way of greeting.

"I've been checking kiwi vines," he said, pulling out a chair and sitting down. "The top end of my property borders on the street out there."

"And where were you yesterday, when the electrician came?" She'd been too distraught last night to mention it. "I thought you wanted to talk to him."

"Unexpected business in Corfu." He grinned, and his eyes warmed. The memory of the kiss they'd shared hung between them like a sensual perfume. Cheeks hot, Leslie looked down, fidgeting with her spoon. "Why, did you miss me?" he added slyly.

"In your dreams," she retorted, embarrassed that he had probably read her thoughts.

He laughed. "You must have had a good night. No more disturbances?"

"Nothing."

"Was anything missing from your room?"

"Not that I can see."

Simon frowned. "Then what were they looking for? Leslie, are sure you're telling me everything?" He made an impatient sound. "How can I help you if you're not honest with me?"

''Why should you help me?''

''Somebody has to. It might as well be me.''

She lifted her chin, pushing aside the uncomfortable reminder that last night she'd been grateful for his help. ''I can take care of myself. I was just upset last night. I overreacted. This morning it seems stupid.''

His expression didn't alter. ''What about the bathtub thing? Someone tried to drown you.''

''Well, they didn't succeed, did they?'' she said tartly. ''Maybe they just wanted to scare me. It's just too crazy. Why would anyone want to harm me?''

''That's a good question,'' Simon said, getting to his feet. ''And I'd like an answer.''

Leslie carried her bowl into the kitchen and put it in the sink. A knock sounded on the front door. Simon strode through the hall and opened it. The glare of sunlight dazzled Leslie's eyes, and she saw only the silhouette of a man.

''Mr. Gage, I presume,'' Simon said, in his best sarcastic tone.

''Who are you?'' the man asked, standing his ground. ''I was told Mrs. Adams is staying here.''

''What do you want with her?'' Simon said belligerently.

''I'd like to talk with her. About her late husband, with whom I had business dealings.''

''Jason's dead. Mrs. Adams has never had anything to do with his business, so she can't help you. Good day.'' Simon turned away, starting to close the door.

Enough of this, Leslie thought. She squeezed past Simon and addressed the man who stood outside. He was neatly dressed in a tan summer-weight suit and a linen fedora. Under the brim his face was pale, his eyes in shadow.

"How may I help you?" Leslie asked. "I'm Leslie Adams."

The man smiled and extended his hand. "I'm so pleased to meet you. My name is Harlan Gage. Please accept my condolences on your husband's unfortunate demise."

His hand felt damp, his fingers limp. Leslie let go, hiding her distaste. His oily smile and polished words were no doubt meant to instill trust in her. It wasn't working. She'd run into plenty of people in her life who were perfectly polite on the surface but stabbed you as soon as your back was turned.

She simply didn't trust Mr. Gage. He was too smooth, his clipped accent too perfect, as if he'd gone to speech school. Not only that, he hadn't removed his hat when he greeted her.

"Thank you," she said under a guise of civility. "Simon is right, however. I knew nothing about Jason's business."

"No matter. All I want is a look around the house. I understand you might be willing to sell it."

"Where did you hear that?" Leslie said sharply.

He shrugged. "Around the village."

"Well, they're mistaken. The estate isn't settled."

"Perhaps you could let me look around anyway?" The man straightened and took a step closer. Behind her, she heard Simon make some sort of noise, and almost laughed. What was he now, her watchdog? "Jason invited me a number of times, but this is my first visit to Corfu and I wondered if you would indulge me."

Leslie stared at him. He had nerve; she had to say that for him. And her first impulse was to send him packing. Especially since she suspected that his desire to look inside the house was motivated by more than architectural interest. "Why not?" she said, swinging the door wider and standing to one side. "Come in."

She could have sworn Simon ground his teeth. Gage stepped inside and made a great show of admiring the curve of the stair banister before going into the living room to check out the hand-carved mantel over the fireplace.

As soon as he turned his back, Leslie elbowed Simon sharply in the ribs. "Smile, you idiot," she hissed. "I want to see what he wants."

"The silverware, probably," Simon muttered darkly.

"More likely the wine cellar," she predicted.

And Gage's next words proved her to be right. "I'm also a connoisseur of fine wines. Would it be possible for me to see the wine cellar? Jason told me all about it, that he even has a couple of bottles of Napoleon Brandy."

Simon, resigned, took the key ring from Leslie. "Maybe I'll lose him in there."

"They're gone," Leslie whispered to Simon the moment they opened the wine cellar door. She stared at the clean square on the dusty floor where the crates had sat.

"They're gone, all right," Simon agreed. "Except for this one." Behind them, Gage cleared his throat. "Let's take care of him first."

"Where are you from, Mr. Gage?" Leslie asked as Simon stepped aside.

"From London, my dear." He sniffed the air like a bird dog. "This is marvelous. Truly marvelous."

"The brandy's out here," Simon said in a repressive tone.

Gage moved after him, prattling about how wonderful it was that all this had been preserved. He gazed at the bottles Simon picked out with the flashlight beam. "Marvelous. Marvelous. If you ever decide to sell any of this, please get in touch with me. I'll be in the area for the next week.''

Simon pulled down a bottle and handed it to him. "Here. A little souvenir of your visit."

Gage's face lit up. "Oh, thank you." Then his expression altered, and the smile slipped. "Uh, thank you."

They went back upstairs. Leslie wasn't surprised when Gage declined to tour the rest of the house. She shook her head. Even scam artists—and she was sure he was one—had no finesse anymore.

In the kitchen the cat greeted them with plaintive meows, as if to say they'd been gone too long.

As soon as the door closed behind Gage, Simon burst into laughter. "Did you see the look on his face? I wish I'd had a camera."

"Yes, what was that bottle you gave him?" Leslie said severely.

"Not Napoleon brandy, that's for sure." Another shout of laughter rang through the hall. "I gave him a bottle of Greek brandy that you can buy anywhere for a couple of thousand drachmas, under ten dollars in your money."

Leslie joined in his laughter, but quickly sobered. "I don't trust that man."

"You too? Then why didn't you let me drive him off?"

"Because I wanted to see what he wanted."

"And we still don't know," Simon said. "It looks as if we can eliminate him from our list of people who may have keys to the house, though. If he'd had one, he could have checked it out the day before you came, at his leisure."

Leslie bit her lip. "When did Gage come?"

"The day before you did. Jason's been dead for two months. If Gage is supposed to be a business associate of his, I wonder why he didn't show up sooner."

"You might say the same about me," Leslie reminded him. "But I didn't know until the lawyer wrote me."

"Could be the same with him. If I were you, I'd check with the lawyer, see if Jason actually had a partner by the name of Harlan Gage, once removed from east-end London, I'd say."

"Pardon?"

"His accent. It's too good."

"Exactly what I thought," Leslie said, pleased her guess had proved right. "Do you think we've seen the last of him?"

"I wouldn't bet on it." Simon glanced at his watch. "Look, I have to get changed and drive down to Kérkira. But first let's check that crate."

Downstairs, he pried up the lid. Shredded paper protected the contents. Simon brushed it away, revealing a row of unremarkable wine bottles. He lifted one toward the light.

"Boutari Red." Leslie read the label aloud. "Bottled in Patra."

*"Vin ordinaire,"* Simon confirmed. *"Très ordinaire.* Considering some of the stuff stored in here, it's completely out of its league. Why would anyone order cases of this, when there's a cellarful of exceptional wine and brandy here?"

"Maybe Jason ordered it for a party. He didn't want to waste the good stuff?" Leslie suggested.

"From what I hear, Jason never had parties."

They replaced the lid without nailing it down. Using the flashlight to poke into corners that the electric light left in shadow, they circled the room. In the wine racks, hundreds of bottles lay neatly on their sides to keep the corks moist.

Deep shadows hid the space behind the barrels. Simon played the flashlight beam around the end of the racks. "Furniture. Must be where they stored what they weren't using."

A couple of overstuffed chairs, a Victorian horsehair settee with some of the stuffing escaping and a lamp table were stacked next to an armoire. Leslie took the flashlight from his hand to get a closer look at the armoire, a heavy piece trimmed with ornate carving. "I wouldn't mind that upstairs. It would hold a television."

Simon made a face. "You don't have a television. Didn't Jason do anything for entertainment?"

"He had his business. And no, he rarely watched TV, even in Canada."

They left the wine cellar and made a thorough search of the rest of the basement. Nothing suspicious turned up. On the other hand, they found no sign of the crates from the wine cellar. Which might have been suspicious, because there appeared to be no way in or out except up the stairs, through the pantry next to the kitchen. The windows were too small to admit anything bigger than a cat, and covered with sturdy wire mesh, besides. An old coal chute was boarded up.

Simon frowned when he saw it. "I wonder when that was done. The lumber and nails look new. But, judging from the boiler, coal hasn't been used as fuel in this house for at least twenty years."

"Maybe it was boarded up before, but the wood rotted and they replaced it." Leslie shivered. "It's damp enough down here."

"Maybe." Simon grasped Leslie's elbow. "Let's get out of here."

"Just a minute. I should take a bottle of wine to Cecil's, to go with dinner."

Simon handed her the flashlight and took the keys. "Wait. I'll get it."

In the kitchen, he paused at the door, the light in his eyes tantalizing her. "Want to come to Kérkira with me?"

Regretfully she shook her head. "I can't. Dinner with Cecil later, remember?"

"Stand him up. I'm much younger, have my own teeth—all around a better bet."

Leslie laughed. "Sorry, I couldn't disappoint him."

"Okay, then." He turned toward the door, then spun around. He pulled her against his hard, sun-scented body, and kissed her soundly. "Think of this, when you're dining, oh, so properly with Mr. Weatherby."

SHE WAS UNABLE to get Simon out of her mind as she sat in the garden. The heat had lost its edge, making the temperature pleasant in the afternoon, when most of the patio lay in shade. A loud wolf whistle startled her, and she dropped her book.

Something fell with a light metallic clink on the flagstones next to her. "Pretty Baby," the mynah squawked from the silk tree over her head.

Leslie laughed. "You've escaped again, I see."

In the fork of the tree where he sat, she saw an assortment of bright objects. Not much of value: several keys, a soda-can tab, a brass curtain ring.

She glanced down, remembering the clink she'd heard. At her feet lay a gold earring. Grasping it between two fingers, she held it up. It was set with what looked like a real diamond, winking as the sun hit it.

"Pretty Baby," the mynah said again.

"Baby, where are you?" Eugenia demanded as she pushed her way through the gap in the hedge.

"It's a great day for gardening, isn't it?" Eugenia inhaled deeply, her formidable bosom stretching her neon pink T-shirt to the danger point. She scanned the trees. "Now where is that bird?"

"Up there." Leslie smiled, watching the bird hop down onto Eugenia's shoulder. She held up the earring. "Is this yours?"

"Oh, good, you found it," Eugenia exclaimed, taking it from Leslie's hand. "It's one of my favorites. I thought I'd lost it. What else did he bring you? He's an incorrigible thief."

Leslie reached up and retrieved the objects from the tree fork. Eugenia looked them over. "The keys aren't mine. Better keep them. They might be for something in your house."

Eugenia pulled an apple slice from her pocket and offered it to the bird. He pecked at it, tilting his head to one side. "Leslie," he said hoarsely, and added another wolf whistle.

Leslie laughed, pushing the keys into her pocket.

Eugenia upended a large clay flowerpot and lowered herself carefully onto it. "Still going to Weatherby's for dinner?"

"I plan to," Leslie said, wondering again why Eugenia seemed so against the idea. "Have you ever eaten at his house?"

"Not me," Eugenia said forcefully. She shrugged her plump shoulders. "He's a good cook, I hear. Just don't let him take advantage of you. He used to come over here all the time whenever Melanie stayed. Of course, he and Jason had some business going together at one time, but I thought he made a nuisance of himself with Melanie. Old enough to be her father, too."

"I thought Melanie was after Simon," Leslie said rashly.

Eugenia lifted one delicate brow. "You've heard about that, have you?"

"Yes. Simon told me." Behind her back, Leslie crossed her fingers, hoping she wasn't betraying Simon's confidence. Although, come to think of it, he'd been questioned about Melanie's disappearance, and everyone knew it. No great secret.

"I don't think he had anything to do with her drowning," Eugenia declared. "Simon isn't a violent person. He took it all very well, and the accusations were completely unjust. Do you know they questioned him again after Jason's accident?"

Shocked, Leslie couldn't speak for a moment. Eugenia rattled on, seeming not to notice.

"Oh, yes. Good thing he was in Kérkira that day, and plenty of people saw him there."

"On what grounds did they question him, then?" Leslie asked in a strained voice. Her stomach was knotted into a chilly lump.

"Motive. Everyone knew about the bad blood between them since Simon's father died."

"What do you think?" Leslie clenched her hands together to still their trembling. After all he'd done for her, was it possible Simon—? No, she couldn't even consider it.

"I don't think Simon had anything to do with either accident. In fact, I'm not convinced either of them are dead. I saw lights on in the house at night a number of times before you came, and it couldn't have been anyone from the management company at that hour. I think the stupid story about all of Jason's family dying at sea made people willing to jump to conclusions.

"I must get home." Eugenia patted Leslie on the shoulder. "Thanks for finding the earring. And don't worry about Simon."

CECIL'S HOUSE was a low whitewashed cottage that conformed to her image of Mediterranean architecture. It stood high enough that it had a magnificent view of the sun setting into the sea, the same view Leslie had from her house. Not that she was given much time to admire it. Cecil opened the door immediately after her knock, as if he'd been watching for her.

"Dear Leslie, I'm so glad you could come." He took her hand in his and kissed her on both cheeks.

"Thank you for inviting me," Leslie said politely, handing him the bottle of wine.

He stood looking at her a moment longer, long enough for Leslie to recall Eugenia's warning. Her misgivings subsided when Cecil nodded, smiling. "Yes, I would like to paint you. I thought I might have been mistaken the other night, but you do have a look about you."

"Thank you," Leslie murmured, not knowing what else to say.

The house was larger than it appeared from outside, a collection of rooms all on different levels. They were sparsely furnished in natural pine and blue-and-white cotton—what Leslie thought of as Greek-island decor. Wide windows made the rooms pleasantly light.

They dined in front of one of them, enjoying the last pink glow of sunset. The table was set with gleaming china and silverware on a lace tablecloth. The meal was a traditional English one—roast beef, roasted potatoes and Yorkshire pudding, which Cecil brought in with a flourish.

"That was delicious," Leslie said an hour later. "Where did you learn to cook like that?"

Cecil's blue eyes twinkled. "I never married. Cooking became a hobby of mine. Can I get you a second serving of trifle?"

"I couldn't eat another bite."

Cecil wouldn't hear of Leslie helping with the dishes, although he allowed her to carry the leftover food to the kitchen. He stacked the plates in the sink. "Why don't you go into the living room while I get us some coffee?" he said.

She did so, wandering about the room and scanning the bookshelves. Cecil was a voracious reader, judging by the variety of books he had, everything from engineering and business to mysteries and science fiction.

A door at the side of the room stood ajar. Curious, Leslie pushed it open. She smelled the pungent fragrance of paint and turpentine and reached for the light switch at her side.

It was Cecil's studio, a room that appeared to have been added to the end of the house. The two walls opposite each other consisted entirely of windows.

Leslie strolled around the room, examining the framed and unframed paintings. While not abstract, they had a surreal quality, giving her the impression that what she saw was not the only image the artist had painted.

On one wall she saw the picture Eugenia had mentioned, a craggy old man, possibly one of the local fishermen. The eyes, half-shadowed by the bill of his cap, were uncanny, possessed of a disturbing intelligence, as if the subject's soul had been transferred to the canvas by the medium of paint.

She turned away from it, her scalp prickling. At the end of the room, near a massive stone chimney, she saw the painting Cecil had to be working on. From a distance it appeared to show a column of dark-clad monks winding down a mountain path. Up close she could see that the hoods hid skeleton faces, and that the sticks they held were scythes. Forty images of Death walking.

Leslie shivered, her gaze moving to the painting hanging above the mantel.

This one was markedly different. A garden, probably Cecil's own. She had noticed that his garden, a riot of flowers in the English manner, rivaled the profusion of Eugenia's. The picture portrayed gay colors and a pleasing composition, showing a section of stone wall and a calm blue sea in the background.

Then she noticed the figure half-hidden in the painted foliage. A young woman, a slender wraith in a white dress, stood between two cypresses that definitely didn't belong in an English garden. The features were not visible, hidden by a wide-brimmed hat.

But the hair was.

It hung down in a straight swath, at odds with the period flavor of her clothing, the color so pale a blond it barely contrasted with the dress. The woman's hands extended in front of her, palms up, as if she were pleading with someone.

"What are you doing in here?"

Leslie started violently, spinning around to face Cecil's furious gaze. "No one enters my studio unless I invite them."

Beside him, the little dog, noticeably absent during dinner, began a high-pitched yapping.

With an effort, Leslie met the blazing anger in his eyes. "The door was open."

She kept her voice calm, controlled, telling herself she'd done nothing wrong. If he didn't want people looking at his work, he should keep the door closed. She would never have opened it. Even now, she couldn't understand the almost irrational rage that carved his face into ugly lines. His breath rasped harshly above the dog's barking, and his face was a dead white except for twin red spots over his cheekbones.

"I'm sorry," she said, hoping he wasn't about to have a stroke or a heart attack. For the first time, she understood the meaning of the term *apoplexy*.

"You saw her, didn't you?" His voice shook.

"Saw who? Oh, you meant the painting. Is that Melanie? Simon told me—"

He cut in. "No, of course it's not Melanie. Why would you think that?"

"The hair. Simon said she was blond."

"Well, so are you, and you're not Melanie, are you?" He sounded a little calmer. He picked up the dog and spoke to it. Scruffy settled into merciful silence. Cecil swallowed, his Adam's apple sharply defined in his stringy neck.

"Please." He held out his hand in a placating gesture. Leslie blinked at the sudden change in him. "Come and have coffee with me."

She preceded him out the door and he closed it firmly behind them. He put down the dog, which gave Leslie a reproachful stare before scuttling off toward the kitchen.

Cecil lifted the silver pot from the table, and poured coffee into two delicate china cups. He handed Leslie one. "Cream? Sugar?" he asked politely, as if the previous scene hadn't happened.

"Just cream, please," she said, knowing how Alice must have felt at the Mad Hatter's tea party.

He brought the silver tray, allowing her to help herself. She declined his offer of cookies, and thoughtfully stirred her coffee. Eugenia had some reasons for her remarks about Cecil. He was unpredictable. Not that Leslie worried about her safety with the old man, in spite of the frisson of fear she'd felt in the studio, when his eyes had blazed at her like twin lasers.

The remaining chill within her rapidly dissipated in the hot room. For some inexplicable reason, Cecil had lit the fire laid in the fireplace. The wood snapped merrily even though they hardly needed the extra warmth.

They sipped their coffee in silence. The little dog poked his head around the corner, as if gauging his master's disposition. Cecil snapped his fingers, and Scruffy leaped across the room onto the sofa beside him.

"More coffee, Leslie?" Cecil asked.

"No, thank you," Leslie said. "That was lovely." Actually, it hadn't been; Cecil's coffee was strong enough to strip paint. Leslie had no intention of abusing her stomach with more.

Cecil poured himself a second cup, liberally adding sugar and cream. Beside him, the dog began to snore.

Cecil extended his hands toward the fireplace. "I like a fire in the evenings, don't you? The air becomes cool after sunset."

Not that cool, Leslie thought, feeling sweat trickle down her sides as she groped for a tactful response. Cecil must have a different internal thermostat from hers.

The old man seemed not to notice her silence. "Did Jason tell you about Melanie's mother?" he asked pleasantly.

It shouldn't have hurt, but it did, a sharp stab reminding her that Jason had been even less honest than she'd thought. "No, he didn't," she said, hiding the brief pain under impenetrable composure. "Simon mentioned her, that she'd died years ago."

Cecil nodded, but she couldn't tell what he was thinking.

"Did you know her?" Leslie asked. "Or was that before you came?"

"I've been here a long time, my dear. Yes, I knew her." Some indefinable emotion flicked through his flat, mud-colored eyes. "But, as you say, she died. An unfortunate accident. She drowned in the bathtub."

# Chapter Eight

Leslie went still, a new chill running up her spine. Her mind flashed back to last night, the black hand pulling her under the water.

Who was it? Some madman determined to make everyone connected with Jason share the same death, drowning? Or was the so-called curse real? She'd never been superstitious, but even she knew events happened in the world that had no easy natural explanations.

"Where did this happen?" she asked, forcing the words past stiff lips.

"Where?" Cecil glanced vaguely around the room. "Oh, in Athens. They lived there so Melanie could attend what Jason termed a good school. Jason tended to be a bit of a snob."

Hearing the reality of Jason restored some of Leslie's equilibrium. Tell me something I don't know, she mused. "I thought Melanie and her mother lived in London."

Cecil's eyes sharpened. "Some of the time they did, but they also had a home in Athens. No matter—it was a long time ago." He leaned forward, his expression becoming as affable as it had been over dinner. "About Jason's house, my dear... If you decide to sell it, would you give me the first chance to bid on it?"

Leslie gaped at him. In two days she'd had three people offer to buy the house from her. "Why?" she asked in a strangled tone.

Cecil shrugged. "I've always been fond of the place. I stayed there once, while my own house was being built."

"Really?" she said. "Seems to me a lot of people suddenly want to buy the house, now that Jason's dead. I understand he tried to sell it in vain two years ago." She shook her head. "But I can't, not right now."

"Well, if you change your mind—" Cecil broke off as a knock sounded on the door. He rose with surprising agility for a man of his age.

"Simon," Leslie heard him say a moment later. "What are you doing here?"

Together they came into the living room. "I came to walk Leslie home," Simon said, glancing curiously at the cheerfully crackling fire. "So many things have happened, I didn't want her walking alone in the dark."

"I would have seen her safely home," Cecil said, in a tone that implied he'd been insulted.

Leslie got to her feet. "I wouldn't want to trouble you, Cecil," she said sweetly. "It was a lovely dinner. Thank you."

"You're going so soon?" Cecil said. Then he shrugged. "All right, then. I'll get in touch when I'm ready to paint you."

"PAINT YOU?" Simon asked incredulously after they left Cecil's. "I thought he didn't do portraits."

Leslie wrinkled her brow. "Yes, that's what he said the day I came, too. But he's got a portrait in his studio, of a fisherman."

"That was painted a long time ago. He doesn't do portraits now, only impressions, as he calls them. Says reality is too restrictive."

"I thought you didn't know him well," Leslie said.

"I don't, but once in a while we talk, usually when Cecil prowls around my orchards, looking for subjects to sketch."

At the beginning of Leslie's driveway, Simon paused and groped in the bushes. He turned with a flourish, a bouquet of yellow roses in his hand. "For you, madame. From my garden. Just to prove I can grow something beside olives and kiwi."

Leslie took them, breathing in the luscious fragrance, her heartbeat lurching. "Thank you. At least I won't have to wonder where these came from."

They reached Leslie's back door. Simon waited for her to unlock it. Leslie heaved a sigh of relief when she saw that the house appeared undisturbed. She glanced back at Simon, uncertain whether she should offer him coffee or tell him she was all right and he could leave.

He solved the dilemma by stepping inside and closing the door behind him. "I'd better look through the house. Wait here."

Leslie put the kettle on the stove while he was gone, making a pot of herb tea. Her stomach burned slightly, probably from Cecil's coffee.

Going to the cupboard, she pulled out the vase that had held the red roses. In the heat, they had wilted rapidly, and that morning she'd thrown them away. And been surprised at the relief she felt when they were gone. She arranged Simon's bouquet, setting it on the kitchen table.

"All clear," Simon said. "Where's the cat?"

"Probably prowling. He's usually out in the evening."
She poured tea into two mugs, handing him one of them.

"Thanks," Simon said, his eyes twinkling as she sat
opposite him, the scrubbed wooden table between them.

Leslie scowled into her cup, unsettled about the whole
evening. "Do you know what Cecil tried to do?"

Simon's mouth curved in amusement. "No, but I'm
sure you'll tell me. He didn't come on to you, did he?"

Leslie smiled briefly. "No, nothing like that. He said
he'd buy this house. Everyone wants to buy this house
now that I'm here. I can understand your offer, for your
mother. But what about Harlan Gage? And now Cecil.
Why didn't they buy it from Jason? They both knew
him." Leslie moved her mug back and forth in random
patterns. "Is it possible that some resort company is again
interested in the land?"

"Could be," Simon said. "But I haven't heard about
it."

"Would you tell me if you had?" Leslie asked gloomily.

Smiling gently, Simon put his fingers under her chin
and turned her face up to his. "Leslie, don't you trust
me?"

Leslie spread her hands, all too conscious of his touch.
"How do I know whom to trust? Eugenia told me earlier
that Melanie was staying here before she drowned, that
Cecil used to visit her. You said you didn't know if she
stayed here until after you found out she was Jason's
daughter."

Simon's eyes narrowed. "Is that why you don't trust
me? The truth is, I was very busy that summer. I didn't
have time to socialize with Eugenia or Cecil. I'd no idea
where Melanie stayed when she was here, until right be-

fore she disappeared. I just assumed she drove back to Kérkira in the evening. Why would I lie to you about it?"

She felt foolish. "No reason, I suppose."

Simon nodded. "As for Cecil's interest in the house, maybe he's decided he likes it better than his own. And he and Jason weren't on good terms when Jason left to go to Canada. Everybody knew that."

"Did anyone get along with Jason?"

"I couldn't say." He frowned. "Funny thing, though, he and Cecil seemed to get along better last summer, when Jason came back. I saw them together in the coffee shop several times." He walked around the table and pressed his lips gently against her forehead. "Good night, Leslie. Lock up after me."

THE SCREECHING of the mynah woke Leslie at dawn. Grumbling, she pushed her tangled hair off her forehead and went to the French doors. He sat on the broad stone balustrade, preening his shiny feathers.

On the balcony floor lay a set of keys. Leslie picked them up, a deep premonition knotting her stomach. Yes, there it was, the wear-softened leather tag with Jason's name on it. "Where did you find this?" she asked.

"Find this, find this," the bird echoed, tilting his head. He spread his wings and awkwardly flapped to the fig tree. From there, he hopped along a branch and made it to a cypress at the edge of Leslie's garden. He disappeared in the direction of Eugenia's house.

Leslie turned the keys slowly over in her hand. They looked identical to the ring that had hung in the kitchen: car keys, house key—which wouldn't fit now—and several miscellaneous keys, a couple of them inscribed with the brand name of a padlock company.

Walking to the end of the balcony, she gazed at the sea. The rising sun, just clearing the horizon, glazed the water. Not even a ripple disturbed its flat surface. Offshore, a yacht swayed at anchor, its sails furled.

Drawing several deep breaths, Leslie went back inside. Maybe the padlock key unlocked the attic. There was one on the other ring, but she hadn't tried it. She squared her shoulders and stripped off her nightdress, replacing it with an old T-shirt and shorts.

It was time she explored the attic, the only part of the house she hadn't seen. Now, while it was still cool. Maybe Jason's secrets were there.

TWO HOURS LATER, Leslie brushed back her hair, which was sticking to her forehead. She plucked the sweat-damp T-shirt away from her chest, grimacing. The heat had risen with the sun's ascent, and had now approached flash point.

As she had suspected, one of the keys on the ring had opened the substantial padlock on the attic door. The attic held a collection of old furniture, discarded lamps, boxes, trunks and suitcases. She'd found old letters and school records for a number of people, indicating that past tenants had left behind some of their belongings. The furniture was old and moth-eaten, giving off clouds of dust when disturbed. Why it had been saved, she couldn't imagine.

She hadn't found Jason's clothes; they might be in one of the suitcases, but she doubted it. The luggage was dusty, the style of it old-fashioned, so it wasn't likely that it was Jason's.

Someone had removed Jason's clothes from the house. Jason himself? Or someone else?

She dragged a box of old papers into the light. The huge room had never been partitioned, which meant that a good many boxes had to be moved to get at those behind. Light bulbs hung at intervals from the ceiling. Even in daylight, they were needed.

Leslie glanced at the shaft of light slanting through a tiny window. She couldn't even open the windows for ventilation. She'd tried, but either they were warped or the paint on the frames had fused the whole unit together.

Sweat dribbled down the side of her face, and she wiped it absently away, concentrating on the papers she pulled from the box. The first one was a land deed, a copy of the title to the house in Toronto that Jason had owned and sold after their divorce. The papers underneath looked like invoices. Jason's business records?

She lifted the corner of the box, gauging its weight. Could she carry it down the narrow staircase? Her mouth felt as dry as cotton and her clothes were soaked with perspiration.

The box was heavy, but she managed to drag it across the floor, leaving a long track in the dust. Sweat dripped into her eyes. She mopped her face with her shirttail. Wishing she'd brought up a jug of water, she licked her lips, dredging up scant moisture. The skin felt dry and cracked; her sweat had no more flavor than plain water and her stomach tilted queasily. She had to get out of there. Heat exhaustion was nothing to fool around with.

Never mind the box. She would come back for it another day.

Halfway to the door, she jumped as she heard a crash below her. She paused, straining her ears. It sounded like glass breaking.

Setting her jaw, she marched to the door. Hadn't she left it open, and propped a box in front of it, thinking even that slight ventilation was better than none?

The box was gone, the door closed.

Renewed sweat trickled between her breasts as she extended her hand toward the handle. The handle turned under her damp, clammy palm, and she let out her pent breath. She pulled on it.

It didn't open.

Her stomach clenched; she couldn't suppress a little whimpering cry. Wrapping both hands around the brass handle, she jerked at it, praying it was only stuck; it didn't move.

And then the clunk of the padlock bumping against the sturdy oak panels confirmed her worst fear.

She let her hands slide off the handle and sank down on the floor, her forehead coming to rest on her knees. Her sweat was drying, her skin turning prickly. How long did it take for a person to die of heat and dehydration?

WHERE WAS THE MAN HIDING? He had to be somewhere in the village. Which meant someone was helping him.

But who? Even two months after the supposed accident, Simon still had no idea. He'd suspected Jason was alive almost from the first day. When he helped Jimmy store the battered windsurfing board in the garage, he'd found Jason's keys in the car's glove compartment. He'd kept quiet about it, knowing Jimmy would take a dim view of what he was doing.

Using the keys, Simon had let himself into the house. Someone had been living there. He'd found freshly used disposable razors in the bathroom. And the clothes in the closet had given off the scent of sweat and after-shave, not the dry mustiness of disuse.

He'd kept an eye on the house, but he'd seen no one. A week before Leslie came, he'd gone into the house again and found the clothes gone. All evidence of anyone's presence had been erased.

Then Leslie had come, and he'd been even more certain. Who but Jason would be harassing her? He couldn't have known Leslie would come. He must have been desperate to get her out of the house.

Simon scowled blackly, kicking a rock out of his path. Leslie, with the soft gray eyes and long, pale hair. Leslie, who was beginning to haunt his dreams and his days. Leslie, who despite the warnings and the attempts on her life, refused to leave, tackling each threat with courage and resolution.

He had to talk to her, tell her what he thought, make sure she understood.

He stamped up the hill toward Leslie's house. Last night, when he hid the flowers—he must have dropped the keys then. He'd taken a handkerchief from his pocket, dampening it with the garden hose, to wrap around the stems. They had to be near Leslie's house.

His shadow followed him, black and distinct under the glaring sun. After one day's respite, the heat had returned with a vengeance. He swiped his forearm over his forehead, drying it on the back of his shorts.

In Leslie's garden, he turned on the water tap. While it ran, he poked around in the mint and chamomile that grew in the damp ground. No keys. No, they wouldn't be here. He'd pulled out the handkerchief earlier, before he'd come this far.

The water soaked his sandaled feet, not cold but no longer hot, as the residue inside the hose had been. He lifted the end of the hose and drank deeply, letting the water trickle down his shirt. On impulse, he ducked his head under the stream, soaking his hair.

Turning off the tap, he went back to the spot where he'd left the bouquet last night. He searched the cool green shadows under the shrubbery, finally settling back on his heels in disgust. They simply weren't there.

WEAK. Dizzy. The edges of her vision turned gray, and she shook her head, fighting off nausea. Pain hammered at her temples. She needed water. What did they do in the Western movies when they were lost in the desert—suck on a pebble or a bullet? Ten minutes ago she had found a mint in her pocket, and that had helped a little. But now her tongue felt swollen, and swallowing had become agony.

For the tenth time she circled the attic, searching for something to pry open the door with. She spotted a rusty metal chair. Crawling to the nearest window, under the sloping ceiling, she swung it and smashed the glass. Hot air drifted in, offering no relief from the heat.

Pushing her face against the opening, she yelled as loudly as she could, "Help! Somebody help me!"

She could see the roof of Eugenia's house, but the singer must have been out. Leslie yelled again, praying the mailman or someone else might be passing by. Her throat ached, and she knew that without water she would soon lose her voice.

She broke another window, but again could see no one. Even the crickets were silent in the oppressive heat. She hauled in a deep, painful breath. If only she could just lie down and let the black oblivion take her.

No! She clenched her fist. She couldn't let him win. She had to find a way out.

The bulb over her head winked off.

Now what? She was about to check the switch when a needle of light caught her eye. It slanted from the wall across a pile of boxes. A window, boarded up in the low eaves—perhaps bigger than the others?

The boards were old, the nail holes dried out. She jerked at them, bending a fingernail. Sucking on it briefly to stop the pain, she gave the board another pull. With a groan of tortured metal, it came free of the nail, setting her abruptly back on her bottom.

She licked her dry lips, uttering a quick prayer. The next board was easier, and the one after that. Leslie crawled inside the space that had been revealed. It was long and narrow, little more than a passage beneath the edges of the sloping roof.

She gave a cry of disappointment, the sound catching painfully in her parched throat. The glazed opening was more of a skylight than a window, too small to crawl through, even if she could have gotten off the roof outside.

Her head felt woolly, and a pungent, dusty smell drifted around her. The confined space was crowded with more trunks and boxes. She sat for a moment, raking her fingers through her sticky hair, her head swimming.

On her knees, she backed toward the hole she'd made in the wall. Her ankle smacked against the metal corner of a large trunk. On impulse, she lifted the lid.

A scream welled up in her throat.

SIMON STRODE across the patio, through shimmering heat waves, to the back door of the house. The sunbaked stones burned his feet through the soles of his sandals. In the narrow bar of shade cast by the roof overhang, the gray cat paced to and fro. Simon spoke to him, but he didn't come over to have his ears scratched, as was his habit. He gave plaintive meows and prowled restlessly, coming back to butt his head against the locked door.

Simon rapped his fist on the panels and waited. If Leslie was upstairs, it would take her a little while to come down.

No one came. Come to think of it, he would have expected her to be outside in the garden by now. He didn't hear a sound from the house. Had she gone out? He walked around the house. No, Jason's little car stood there.

"Could she have gone to the beach?" he asked the cat.

The cat yowled and batted at his ankles before going back to the door. He crouched, lifting his front paws. He dragged them down, leaving long scratches in the paint.

"What's wrong, cat?" Simon asked him. "I've a good mind—"

He broke off, the hair rising on his skin. Somewhere in the house, a woman was screaming.

HER SCREAM echoed around the attic. Leslie felt as if her eyes were bulging from her head as she stared at the open trunk in front of her. The sweet musty odor she'd noticed before stole her breath.

*They say she drowned, but they never found a body.* The words echoed through her head as nausea swam in her stomach. She swallowed the bile in her throat.

The body was found.

Definitely a woman. She wore a flowered dress, and her long blond hair mercifully covered what was left of her face. She lay on her side, her knees drawn up slightly to accommodate the short length of the trunk. The hand that rested on her thigh was wrinkled and dry; the fingers looked like leafless twigs.

With a shudder of revulsion, Leslie scrambled back. She stood up, scarcely feeling the pain when she cracked her head on the low ceiling. She ran to the door and pounded her fists on it, yelling, "Help! Please help me!"

Not that anyone was likely to hear.

She coughed and swallowed, her mouth parched. She shivered, cold and hot at the same time. She was no longer sweating, and goose bumps feathered her skin.

Her hands began to ache from beating on the door, and her throat felt as if she'd swallowed ground glass. She sank down on the floor, her cheek against the door. Red and black dots floated behind her closed eyelids.

She forced them open, concentrating on settling her roiling stomach. She couldn't faint, she couldn't give up.

She refused to end up like that poor woman in the trunk.

Her ear, pressed to the door panel, registered a vibration deep inside the house. She sat up. Was that a shout she heard? The vibration was someone pounding on an outside door, two or three thuds, silence, more thuds.

The kitchen door. Hope surged through her. She got clumsily to her feet, shaking her head to clear it. She had to be quick, before they went away.

Her gaze skittered around the room, finding the chair. Fighting dizziness, she slammed it against the window she guessed overlooked the kitchen door. The glass broke with a satisfying crash, the pieces clinking as they rained down on the patio below.

The window was smaller than the others, barely allowing her to poke her head out. "Help!" Her voice came out as a hoarse croak. Would anyone hear? She coughed and tried again. "Is anyone there? Help!"

"Leslie? Where are you?"

She nearly fainted in relief when she recognized Simon's voice and saw his dark head below her. "I'm here, above you. In the attic. Break a window or something. Just get me out of here." Her voice broke in a racking cough.

"Right away."

She heard glass shatter, and headed back to the door. The room tilted under her feet. She swayed dizzily, her tongue sticking to the roof of her mouth. Next to the door, she huddled on the floor, counting the seconds. One thousand and one, one thousand and two, one thousand and three... Dark shadows swirled in her brain, and she concentrated on the numbers. She couldn't pass out. She couldn't.

Only half-conscious, she barely moved when an odor prickled her nostrils. She coughed painfully and ran her tongue around her teeth, trying to dredge up a little saliva.

Suddenly it didn't seem to matter anymore. The heat was gone, and cold shivers enveloped her. Chest heaving, she coughed miserably, clutching her aching stomach.

Smoke. Letting out a hoarse croak, she put her face against the bottom of the door. She smelled smoke, and this time it was in the house.

Where was Simon? Horrible doubts began to penetrate her mind, sluggishly coalescing into certainty. Simon wasn't coming. He, too, wanted her dead.

She lay down on the floor, uncaring that it was dirty and hard and rough with splinters. She told her mind to stop fighting. At least if she passed out, she wouldn't feel the pain when she burned to death.

She sank into a black void where nothing mattered.

SIMON HOISTED HIMSELF up on the windowsill. His shoulders barely fit through the frame. He cursed as a shard of glass in one corner ripped his shirt and laid a long, burning scrape on his shoulder.

He curled himself into a forward roll and pushed himself through, painfully bruising the other shoulder when he landed. The cat jumped in after him, dropping gracefully on four silent paws. It ran to the kitchen door, then stopped, letting out an earsplitting yowl.

Then Simon noticed it. The smell of something burning. He crossed the kitchen. Near the door, his foot slipped. He grabbed the corner of the table, scrambling to keep his feet under him.

Shards of pottery from a broken vase lay smashed on the quarry-tile floor. Around it, his yellow roses were scattered in a litter of crushed petals and broken stems. He forgot the smoke for a moment as he focused on the table.

Another vase stood there, filled with red roses.

"Damn," he muttered, coughing.

The pungent smell of smoke was stronger, gray tendrils floating around the room, dissipating out the open window. The cat howled again.

Simon ran into the front hall. More smoke. There, in the living room. The fire burned on the hearth, but the chimney had to be plugged, because the smoke blew back into the room.

An embroidered runner on the mantel hung down low enough that the edges were beginning to scorch. Simon ran back to the kitchen, and yanked the roses out of the vase on the table.

Coughing, he crossed the living room and dumped the water on the fire. It hissed and subsided. Just to be sure, he refilled the heavy glass vase and soaked the fire again, using the poker to scatter the soggy ashes.

Poker in hand, he dashed up the stairs, his mind racing as fast as his feet and his heartbeat. Who would build a fire on such a hot day? And what was Leslie doing in the attic on that same hot day? It must be an oven up there. Didn't she know about heatstroke, and how fast it could kill?

At the top of the attic staircase, he found the cat waiting for him, clawing at the door. The padlock hung from its hasp, neatly closed. Simon's blood turned to ice, despite the suffocating heat.

No accident, then. This was outright murder. Leslie dead of heatstroke, the house burned down, and no one the wiser.

He clenched his fist around the poker, the metal handle digging into his palm. If he caught the person who'd done this—

"Leslie, are you there?"

No answer. He inserted the end of the poker between the hasp and the lock, frantically calling to her again. "Leslie!"

With a high-pitched groan, the hasp came out of the frame. Simon shoved open the door and lunged inside, nearly tripping over Leslie's prone body on the floor.

His heart stopped as he saw her. Her face was as white as paper and she wasn't breathing.

# Chapter Nine

The cat meowed plaintively and patted Leslie's face with a gentle paw. Her chest heaved, and she coughed harshly. Simon groaned with relief, pushing the cat aside. He gathered Leslie into his arms. She felt alarmingly light and fragile, her skin hot and dry.

He had to get her out of here.

Wisps of smoke still lingered in the hall as he carried her down the two flights of stairs and outside. His own lungs felt parched, oxygen-starved. He gulped in fresh air, laying Leslie down on the mossy stones near the water tap.

Stripping off his T-shirt, he soaked it with water and bathed her face. He let the hose spray her T-shirt, to cool her off, closing his mind resolutely to the sight of her nipples pebbling under the thin cotton.

He had to get water inside her, as well.

Running quickly to the kitchen, he grabbed a glass and took it out to her. To his surprise, Leslie was struggling to sit up, hindered somewhat by the anxious ministrations of the cat as he licked her face. "Stay down," Simon said. "You have to rest."

Her gaze skittered around the garden, her eyes dark and wild. "How'd I get here?" she asked in a hoarse voice.

"You're safe now," he murmured reassuringly, filling the glass and holding it to her lips. She grabbed it with one hand and gulped greedily. Simon pulled it back. "Slowly. You have to drink it a little at a time or you'll be sick."

She lay back, her eyes falling closed. He could see the thin blue veins on her eyelids, the dark lashes against the pallid white of her cheeks. What else could he do? Her breathing was rapid and shallow, her skin still hot when he picked up her wrist to check her pulse.

Suddenly she cried out, her fingers gripping Simon's arm. The cat leaped away as she sat up. "Simon, there was a woman." Her voice broke in a racking cough, and Simon allowed her another mouthful of water.

"A woman?" he asked, wondering if she was hallucinating. "Where was this woman?"

Her body jerked. Color flooded her cheeks, and she clawed at his arm. Her nails left sharp, stinging scratches on his skin. "In the attic." She shuddered, her feet sliding on the wet moss as she struggled to get up. "I have to call Jimmy."

"We'll call Jimmy," he said soothingly. "As soon as you're feeling better.

She sagged in his arms, like a doll that has lost its stuffing. "He locked me in, didn't he?"

"He?"

She shook her head impatiently, her eyes desperate. Simon frowned. Something had scared her, something more than the danger of being locked in. "Yes, he wanted me dead." Her voice became clearer, insistent. "Just like the woman was dead."

Simon gathered her up in his arms and sat her in one of the chairs next to the patio table. He refilled the water glass and put it in front of her. "Half now, half in five minutes."

Good thing she hadn't been up in the suffocating heat of the attic longer. Heat exhaustion could be deadly, he knew, but if it was caught in time, it was relatively quick to reverse. She already showed signs of recovery, and he didn't think she'd need a doctor.

What bothered him more was her mental state.

"Where was this dead woman?" he asked in a calm voice, willing her to settle down, not perch on the edge of the chair as if about to take flight.

"In the attic. She was in the attic." Leslie gave a whimpering cry and covered her face with her hands. "She had blond hair. Like me."

"What?" A cold fist seemed to squeeze his heart. He stared at her. Had she been having a nightmare? Dehydration could do odd things to the mind.

"There is a dead woman in the attic." Eyes closed, Leslie spoke with the exaggerated patience of one explaining something to a child. "In a trunk, under the eaves. She's been dead a long time." A shudder lifted goose bumps on her skin. "She looked like a mummy. Call Jimmy." She braced her hands on the arms of the chair, pushing herself up.

Simon gently pressed her down. "Sit. I'll have a look." He hesitated, placing his palms on her cheeks and tilting her face up. Some color had returned to her skin, and her eyes no longer had that sunken look. "Will you be okay here?"

She picked up the water glass and sipped from it. Her hand shook, the glass clicking against her teeth. Jerkily, she nodded. "I'll be okay."

Simon ran up the stairs, taking them two at a time. Dust motes shimmered in the light from the dusty windows in the attic. The heat, dense and heavy, drove the breath from his throat. His stomach rolled. If she had been up here any longer—

He raised the lid of a nearby trunk. Folded clothes and the smell of mothballs. He looked around. There it was, the space under the eaves. He picked up one of the loose boards, his heart clenching. She'd torn them off, looking for a way out.

Cautiously he crawled into the space. Another trunk stood open. With a feeling of dread, he looked inside. And recoiled. A sweet, musty smell enveloped him, along with the ghost of cedar.

Simon swallowed down nausea as he gazed at the dried-twig fingers. He knew that dress, a small floral print on a cream background. He'd seen her wear it a number of times that summer two years ago.

Driven by a need he couldn't control, he lifted the strands of hair that covered her face. The skin had shrunken on her bones and pulled back from her teeth. Yes, it was Melanie. He recognized the slight overbite, the faint crookedness of one front tooth.

For an instant, impotent anger swamped him. He'd been accused of her murder, at least unofficially, and all the time she'd been here. Dead, but not at his hands.

Shame overwhelmed his anger. And guilt. She had been murdered. The realization slapped him in the face. Someone had shut her up in the attic to die. Or, at best, had hidden her body. Her death could not have been a natural one; she'd been in perfect, robust, angry good health the last time he saw her. She'd screamed insults at him as he walked out of this very house that night.

Leslie had almost died here, too. His anger returned, burning through every other emotion. Whoever had killed Melanie must be behind the attempts to drive Leslie from the house. He probably feared she would discover the body.

Simon had to find him before he killed again.

SIMON RAN down the stairs and into the kitchen. Leslie still sat on the patio, the cat in her lap. Her eyes were blank, her face was pale, as she stared out at nothing.

Simon's heart twisted in pain at her stillness, and he almost went to her. No, this had to be reported. And resolved.

Turning, he went into the living room, where smoke and the smell of wet ashes hung in the still heat. Picking up the phone, he dialed the police station.

Jimmy answered.

"Simon here. Could you come over to the Adams house?" With a terse economy of words, he explained about Leslie and the body.

Jimmy didn't ask questions. "I'll be right there."

Simon sat beside Leslie, offering her sips of water, until the battered Land Rover chugged into the driveway. She hadn't said a word, merely nodding when he told her Jimmy was on the way.

"Is she all right?" Jimmy asked, jumping out of the vehicle.

"She will be," Simon said, although the continued blank look on Leslie's face bothered him. "I'd like to get her away from here."

"Just let me look around first. The attic, you say?"

Jimmy loped into the house. Simon shook his head at his eagerness. This would probably be the highlight of Jimmy's tenure in Platania.

To his surprise, Leslie lifted her head, the beginnings of a smile tugging at the corner of her mouth. "I still think he looks too young to be a cop," she said. "Yes," she added, the smile widening, "I'm alive again. The water did the trick."

"Thank God," he said fervently. "I was worried."

She reached out and touched his cheek, her fingers rasping over the beard stubble, reminding him that in his rush to find the missing keys he hadn't taken time to shave that morning.

"As soon as Jimmy comes back, I'm taking you to my house. Close to the sea, it's cooler. And you'll be safe."

"Simon, there's a box in the attic I'd like to look at, near the door. Could we get it out?"

"I'll find out."

Jimmy emerged from the house and threw himself down on a chair. He raked his fingers through his hair, making the closely trimmed strands stand on end. Sweat left dark patches on his pale tan uniform shirt. "She's been there for a couple of years, I'd say. I've called for a forensic expert. He'll have to come from Kérkira. It'll be at least an hour. I'll have to wait for him." He looked at Leslie. "Could you give me a statement, Mrs. Adams?"

"Later?" Simon suggested.

"Later is fine." Jimmy indicated the house with a toss of his head. "She's not going anywhere."

"Is it all right if I take Leslie down to my place?" Simon asked. "The house is going to be in an uproar when your expert comes."

"Fine." Jimmy smiled faintly. "Just don't leave town."

SIMON DROVE the little Renault through the outskirts of the village and down a side street before turning onto a rough track lined with drying grass. The car bumped through an olive grove heady with the fragrance of Spanish broom.

Leslie leaned back in the seat, gazing out at the pattern of light through dusty green leaves. They rustled like the distant whisper of voices, and she shivered.

Shaking off the gloomy thought, she glanced over at Simon. Without his T-shirt, which he'd tossed in the trash as soon as she recovered, the hard muscles of his shoulders were visible, flexing when he shifted gears and steered down the twisting road. Glossy black curls covered his chest, and her palms suddenly itched to feel the contrast between the brown satin skin and the crisp hair.

She tore her gaze away, instead studying his hands; they were broad across the palms, with long, slender fingers. He handled the steering wheel with the easy skill of a racing driver, but the grim set of his jaw betrayed his tension. His silence made her nerves scream.

They came out of the trees, emerging onto a narrow track running parallel to the beach.

"This is where I live," Simon said, stopping the car under a grape arbor.

The whitewashed house hugged the land, the varied angles of the red-tiled roof showing how rooms had been added on as needed over the years. A profusion of flowers grew in the small courtyard behind a low stone wall separating the garden from the beach.

"Your garden is lovely," she said inanely, in a effort to banish the feeling that nothing would ever be normal again.

"Thank you." He stopped the car and killed the engine. "Let's get you inside, where it's cooler."

To her chagrin, she nearly fell on her face when she stepped out of the car. Her legs felt like overstretched rubber. Simon's face tightened, and he swung her up into his arms.

He took her inside. She had only an impression of cool halls and the scent of orange blossoms before he deposited her on a wide bed in a room darkened by lowered shutters.

"My room," he said. "The guest room isn't made up. You'll be fine here for a while. Take a nap. I'll bring you something to drink."

He pulled a sheet over her, ignoring her token protest. A ceiling fan wafted fresh air around the room, and her eyelids fell closed, as if weighted. "Thanks." Her lips formed the word, but she was asleep before it found utterance.

SHE WOKE SLOWLY. For a moment, she lay without moving, breathing deeply and savoring a feeling of well-being. Where was she? It didn't seem to matter as she turned, wrapping the sheet around her.

She sat up, realizing she was dressed. It wasn't night, although the light in the room had dimmed. The events of the morning flooded back. The attic. The heat. The body.

Her eyes skittered around the room. Simon's room, she remembered now. On the night table stood a glass of fruit juice, condensation trickling down its sides. She lifted it, drinking deeply. Ice cubes clinked against the side of the glass, and she sucked one of them into her mouth, welcoming the cold.

Getting up, she pulled the strap that raised the shutters. The sound of voices drifted through the open window. She leaned out, but saw no one.

Going into the well-equipped bathroom, Leslie rinsed her face with cold water. She found Simon in the kitchen, a small, homey room lined with beautifully crafted pine cabinets.

"How are you?" he asked.

"Okay. Were you talking to someone?"

"Jimmy came by. He says you can go back to the house if you want. It'll be a few days before he has an autopsy report."

A chill ran through her, and she shivered, her face paling. "They took away the body, then?"

"Yes. He said not to disturb the attic, though, in case an investigator wants to have another look." Simon opened the fridge door. "How about a drink? I've got orange juice, lemonade, white wine."

"Lemonade will do, please."

As he poured it out and handed her a glass, he searched her face. Gently he laid one finger beneath her eyes. "You've got black circles. You need more rest."

"Thanks," she said, with a faint edge to her voice.

"You can stay here tonight." The words were casual, but a flicker of emotion in his eyes told her the invitation was not.

She grasped the lemonade glass between her palms, anchoring herself to the cold wetness. She was acutely aware that Simon's invitation carried more than an offer of a bed. He was offering himself, as well, and asking her to accept that offer.

Was she ready for this? She and Jason had formally separated two years ago, but they hadn't shared the same room for at least a year before that. Sex had not been a priority in her life, but Simon stirred feelings in her she didn't understand. And it was tempting to bury herself in them, to forget the horror of her discovery.

And yet she was scared. Could she really give herself to another man, share that intimacy of body and soul with him?

"You didn't happen to see a stray bunch of keys, did you?" Simon's voice cut through her indecision.

She almost gulped in relief that he wasn't going to push it.

Groping in her pocket, she pulled them out. "These? Baby brought them to me this morning." The color abruptly drained out of her face, her skin turning icy-cold. "How did you know about the keys?"

She struggled to her feet, her balance shaky, and braced her hands on the table. "What's happened to Jason?" Her voice rose. "You know something, don't you? That's why you asked all the questions, isn't it?"

Simon let his eyes fall closed, and pinched the bridge of his nose. "Leslie, please. I found the keys. In the car, after Jason's accident."

"So you could have gotten into the house." Her strength gone, she sat down again. "I knew I shouldn't have trusted you."

"Leslie, it wasn't like that—" He swallowed hard, visibly fighting for control. "Look, Leslie, if I'd had a key this morning, I wouldn't have had to break into your house." He dragged the collar of his shirt aside, revealing the jagged red scrape on his shoulder. "This didn't exactly tickle, you know."

Remorse filled her, but not enough to drive out the demons of distrust formed during her childhood and reinforced by Jason. "I'm sorry," she said. "But I have to go. Goodbye, Simon."

She walked briskly out the door to her car, a rush of adrenaline overcoming the shaking in her legs. Thrusting the key into the ignition, she cranked over the engine. It coughed and stalled. She tried again, and it started. She glanced over at the house. Simon stood in the doorway, his expression unreadable, making no move to stop her. She stepped on the clutch. Gears grinding harshly as the wheels spun in the loose gravel, she drove off.

LESLIE SAT on the window seat in the bare dining room long after dusk stole across the sky and shrouded the garden in gloom. Her stomach felt hollow and empty, but she ignored it, knowing she would never be able to force a bite of food past the constriction in her throat.

The house gave her a creepy, spooky feeling, but where else could she go?

The gray cat crept across the hardwood floor on silent paws. He meowed inquiringly before jumping up beside her. She lowered her knees and gathered him onto her lap. "Oh, cat," she murmured into the velour-soft fur, "What am I going to do?"

She had been ready to trust Simon. More than trust him.

And now she realized he could be behind the attempts on her life.

No! Her logical mind rebelled. No. If he intended to kill her, he wouldn't have rescued her from the attic.

But the fact remained that he knew more about Jason's death than he'd told her. And he'd had a key to the house all along. She couldn't help but feel betrayed.

The cat purred in her arms, but she drew little comfort from his warmth. It was starting all over again, her involvement with a man who couldn't be trusted. She'd begun to like Simon, to believe in his integrity.

But she'd been wrong before, hadn't she? She'd given Jason her trust and her loyalty. And he'd eventually counted both as no more valuable than dust.

Hadn't she learned? Not a hell of a lot, apparently.

SHE STOOD AT THE STOVE, scrambling a couple of eggs for a late supper, when the cat ran, meowing happily, to the door. A moment later, a heavy fist landed on the panels.

She opened it, scowling, hoping to discourage him. She might have known Simon wouldn't stay away, not only because of her precipitate departure, but also because of his protective instincts, because he knew she was all alone in the house she was beginning to think was haunted.

"Yes?" she said coldly.

"May I come in?" Steady eyes, no hint of apology.

The absence of guilt in his demeanor shook her resolve.

"Why?"

"Because we have a number of things to talk about." He picked up the cat, who was fawning at his feet.

"And if I say we don't?" The sight of those strong fingers gently kneading the cat's fur reminded her of how they'd felt on her face, gently washing moisture back into her skin, checking her pulse.

He must have sensed the falseness of her bravado. A smile tugged at his mouth. "I'm bigger than you, so if I want to come in, you can't stop me."

His humor sent some of her demons into hiding. "I guess that's true." Not allowing herself to smile in return, she stepped aside. But she wasn't going to fall for any sweet talk, she reminded herself, stiffening her spine. Not ever again. "Have you eaten?" she asked, gesturing at the pan. "I can add a couple of eggs."

"Thanks. I'm okay. I ate a while ago." He pulled out a chair and straddled it, resting his arms on the back. "Have you heard from the solicitor?"

"Not so far." Leslie transferred the eggs to a plate, added tomatoes she'd sliced earlier, and a couple of slices of bread. She set them on the table and sat down to eat.

"Why don't you call their office and see if they've made any progress?"

"Yes, I'll do that." Leslie swallowed the last mouthful of salad. "Did you get the box from the attic this morning?" she asked, casting a troubled look at the ceiling.

"Yeah. Jimmy said it was okay. Do you want me to bring it in here?"

SHE CLEARED AWAY her dishes and spread the contents of the box on the table. Within twenty minutes, she knew she'd been right about the box. The papers detailed Jason's business—at least that was what she assumed because of the dates and amounts of money listed. No words appeared anywhere, only cryptic combinations of numbers and letters that didn't appear to follow any set pattern.

"Some kind of code," Simon suggested. "Not that it matters, if he's dead. The business died with him."

"Except for Harlan Gage," Leslie said slowly. "If it's true what he said. And unless we know for sure whose side he's on, I can't ask him what this all means."

She closed the last ledger and lifted it to return it to the box. It was then that she noticed the corner of an envelope protruding from the crossed flaps at the bottom of the cardboard box. She dropped the ledger and pulled it out.

"What's that?" Simon asked, tiredly rubbing his eyes.

A broad smile spread over Leslie's face. "No wonder that solicitor in Athens was so vague about Jason's affairs, mumbling something about an incomplete will. I think we just found the will, and I'm sure they'll be most pleased to have it."

To her disappointment, Simon didn't look impressed. "Tomorrow. We'll call him tomorrow." He got up, yawned, and stretched. "It's late."

He paused, looking straight at her, and added in a tone she knew better than to argue with. "I'm staying tonight." Going to the kitchen door, he opened it and brought in a small duffel bag. "And before you go all Victorian-maiden on me, I'm sleeping down here, where I'll know if anyone tries to get in any of the doors."

TO LESLIE'S SURPRISE, when she called the law office the next morning, the receptionist told her that Christos Papadopoulos was presently in Kérkira checking out some of the aspects of Jason's estate. She recited his phone number.

Excitement rising, Leslie dialed it. Another receptionist, again speaking excellent English, confirmed that Mr. Papadopoulos was presently there. Would it be convenient for Leslie to see him at four? It would.

Simon nodded when she told him. "We can drive to Kérkira now, if you like." He grinned. "I'll show you the sights."

THE ADDRESS Leslie had scribbled down indicated a street near the Esplanade. At Simon's suggestion, Leslie parked the car in a quiet little square in the Old Town. "There's never any space near the park," he explained. "It's not far to walk."

White-clad cricket players stood on the lawn, like a scattering of sea gulls on a meadow. Leslie heard muted applause as someone scored a point. She brushed her hand over her sweat-beaded forehead, wondering how they could play under the intense afternoon sun.

Simon had taken her around the Old Town, where she'd bought kumquat preserves and a wildly decorated T-shirt. After lunch they'd gone out to Pontikonissi, finding respite from the heat in the cool, dark church. Later, Simon had laughed at her as she sat on the seawall, dipping her feet in the water. Then he took off his shoes and joined her.

She couldn't remember when she'd enjoyed a day more. Or been with a man who could make her laugh and briefly forget her problems. They would return soon enough, she knew.

PAPADOPOULOS, a short, bespectacled man with thinning hair, greeted them with a cordiality that changed to enthusiasm when Leslie handed him the will she had found in the attic. "Your husband's affairs have been, ah, difficult," he said in passable English. "I understand you work in the financial field?" She nodded. "Then you know that this may take some time to finalize. But having the will is going to facilitate matters."

He tapped the envelope on the desk. "In the normal execution of these matters, I would study the document and call you back for an appointment. But as I am already working on the estate and I have ascertained that you are the only relative, I will open it now. You will understand, if there are irregularities or other beneficiaries, I may have to ask you to return at a later date."

"That's fine," Leslie assured him. She waited, perched on the edge of her seat, while he slit the envelope and read through the two sheets inside.

He laid down the papers and looked at her, lips pursed and fingers steepled under his chin. "What is it?" she asked.

"I believe this is your husband's final will, since I have no other documents to dispute that. And it is dated the third of April, this year."

"Three weeks before he died," Leslie said.

"That would be correct." Papadopoulos's dark gaze moved to Simon, sitting silently beside her. "This may also be irregular, but do you want Mr. Korvallis to stay while I read it?"

Leslie glanced at Simon. She shrugged. What difference did it make? Sooner or later, he was bound to find out what was in the will. "Let him stay," she said.

Papadopoulos nodded, picking up the will. "It's very simple, so I will dispense with the legal jargon. What it comes down to is that Jason Adams has left you, Leslie Adams, his entire estate, consisting of one house in Plantania and the contents of the wine cellar in that house."

"Oh." Leslie felt numb, overwhelmed. The house was hers. But what was she going to do with it?

"I'm afraid, my dear Mrs. Adams," Papadopoulos went on, "that that's the good news. The bad news is that the house has a mortgage on it, the payments and the taxes are in arrears, and if it was sold at anything near the market value, there would be little left."

So, Jason *had* been in trouble. A chill suddenly enveloped her. Was it possible that his death had been not an accident, but suicide?

"Do you have any idea what the market value of the house is?" Simon asked.

The solicitor pursed his lips. "Not offhand. A real estate agent would be happy to tell you."

"What about Jason's business?" Leslie asked.

"That's why I'm here, Mrs. Adams. We're trying to straighten that out. We have very few of his records, although he's retained me as his solicitor for a number of years. But he did most of his business in cash and in person. And it appears to have died with him."

Simon leaned forward. "Have you heard of a man named Harlan Gage? He claims to have been Jason's partner."

"Harlan Gage." The lawyer riffled through the papers on his desk. "Yes, that name is mentioned. I'm not sure what their connection was."

"Maybe I can help," Leslie said. "At the house, there's a box of papers. I think they document at least some of Jason's business. I've also had several offers to buy the house. I don't know how serious they are."

A ghost of a smile crossed Papadopoulos's face. "If you get a serious offer, I'd take it, if I were you. Jason had the house on the market two years ago, but didn't sell."

His smile grew wider. "Actually, if the house burned down, you'd be in the clear, unless you were charged with arson. It's very well insured, and the policy is paid up until Christmas. But that's hardly a solution." He looked at his watch. "I'm afraid I won't have time today, but could I pick up that box of papers tomorrow morning?"

"Of course."

In a daze, Leslie walked out into the breathless heat of late afternoon, barely aware of Simon beside her. It was just typical of Jason, after years of shutting her out, to die and dump his mess squarely in her lap.

"What are you going to do?" Simon asked, jarring her out of her disquieting thoughts.

"Do? I don't know. Sell, I guess. I wonder how much the wine cellar would bring."

"Plenty, I'll bet. Some of that Napoleon brandy is worth a fortune."

"Enough to cover the debts?"

"Probably more than enough."

"Not that I want anything for myself, you understand," Leslie said. "I just want to clear this up."

Simon took her arm as they crossed a street. "Then let's find a place to have dinner. Matters always look better on a full stomach."

THE NARROW, meandering streets of the Old Town were virtually deserted at ten that evening, except for lean, half-wild cats slinking away into the shadows. From a window above them, a clarinet wailed a plaintive melody.

"It's so sad," Leslie said as the last note quavered and died on the night air.

"What?"

"The music," she explained. "It's so sad, and so Greek."

"Our history is full of turmoil."

She laughed, half-bitterly. "So was—is—my life. I should have been Greek."

He stopped and faced her, his hands coming up to grasp her shoulders. "Let it go, Leslie. Leave the past behind. Jason's gone. You can't change what's happened, but you can determine your future. Give me a chance."

"I can't change it," she said bitterly. "But I'd be stupid if I didn't learn from it, wouldn't I?"

And for that, he had no answer.

LESLIE OFFERED Simon the car keys, but he said she had to learn to handle the road at night, as well as in daylight. She drove carefully, guiding the little car around the tight loops, through olive groves. The pale leaves of the trees appeared as insubstantial as ghosts in the glow of the headlights.

On a short straight stretch, a rusting Fiat passed her, then braked sharply at the next curve. Leslie slammed her foot down on her own brake. The Fiat roared away, leaving her coughing in the dust its wheels spun up beside the pavement.

She braked again, slowing down in anticipation of a long downgrade.

She held her foot on the pedal. Odd—it felt soft. Frowning, she tried again, lifting her foot and setting it down firmly. The car jolted, slowing, but the pedal again sank to the floor. Definitely mushy. A red light on the dash blinked a warning, then went out.

"What's wrong?" Simon asked, with that uncanny perception that never failed to surprise her.

"The brakes—they feel funny."

"Then stop, and I'll have a look."

"Here?" she asked, gesturing toward the olives crowding the road, and the ditch guarding them.

"As soon as you have a chance."

She pressed the pedal to slow for a curve. "They seem all right now. I think we can make it to the village. It's just ahead."

The road leveled off, ran up another hill, then descended again, toward the village. Leslie stepped on the brake again, and this time she was horrified to find her foot sinking to the floor with no resistance. The dash warning light filled the car with a wash of crimson.

"Oh, hell," she muttered. Frantically she pumped the pedal. No use. She'd lost them. And from here it was all downhill to the village.

*Chapter Ten*

One hand on the wheel, the other on the gearshift lever, Leslie swallowed the panic that dried her throat. Movie scenes notwithstanding, there was more than one way to stop a car, especially one as small and maneuverable as this.

Luckily, there were no tight hairpin curves between here and the village. Risking a glance at Simon, she saw that his face was grim as he braced one hand on the dash.

"If you go straight down, you'll end up in the sea," he muttered.

"Soft landing, at least," she said darkly.

She stepped on the clutch and shifted from fourth gear to second. The engine lugged ominously, a grinding roar echoing in her head. The car slowed.

Gratified that it was responding, she gently pulled up on the hand brake. If she could slow the car a little more, she knew she could stop it by turning into the track used by tractors entering the olive groves.

Her headlights picked out the break in the trees. She spun the steering wheel, narrowly missing a thick olive trunk. She jerked up the hand brake. The car shuddered to a stop, the engine stalling with a harsh cough.

Leslie rested her forehead against the steering wheel, dust settling around the car and drifting into the open window. Her heart pounded in her throat. It felt as if it would never beat at its normal place in her chest again.

"Leslie, are you all right?" Simon's voice seemed to come from a great distance. "Where'd you learn to drive like that?" His voice cracked, and he grabbed her shoulder, pulling her against him. "Don't you ever scare me like that again."

"I don't want to scare myself like that again, either, thank you very much," Leslie said shakily.

He hugged her close, and she let herself fall against his chest. His warm, hard chest, where she could hear his heart beating in double time. The gear lever dug into her thigh, but it was a minor discomfort compared to what could have happened.

Still holding her, Simon reached forward and turned off the Renault's headlights. "No use draining the battery. You must have lost the brake fluid. I saw the brake light come on."

Leslie nodded. "Yeah, it blinked before, but it stayed on just before the brakes died."

"Can you stand?" Simon asked.

She laughed unsteadily. "How did you guess?"

"Oh, I've had a few mishaps in my life. Fell off a roof once. Lost my lunch, and couldn't stand alone for half an hour."

He got out of the car and came around to her side to help her out. For a moment, Leslie clutched the roof of the car, until the trembling of her legs subsided. "Wasn't there a flashlight in the glove box?" Simon asked.

"I think so."

He got it out and knelt beside the car, shining the light underneath. He groped with his hand, then stood up and showed her his fingertips, shiny with oil. "You lost your brake fluid. Whether by accident or not, I can't tell, not until the car is towed and put on a hoist."

A chill ran over Leslie's skin. She shivered, hugging her arms around her chest. "It could have been an accident." Even to her own ears, the statement sounded hesitant, as if she needed to reassure herself. The alternative was too horrifying.

"It could have," Simon agreed. "But the mechanic checked the car over thoroughly the other day, and it was okay. Brake seals can deteriorate, but that doesn't cause entire system failure all at once. It's a gradual process, and you'd notice."

"The brakes were fine this morning. If it was tampered with, it had to have happened in Kérkira today."

"I think we'd better report this to Jimmy tomorrow morning," Simon said grimly. "In the meantime, I guess we walk. Good thing it's not far."

THE HOUSE appeared undisturbed, but Simon walked through all the downstairs rooms anyway, checking the locks on the doors and windows. The gray cat wound himself around his ankles, purring, apparently at ease.

Leslie picked up the cat, hugging him close. He nuzzled her, his whiskers tickling her chin. "I'm going upstairs. I need a shower."

"Just let me look around first." Simon walked past her, loping up the stairs two at a time. After a moment, he called to her. "All clear. I see you're being careful about locking your balcony door."

She went slowly up and entered her room, aware of Simon standing on the landing. Was he waiting for an invitation to stay? She was tempted; the brake incident, on top of everything else, had shaken her and she didn't want to be alone. But having him here would lead to complications she felt in no condition to handle.

Not that he would force himself on her. He hadn't last night, had he? No, she was more afraid that she would fling herself at him, and never let him go home again.

In the glow of light from the hall, she could see the bed sheets in disarray, attesting to her haste that morning. She set down the cat. He stopped purring and stood in the middle of the room, ears pricked but tail down, growling faintly. Shaking her head at him, Leslie crossed over to the dresser to turn on the lamp.

In front of the mirror, she slipped off her earrings and unhooked the shell necklace she'd worn. Her white sundress was wrinkled, and an oily smudge decorated the front of it. She grimaced at her reflection. She looked like a ghoul—dead white face with hectic dots of red on the cheekbones.

As red as— Her throat closed over her scream, and all that came out was a thin, despairing wail. "Simon!"

SIMON HAD REACHED the foot of the stairs when he heard her cry out. The sheer terror in her voice congealed his blood and made the hairs rise on his nape. He whirled, found himself upstairs without being conscious of moving.

Leslie stood next to the bed, her hand pasted over her mouth. Behind her, the cat crouched against the headboard, his fur bristling. He growled deep in his throat and launched himself toward the door, nearly tripping Simon in his rush to escape.

"What is it, Leslie?" Perplexed, Simon swept his gaze around the room. The French doors were firmly closed; nothing appeared to have changed from five minutes ago. He focused back on Leslie. Her eyes were wide with horror. He followed the direction of her gaze, realizing she was staring at the vase of roses on the nightstand as if it were a coiled cobra.

"Another unsolicited gift, I take it," he said tightly. "I saw them, but I thought you'd put them there."

Impotent rage flared within him. Who was tormenting her? And how was he getting into the locked house?

"Look at the note." She gulped for breath.

A white square lay on the floor. He picked it up and read the neatly typed words on it aloud. "'I'm sorry, Allegra. I didn't want you to die.' What the hell?"

"Don't you see?" Leslie cried. "He meant me to die when the brakes failed!"

"He has you mixed up with someone else," Simon said, his jaw clenched. "Who the hell is Allegra?"

"You'd probably know better than me. Maybe she used to live in this house."

"Not in recent years." Simon shook his head. "It could have been one of the summer tenants, but I don't recall the name. Are there any other beds? I'm not leaving you alone. And that couch last night was torture."

"There's a bed in the next room," she said, her voice still shaking. "It's not made up, but there are linens in the hall cupboard. I'll get them."

"Don't bother. I can manage." He picked up the vase of roses. "Would you like me to get rid of this?"

She gulped. "Please."

He took it downstairs, pausing at the kitchen table to put down the note. It was too late tonight, but tomorrow they had to talk to Jimmy again, about the brakes, the roses, the note, everything. And this time Jimmy would have to do something.

Unlocking the back door, Simon set the vase outside. The cat moved past him, silent as a shadow, and disappeared into the bushes.

Going back into the hall, Simon paused at the bottom of the stairs. How could he spend the night here again, alone, when he wanted nothing so much as to sleep beside her, all night, holding her, protecting her?

Loving her.

Ah, hell, he might as well admit it. He was more than halfway to loving her and he wanted to show it. Last night had been the purest torture; tonight would be worse.

He couldn't take advantage of her. She was frightened, uncertain, and possibly grieving for Jason, even if the emotion was inspired by guilt. He had to give her a chance to get over that first.

CLUTCHING a couple of towels to her chest, Leslie turned from the linen cupboard and found herself looking into Simon's face. Her heart stumbled when she saw the yearning in his eyes.

He touched her as if he couldn't help himself, pulling the clip out of her ponytail. Gathering the long waves in his hands, he spread them on her shoulders. "So soft, like satin moonbeams. I've waited so long to touch you like this. I want to feel your hair brushing over my body when we're alone and naked together. I want—"

"Simon!" Heat flooded Leslie's face and slid down her body, leaving scorching awareness in its wake.

Simon laughed softly. "Leslie, you know I want you. I've wanted you from the beginning, when I fell into those mist gray eyes and knew nothing would ever be the same again."

"It's still not right."

"What's not right?" Simon demanded. "Jason's dead."

"We're in Jason's house." She groped for a reason that would convince him. "And even you said Jason could be alive. I want to find the truth first."

"Whatever the truth is."

"The truth is, I'm not ready," she blurted, then clapped a hand over her mouth in horror.

He smiled, a smug male light in his eyes. "Yes, that's the truth, isn't it, Leslie? You're afraid to have a relationship with another man. Well, I can change that, if you give me a chance."

She held her breath, waiting for him to grab her, kiss her brutally in an effort to convince her she needed him, like a couple of the men she'd dated after the divorce was done.

"When you're ready," he whispered. Then his mouth came down to cover hers and she forgot her protests, her misgivings, her common sense.

His lips were soft, hot, moving over hers, cherishing rather than coercive. In a moment she was burning, as he filled her whole world, driving out all memory of Jason's perfunctory lovemaking.

Simon kissed her as if it were the most important thing in the world, as if everything else could wait until they were satisfied. His hand slid down to her hips. He was aroused, hard and hot against her, and she reveled in the feeling that she could do this to him. She moaned and tangled her fingers in his hair, wanting more.

Wanting all of him.

He lifted his head, his eyes amused, although she could also see the need in them, the desire. "Let's call it a deposit on account," he said, his voice faintly breathless.

He studied her intently for a moment longer, running a gentle fingertip over her hot cheeks. "Just let me know when you're ready," he said quietly. "I'll be waiting." Then he turned and walked into the other room.

Leslie sank down on the floor, burying her face in her hands. She'd never felt like this, and for a wild moment she reveled in the feeling.

Was it love? Or was it only a powerful chemical attraction fueled by danger and Simon's proximity? She'd heard of women falling for a handsome man they met on holiday, and she'd always thought them foolish. Was that what was happening to her?

No, she told herself. If she'd met Simon in Toronto, or London, or anywhere else, she would have felt the pull between them. But could she trust that feeling, when she wasn't sure she could trust the man?

She got up and briskly straightened the stacks of towels in the cupboard, picking up the ones she'd dropped. Going into her room, she began to get ready for bed, resolutely banishing thoughts of Simon.

THE DAY'S HEAT hadn't abated at nightfall. Simon lay naked on the bed in the room to which Leslie had banished him. Not a breath of air came from the open window. It had to be hours since he'd gone to bed. He was thinking of getting up and taking another shower when he heard a sound from the other room.

His heart leaped into double time. Someone had broken in and was attacking Leslie. The French doors—he knew he shouldn't have let her open them.

He catapulted off the bed, through the door and into her room. Good thing her door hadn't been locked; his momentum would have broken it down.

She was alone—no one else in the room. Relief nearly flattened him. He gulped in a breath and willed his heart to slow.

"No. Please, no." He jumped. The voice trailed off in a high, keening cry.

He sat down next to her, gently shaking her shoulder to wake her. Startled, she batted his hand away, opening her eyes. They were wide and terrified.

"Leslie, wake up. You're dreaming." He kept his voice low, soothing.

Recognition came into her eyes, and the tension left her limbs. She pushed back her tangled hair. "Simon, what are you doing here?"

"I heard you cry out," he said, lying down beside her. "Bad dream."

She went into his arms as if they'd been lovers forever. He lay beside her, simply holding her until her trembling subsided, until she relaxed. Just when he thought she had fallen asleep, her hand began to stroke restlessly over his arm.

"Do you want to talk about it?" he asked.

Her fingers stilled. "The car. Like tonight, only I couldn't stop it. And I dreamed about my parents' funeral. I was six when they died." She sighed, her hand resuming its mindless motion. "I haven't had that dream in years."

Her face was inches away from his, her eyes soft, sleepy. He began to be painfully aware of his nakedness, even though a sheet lay twisted between them. "Thank you."

"For what?" he asked.

"For being here."

He ducked his head. "You're welcome." How the hell was he going to get out of there without embarrassing her?

She lay half on the sheet, preventing him from dragging it around himself. And if he stood up as he was . . .

He shunted himself back until he felt the edge of the bed. He'd never been self-conscious about his body, but that quality of innocence in her made him want to protect her. When they made love, he wanted it to be romantic, not stark and carnal.

He smothered a laugh. Maybe he should tell that to certain parts of his body. The moonlight had brightened. There was no way he could hide his rampant arousal.

"Simon, please stay." Her low murmur cut through his discomfort.

"What?" His voice rasped in the silent room. Stay? He couldn't believe she'd said that. No, he must be dreaming.

"Simon, stay. Make love with me."

He felt as if a fist had clenched his heart and then let it go. "Leslie, are you sure?" he whispered, hardly aware of what he was saying.

She gave a throaty laugh. "No, I'm not. But I think I soon will be. Please, Simon. I want this. I wanted it all along, but I kept trying to convince myself I didn't."

Convoluted logic, if he'd ever heard it. But who was he to argue? A fierce tenderness overwhelmed him. He would take care of her. Yes, he would cherish her. They had tonight. He bent his head and began to kiss her.

Passion ignited within Leslie, sending incandescent sparkles through her body. She leaned into the hand that Simon laid on her cheek, nuzzling it with a soft, open-mouthed kiss. The car, the other things that had happened—was danger arousing? She'd never felt like this, aware of every pore in his skin, every nerve in her own.

"Sweet," he murmured. "You're so sweet." His breath kissed her lips just before his mouth came down on hers.

After an eternity, he pulled away, plainly reluctantly, his fingers trailing a hot path down her throat before he lifted himself off the bed. "I'll be right back." He turned before she could get a good look at him, almost running out the door.

Leslie closed her eyes, her limbs heavy with a lassitude almost as profound as the aftermath of love. In a moment he was back, dropping something on the night table. When he didn't come down on the bed, she opened her eyes. His expression was troubled, uncertain.

Seeing it, she knew this was more than just a summer conquest to him. If she hadn't been sure it was right before, she was now. No matter how long this lasted, and where it led, he would not willfully hurt her. In fact, his brief visit to his own room proved it. In spite of the overpowering desire he felt, he had put concern for her first.

She lifted the sheet, pushing it to the end of the bed. Grasping the bottom of her nightgown, she pulled it over her head and tossed it aside. A fine tremor roughened her skin. Nervous sweat trickled between her breasts, cold against her hot skin. Amid the turmoil in her mind, she could isolate only one fact. She wanted Simon. She wanted to lie with him, explore him, love him. So much that it terrified her.

"Come. Simon, come to me." The ragged edge of her voice betrayed her.

Simon knelt beside the bed. "Leslie, don't be afraid." Gently he caressed her cheek, the heat of his hand annihilating the shivers in her body.

She closed her eyes, inhaling his clean scent as he pulled her against his chest. His body was hard, solid, a bulwark against danger. "Please, Simon."

He kissed her mouth, her throat, her breasts. For a brief second, he laid his cheek against her waist, his hands running softly up and down her thighs. "Leslie, why did we wait so long?"

Why indeed? From the first moment she met those fathomless chocolate eyes, Leslie had known this would come. And suddenly she couldn't wait.

She pulled him up beside her with surprising strength, feeling the roughness of his chest hair against her nakedness, an erotic contrast that heightened her arousal.

For a long moment they lay together, savoring their closeness, listening to each other breathe, absorbing the essence of each other through their skin. But soon that wasn't enough.

Simon ran his hand up her back, aligning her precisely against him. Leslie shifted so that one of her thighs lay between his. At the intimate pressure, he groaned. "Yes, like that. Oh, yes."

He kissed her, and her mouth flowered under his, their tongues meeting intimately. Leslie felt the last of her nervousness float away. She responded with the passion that had lain dormant in her. She kissed him all over his body, until he shook with the need to bury himself in her. And when it came time, she helped him roll on the condom and positioned herself to receive him.

He whispered passionate words in her ear, words that would never have passed Jason's lips. Erotic words that had the power to arouse her unbearably. Then all thoughts of past or future faded. She cried out in joy and relief when he joined their bodies. And she was with him all the way on a journey that culminated in a crashing pleasure that left them exhausted and giddily euphoric.

"GOOD MORNING, Simon." Despite her efforts at nonchalance, her voice sounded breathless as she walked into the kitchen the next morning.

He turned from the eggs he was frying, dropping the spatula. His eyes twinkled. "Yes, it is, isn't it?" He pulled her close and kissed her. Her mind and body went into an instant replay of the night before. Where the renewed kindling of passion would have led, they didn't find out, as a thin column of smoke began to rise from the frying pan.

"Damn." Simon let her go and dragged the pan off the burner.

"You may have created a monster," Leslie muttered. "I don't know this person I've become overnight."

He laughed. "I guarantee you'll see more of that person." He sliced bread and put it on a tray to toast under the broiler. "How about setting the table?"

She pretended to sigh. "Oh, what happened to romance?"

He laughed again. "We'll find out later. First we have to see Jimmy. Oh, and maybe Eugenia. She might know something."

"Where did you put the note from last night?" Leslie asked, setting plates on the table.

"Isn't it there, under the salt and pepper shakers?" He opened the oven door and pulled out the bread, turning the slices to toast the other side.

Leslie pushed aside the items, and a magazine she'd bought yesterday. No note. "It's not here."

"Has to be." Simon came over and did his own search. "That's strange." He frowned. "I know I put it there. Hang on."

He strode to the door and threw it open. The cat came in, tail waving jauntily. "Damn," Simon said. "The roses are gone, too." He slammed the door. "That does it. We're going to see Jimmy and have someone watching this place every night. Maybe then we'll catch him."

Leslie sank down on a chair. "It would do more good if we could find out how he's getting into the house."

Simon yanked a tray of toast from under the broiler in the nick of time. "Only one piece a little scorched." He took it to the sink and scraped the black bits off. "There, can't even tell."

He sat down, pushing the dishes of butter and honey toward her. "Eat. It won't do any good if you starve yourself."

"Easy for you to say," she muttered, picking up her fork. "No one's attacking you or your house."

"What's so frustrating is, we don't know what this person is after. Unless he just gets his jollies from scaring you. Wait a minute." His knife clattered against the edge of his plate. "That box from the attic. Where did you leave it?"

"In the dining— Oh!"

"Yes. Oh."

They nearly collided going through the door. As they'd feared, the box was gone, but the French doors leading to the patio were still locked.

"This isn't how he got in." Leslie didn't know whether to be relieved or disappointed.

"The fact remains, he got in. And took the box. You'd better call Papadopoulos, save him the trip, at least until we find it."

"If we find it," Leslie said gloomily. "Good thing we took the will with us."

"Yeah." Simon headed back to the kitchen and their cooling breakfast. "You know, I've been thinking. What Papadopoulos said about insurance. I wonder if Jason is alive and set that fire the other morning."

Leslie's mouth dropped open. "I can't believe Jason would have tried to kill me."

"Maybe he didn't. Maybe the person who's sending the roses and so forth and shot at you locked you in the attic. Whoever set the fire wouldn't have known. And if the house burned down, Jason has the perfect alibi."

"But as long as he's supposed to be dead, he can't collect, can he?" Leslie pointed out.

Simon shrugged, grinning ruefully. "I never said my scenario was perfect."

THEY HAD just put the dishes in the sink when Leslie heard someone call her name outside. She opened the door. Cecil stood on the patio, an enormous bouquet of red roses clasped in his arms. "Good morning, Leslie, Simon. The roses looked so lovely this morning, I thought you'd like to have some."

Hiding her reluctance, Leslie took the roses, staring at the dew-sprinkled petals. Had last evening's bouquet come from the same garden?

Behind Simon, the gray cat poked his head around the doorway. Cecil spotted him and scowled. "My Scruffy chased your cat out of my garden last night."

Chased the cat? Leslie almost laughed. Scruffy was such a coward, the cat was more likely to chase *him*. "Are you sure it was my cat?"

"I'm sure. Not that I mind him coming around, you understand. It's just that he disturbs Scruffy." Cecil extended his hand. "Here, kitty."

To Leslie's astonishment, the cat let out an angry squall and streaked across the patio toward Eugenia's garden. A moment later they could hear the mynah bird giving his trademark wolf whistle. "It's a zoo," Leslie muttered. "I hope Baby stays out of the cat's reach."

"Always has before," Simon said. "Cecil, you're sure no one's been in your garden, stealing your roses?"

"Stealing?" Cecil's gaze darted around the patio, as if he were searching for the thief. "No, no one's been in my garden."

Simon realized it had been a long shot at best. Almost every garden in Platania had roses blooming this time of year, including his own. But Cecil's was the closest.

"It's all right, Cecil," Leslie said hastily as the old man's color began to rise. She smiled at him. "Thank you for the roses. They're lovely."

Cecil's testiness vanished. He smiled. "Not as lovely as you, my dear." His eyes remained fixed on her, disconcertingly watchful. Leslie felt her smile freeze on her lips. "You should wear your hair like that more often. I'll let you know when I'm ready to paint you. Good day." He lifted his hand in farewell and walked off.

The mailman came up the driveway and handed Leslie a package.

"Thank you," she said in surprise, turning the flat box over in her hands. No return address.

"What's that?" Simon asked. "Could I look at it?"

Her first impulse was to hang on to the package, but the hard set of Simon's jaw told her not to argue. "You never know what might be in it," he said grimly.

He examined the plain white paper, running sensitive fingertips over the lapped ends. "I think it's safe." He inserted one finger under the tape and pulled it off.

Another anonymous gift? The box was covered in burgundy leather, with a thin gold clasp. Heartbeat tripping erratically, Leslie watched as Simon carefully unclipped it. He held out the box to her.

Inside, on a bed of age-yellowed satin, lay a necklace.

Leslie lifted it out of the box. On a heavy gold chain hung an ornate cluster of flowers, petals formed of sparkling blue stones, trimmed by leaves of green. Forget-me-nots.

Simon took the necklace from her. "Sapphires and emeralds." He laid it back in the box. "This is a valuable piece. Looks like somebody's family heirloom. Is there anything else with it?"

Her mind numb, Leslie turned over the box. Taped on the bottom was an envelope. She thrust it at Simon, her stomach churning. "You open it."

He unfolded the flap, drew out a single sheet of heavy paper. He read it silently, then handed it to Leslie. "It's not a threat."

Leslie took the paper. The words were handwritten, in a fancy, stylized script.

Dear Allegra,
I love you. Please remember what we were to each other.

There was no signature.

"Who is Allegra?" She forced the words from a dry throat.

"As I told you, I don't know," Simon said. "I'm going to ask around. It's obvious, though, that someone thinks you are Allegra."

"That means someone is suffering from serious delusions." Leslie twisted her cold fingers together. "We'd better take this to Jimmy, as well."

"DID YOU get the impression he thinks I'm nuts?" Leslie asked as they left the police station several hours later.

"I wouldn't say that," Simon said sympathetically. "I think he took it seriously, especially when the mechanic came in about the brake failure." Simon had phoned early in the morning to have the Renault towed in and checked over as quickly as possible by the same mechanic who'd serviced it previously. "And Jimmy agreed there could be a connection between the roses and the brake failure, although the note doesn't refer to it directly. But you have to understand his position. There are no leads at all, no clue to who's doing this."

"What happened with the brakes? I didn't understand what he said."

"It looks like deliberate sabotage. One of the lines that carry fluid had been cut with a hacksaw, not all the way through, but just enough that the pressure of braking several times would cause the fluid to leak out."

Leslie shivered. So it was true. Someone had tried to kill her.

They reached the garage, where the little car sat waiting. Simon, overriding Leslie's vigorous protests, paid for the repairs. "It's the least I can do. You must be developing a very bad opinion of us by now."

He held out the key. She shuddered. "You drive," she said, feeling like a coward. "I'll try it later, on a level road."

Simon pulled her into his arms. "The brakes are okay now. You know, except for the note with the roses, I would think whoever did it was only trying to scare you. It's too inefficient as a means of murder."

Murder. The trembling started in Leslie's knees and spread through her body. Only Simon's warmth and solidity felt secure—and perhaps that was an illusion.

This was insane. She breathed in the sunshine smell of his skin and wanted to immerse herself in him and never surface. The voice of reason nagged her, and she pushed herself away.

"Somebody murdered Melanie. That means the killer may be someone we know." Leslie wrapped her arms around her waist, shivering, horrified at the question that hammered in her brain. Was she safe with Simon?

With her wide eyes on him, Simon couldn't help but know what she was thinking. He reacted with more exasperation than anger. "Come on, Leslie. You can't still suspect me. Not after all this. Not after what we've been to each other. What we are to each other."

Her features seemed paralyzed. She had to open her mouth several times before the toneless words emerged, and then her voice cracked as she said them. "What have we been to each other? Two people drawn together by mysterious circumstances."

"Lovers, you twit," he said, his hands balling into fists, as if he were thinking of shaking her. "Or do you jump into bed with every man you meet?" He hauled in a deep breath. "Look, Leslie, we've been through this before. I know you have a bit of a problem trusting men, but it's time you got over it."

He broke off, raising his eyes to the ceiling as if begging for patience. "Leslie, you might as well know. Melanie's killer is more likely to be someone we don't know. There were plenty of people around that summer, people Melanie had invited, who came on a yacht. You know how it is when you live on a resort island. Hordes of people you don't even know descend on you and expect hospitality."

He frowned. "You know, I've just remembered something. I saw Cecil that night, at the end of the garden, when I left. He didn't say anything to me—he was calling Scruffy. But he must have seen me. Yet he never said anything to the police. And Melanie was standing in the doorway, screaming at me to come back, so he had to have heard her and seen that she was alive and well after I left." He shrugged. "It hardly matters now."

"They suspected you of drowning her then. Aren't you scared someone will decide you shut her up in the attic instead?" Even to her own ears, her voice sounded strained.

"I told you everything. I didn't drown her, and I didn't kill her and stuff her body in the attic."

Who had? Leslie turned on the stairs and looked at Simon. "Do you realize we still have an unsolved mystery on our hands?"

"Jimmy's working on it." Simon's voice was cold and distant, a stranger's. "By the way, he says she died of suffocation and dehydration. It was murder. Look, if I'm guilty, why did I rescue you from the attic? If I knew the body was there, I would have let the house burn."

Her back to him, she leaned against the car, her hands shaking, tears burning in her eyes. No, Simon was the last person she should be afraid of.

She heard him utter a shaky, incredulous laugh. "As for the gifts—I don't know any Allegra. To call you Allegra would be crazy."

Leslie closed her eyes, clawing her fingers through her hair. "I'm crazy. This is making me crazy." She whirled and stared at him. "I'm sorry, Simon. I didn't mean what I said. You're the last person I should distrust. You've helped me so much."

He shrugged. "It's all right, Leslie. I don't blame you." He held open the car door. "Let's get going, okay? Jimmy's on the case, tracing people who were here that summer and questioning them. But that might take some time."

"Yes," Leslie said firmly. "I think it's time we stepped up our own investigation."

"Exactly." Simon nodded in satisfaction. "And we'll start with the basement. There has to be something we're missing."

THE CAT was noticeably absent when they got out of the car, which was odd, since he usually liked to spend the hot afternoons in the house. Leslie called to him, but there was no answering meow.

"He'll show up," Simon said, using her keys to unlock the door. Leslie walked past him into the kitchen, slipping off her sandals and wriggling her toes against the deliciously cool tile floor.

"Shall I close it?" Simon asked. "Or wait for the cat?"

"Close it. It's cooler, and he'll let us know if he wants in."

Simon rummaged in a kitchen drawer for a flashlight, testing it first. "We're not going to take any chances of being stranded in the dark if the lights go out again."

Suddenly, inexplicably, the back of Leslie's neck prickled. She whirled around, expecting to see someone behind her. Nothing.

"What is it?"

Leslie shook her head. "I don't know. Just a weird feeling." She followed him into the pantry.

A sharp crack made her jump. "What was that?"

"Outside." Simon grasped her by the shoulders, setting her to one side. "It came from outside."

A heavy thud shook the outside door. Leslie felt her jangled nerves settle. The cat. He must have knocked over a flowerpot, and now he wanted in.

She pulled open the door, and screamed.

Jason lay on the step, blood pooling in an obscene crimson lake around him.

# Chapter Eleven

"Quick, Simon, bring me some clean tea towels from the drawer by the sink. Then call Jimmy and an ambulance, if there's such a thing here." Leslie never knew how she managed to get out the words, but after that one panicked scream, her mind inexplicably cleared and she knew exactly what to do.

Simon didn't waste time with questions. He tossed her the towels and ran back inside. Leslie wadded up the linen and pressed the makeshift pad to Jason's chest. Miraculously, considering the quantity of blood pooling around him, he was still alive. His chest rose and fell, and his breath emerged raggedly from his mouth.

He wasn't going to make it, she realized with a strangely dispassionate fatalism. Pink bubbles burst on his lips, and she could hear a rattle in his throat.

"Leslie." She had to lean down to hear him.

"Yes, Jason, what is it?"

He coughed, and more bubbles, a brighter pink, appeared from his mouth and nose. Lung damage. "Leslie, I'm sorry."

"It's all right," she said gently. "Don't tire yourself. A doctor will be here soon."

He closed his eyes, seeming to rally his strength. Leslie pushed down on the pad, but blood had already soaked through it.

He muttered something else, something unintelligible to her. She became aware of Simon crouching down beside her, bringing more towels and a blanket, which he used to cover Jason. He replaced the pad on his chest, but as his eyes met hers, he shook his head.

The hot sun blazed down on them, but Jason's skin felt cold, and a violent spasm shook his body. He spoke again, the words garbled. By placing her ear against his mouth, Leslie could make out some of them. "That crow... Keys... cellar. Tell Gage..."

"Gage?" Simon lifted Jason slightly, which seemed to ease his breathing. "What about Gage?"

"Tell him— Please, Leslie, forgive me."

His eyes rolled back and glazed over, and his breathing stopped.

"Leslie, I'm sorry."

She lifted her stunned gaze to Simon's, saw the genuine sympathy on his face.

She gulped, and tears welled up in her eyes. Dabbing them away, she looked down at the man lying on the ground, his face strangely peaceful. "Poor Jason. He didn't deserve this."

A muscle jerked in Simon's jaw. "No, and I wonder who was responsible. I just realized we've been sitting out here, a perfect target for whoever shot him."

"Shot him?"

"Yes, that was the first sound we heard, a gunshot. My guess is he was shot in the back. That hole in his chest is the exit hole. It's always bigger. And since there were no more shots, I guess they've decided to let you live after all."

"Unless the person after me is someone else," Leslie said somberly.

"Yeah, that's possible. What did he say about Gage?"

"I'm not sure. 'Tell Gage.' Tell Gage what?"

A car ground up the hill, and a moment later Jimmy braked at the edge of the patio. Behind him, another vehicle pulled up, something that looked like a large army jeep on a high frame.

Jimmy gestured toward the vehicle. "This is the nearest thing we have to an ambulance. Most of our accidents happen in the mountains."

A man carrying a medical bag emerged from the jeep and hurried over to Jason, impatiently gesturing them away. Leslie found she couldn't watch as he cut away the blood-soaked shirt and examined his chest. A moment later, he spoke. Simon translated, pulling Leslie into his arms. "Just as we thought—he's gone. He wants your permission to remove the body."

Fresh tears threatened. Jason wasn't Jason anymore; he was just a body. But no matter how cold and worn-out their relationship had been at the end, she felt a deep remorse, much more acute than any grief she'd felt upon receiving the letter telling of his sailboarding "death."

She shook herself. There was no time for tears. She could indulge herself later. Now she had to deal with Jimmy and his questions. And what to do about Jason. She supposed she would have to arrange a funeral. Good thing Papadopoulos was still on Corfu; he would be able to advise her.

"Thank you, Simon," she said, pulling away. "I'm fine now. Jimmy will want to talk to us."

Simon studied her pale face for a moment. "Yes," he finally said. "I expect he will."

Leslie looked down at the flagstones, at the pool of blood that was all that remained of Jason. The doctor had ordered his body put into the ambulance and was waiting for Jimmy's okay to leave.

"Did you find anything?" Simon asked as Jimmy emerged from the dense shrubbery at the edge of the patio.

"Not much. He hid in the bushes and used a rifle. I found a shell casing, but it's a common type and doesn't tell us much, unless he was careless enough to leave fingerprints."

"That's all?" Simon asked, disappointed. Yet what had he expected? The killer to leave a calling card?

"I'm afraid that's it," Jimmy said. "But I'm marking off the area until I can get an expert from Kérkira to have a look. So I'm asking you and Leslie to stay out of that part of the garden."

He turned and spoke to one of his men. "Would you ask Cecil Weatherby not to use that path?"

"You mean he's been coming into this garden?" Simon asked.

"What is it?" Leslie said.

Simon repeated Jimmy's words, realizing Leslie hadn't understood the Greek. "How do you know he's been using the path?"

"Flattened grass," Jimmy said in English. "That path is used regularly. It's well-worn."

"I wonder why," Leslie said slowly. She shivered as a creepy chill crept over her skin. Had Cecil been hiding in the bushes, spying on her? "Each time we've seen him here, he's come up the driveway."

"Yeah, he has," Simon said. "But maybe we should talk to him anyway."

"Does Cecil have a rifle?" Leslie addressed the question to Jimmy. "I understand he and Jason had a falling-out years ago."

"That's true," Jimmy said. "But last summer, and in the months before Jason's sailboarding accident, they appeared in public on apparent good terms. But I'll check whether Cecil has any weapons." He pulled out a handkerchief and mopped his face. "Why don't we go inside, and I'll take down your statements?"

BY THE TIME Jimmy drove away, leaving a young officer on guard until the forensics expert could arrive, the afternoon was far gone. Leslie rubbed the bridge of her nose, feeling a headache coming on. Simon came up behind her and gently massaged her temples. She rested her head against him for a moment, giving in to her exhaustion.

"What are you going to do now?" Simon asked.

"I wish I knew," she said wearily. Nerves were jumping under her skin, and not even his touch could soothe them. "I'd better let Papadopoulos know."

She'd called him that morning, and he'd taken the loss of the box of Jason's papers with surprising equanimity. But how would he react to this, the news that Jason had been alive up until now, and obviously hiding somewhere?

"This is most irregular," Papadopoulos said after she had filled him in. "Most irregular."

"I would say that's an understatement," Leslie said. "I suppose we'll have to arrange another funeral. Would you help me with that?"

"A funeral." Papadopoulos's tone was dry. "Jason didn't have a funeral before. Since there was no body and no relatives to mourn him here, it didn't seem necessary.

I believe the village priest said prayers on the forty-day anniversary. Have the police taken the body? I take it you're still at the house?''

"Yes," Leslie said. "The police have a man in the garden, but since he died outside, they don't need the house for evidence." She closed her eyes, feeling momentarily sick. In her ordered life in Canada, she'd never thought she'd be part of a violent crime. Two crimes, if they counted Melanie.

"Well, then, I'll come down to Platania when they release the body. Oh, and please accept my condolences."

"Thank you," Leslie said faintly, not sure she deserved them. "I'll be in touch."

She had just put down the phone when there was a knock on the front door. Simon laid his hand on her arm, stopping her from rushing to answer it. "Wait a minute. Jimmy's man is watching the garden. He can't see the front door."

Another knock, a loud pounding that reverberated in Leslie's aching head. "Go see who it is, Simon. By the sounds of it, he's not going away."

Scowling, Simon opened the door. "Oh, it's you."

Harlan Gage stood outside, oily smile firmly in place. Behind him stood another man, dressed in a raw-silk suit. "I understand you had some trouble here earlier."

"You might say that," Simon said dryly. "What do you want?"

Gage looked past him at Leslie. "Please accept my condolences, Mrs. Adams. I know how you must be feeling. Jason was a friend of mine, too."

Simon made a mental note to have Jimmy check whether Gage owned a rifle.

"I was as surprised as you to find Jason alive," Gage said. He gestured toward the man with him. "This is Mr.

Wheeler, an associate of mine. He's considering purchasing a house here, and would like to look at yours."

Wheeler nodded at them without offering to shake hands.

Leslie pushed past Simon. "When did you learn he was alive?"

"Why, late yesterday evening, dear lady. Jason came to me at the inn, wearing dark glasses and a hat and scarf that concealed most of his face. He said he'd received a delivery for me that is being held at the house."

"I received nothing," Leslie said.

"Perhaps it came before you arrived. Jason gave me this."

Gage reached into the pocket of his wrinkled linen jacket and produced a folded paper that he handed to Leslie. She read the scrawled words, going down to the signature.

"Is it real?" Simon asked.

She gave him an annoyed look, chastising him for his nosiness. "It looks like Jason's signature. And the date is yesterday's. We know he was alive then, so he could have written it. I guess we have no choice."

She turned to Gage. "Why didn't you come sooner?"

"Jason gave it to me late last evening. I didn't think you'd appreciate a visit then. And when I came by this morning, you were out."

"This morning?" Simon said. "What time?"

"Early. The car wasn't here."

The car hadn't been there all night. Simon stood aside, holding the door open. "Okay, I guess you can come in and have a look. But I haven't seen anything in the basement."

THE CRATE OF CHEAP WINE had disappeared from the wine cellar. Only a cleaner spot on the dusty floor showed where it had stood. The place where the other crates had been was wiped clean, all traces of oil gone.

"Someone's been down here," Simon said angrily. "And that might be how the roses were left and the notes taken."

"But how could they get up there, when I kept the door at the top of the stairs locked?" Leslie asked. A knot tightened in her chest; someone could have been spying on her, not only from outside, but from inside as well.

"Did we have a good look at it?" Simon asked. "I think the lock can be released from the stair side, although it's a little tricky."

"Can we get on with it?" Gage had dropped all semblance of affability, and stood shifting impatiently from one foot to the other.

"Oh, by all means," Simon said sarcastically. "Where would you like to look?"

"Jason said there's an old armoire in here. The box I'm supposed to pick up is in it."

"Is it? Then I trust you have a key. It was locked the last time we looked."

Simon led the way to the back of the wine cellar, swinging the flashlight from its cord. The lights remained on, however. Leslie brought up the rear, keeping her eye on Wheeler. If he was anything like Gage, she wouldn't put it past him to swipe a bottle or two when no one was looking.

To their surprise, the armoire was not locked today. Gage swore when he saw what was inside, his tone so vicious that Leslie winced. "Well, what did you expect?" Simon asked. "The crown jewels?"

The box inside the ornate cupboard was the very crate of cheap wine that had been near the wine cellar door a few days ago. "You're welcome to take it, Mr. Gage," Simon added.

Gage swore again. "He lied to me. He lied." With that, he turned and stamped out of the room and up the stairs, his footsteps echoing eerily. Wheeler cast them a speculative look, then turned and followed him.

Simon waited until the back door slammed, then went up and locked it. Through the window he could see the two men striding off down the driveway.

"Is he gone?" Leslie asked from the top of the stairs.

"Yeah, and I don't think he'll be back," Simon said with grim satisfaction.

"His friend didn't see much of the house," Leslie said.

"You mean you believed that story?"

"No, of course not." Leslie turned around. "D'you think we should have another look around the basement? The lights seem to be pretty stable."

"Let's go, then."

They explored the cavernous space, searching out walled-off storage rooms. A couple of them were locked, but the keys on Jason's ring, which Simon had lost and Baby had brought to Leslie, opened the doors.

Inside one they found enough canned goods to let someone withstand a siege. "Somebody must have been expecting a famine," Simon said.

He unlocked the door next to it, and let out a long whistle. "I think we've found where Jason was holing up. Or at least where he kept his clothes. Look, there in the corner. Isn't that the box from the attic? Someone's been busy."

"Papadopoulos will be pleased," Leslie said flatly.

"At least that explains the noises we kept hearing. Do you suppose he brought the roses?"

Leslie gnawed on her lower lip. "I don't know. It's not the sort of thing Jason would do, unless he changed a lot. But then, there was so much I've recently found out about him, he could have, I guess. But why would he call me Allegra?"

"The key question in all of this, I'd say."

"Another question would be, did Jason go in and out through the house, or did he have some sort of secret way to get in the basement? I'd say there must be a way in here without going through the house, because someone's been coming in after I changed the locks."

"Let's look," Simon said.

"You know," he said ten minutes later, "this section is next to the wine cellar, but it seems longer." Beginning at one end, he paced it off. "Okay, let's go inside."

Inside the wine cellar, he counted the steps to the opposite end. "Yes, it is shorter. There has to be another room behind here, probably hidden by the furniture."

Together, they shifted the smaller furniture between the wine racks. Dust rose around them, a clear indication that this stuff hadn't been moved in years. Leslie sneezed as she lifted one end of the ugly Victorian settee, and let out a little shriek when a huge black spider scuttled over her arm.

The settee out of the way, she stood back, her hands on her hips. "That leaves the armoire. I think we might need a block and tackle to get it out of there."

So far they had only uncovered a sturdy wooden wall that matched the walls around the rest of the wine cellar. And there wasn't enough space for a mouse to get behind the armoire.

Leslie suddenly snapped her fingers. "A secret door."

To Simon's surprise, she snatched the flashlight from him, opened the door and clambered on top of the wine crate. A moment later, she cried out in triumph. "I knew reading all those mysteries would come in handy someday. I found something."

She jumped off the crate, swiping at the cobwebs draped stickily across her face. "I suppose those don't mean no one's been here."

Grinning, Simon shook his head. "That many cobwebs can be rebuilt overnight. What did you find?"

"Help me move that crate, and we'll see."

They set the crate on top of the settee, raising new clouds of dust. Reaching into the armoire, Leslie tugged at the back panel. It moved outward in eerie, well-oiled silence, revealing a door fitted with a shiny brass cylinder lock. "Now what would that be?"

Simon crowded in beside her, the clean scent of him tickling her nostrils and setting up little shock waves in her belly. "Could be a passage," he said. "These houses often had hidden exits, in case of war or revolution. Or it's the entrance to a bomb shelter. Lots of people built them in the fifties."

"But the lock is new."

"So are several other things in the house," Simon said. "Jason lived here openly before his sailboarding accident. He might have done some repairs. Do you have the keys? Let's try them."

None of them fit the lock—not even close. "I wonder if Jason had another set of keys, besides the ones I found," Simon said. "Maybe we should give Jimmy a call. Oh, and let's bring up that box with Jason's papers in it."

With a cursory look at the rebuilt coal chute, they went upstairs, locking the doors after them.

"Of course, with Jason dead," Simon said, "there may be no need to lock everything all the time."

"*If* he was the one coming in, and *if* no one else has a key," Leslie pointed out.

Simon's eyes softened. "You're right. It's better if you don't take any chances, Leslie."

He moved to the telephone and called the police station. When he came back, he found Leslie standing in front of the open fridge door, contemplating its meager contents. He reached around her and closed the door. "I'll take you out for dinner."

"What did Jimmy say?"

"He said whatever personal effects they find in Jason's pockets will be returned when the body is brought back here from Kérkira."

"How soon will that be?"

"A couple of days, he figures. Oh, and Cecil's not in. We'll get him tomorrow."

Leslie plucked her dusty shirt away from her chest. "Just let me take a shower before we go out."

"Want me to scrub your back for you?" he asked, grinning.

Heat kindled in her eyes, then died. "I want to see Eugenia before we go, return her watch."

Simon's grin slipped. "Last night happened, Leslie. It's too late for regrets."

"It's also too soon after Jason's death."

"You didn't love him."

"I cared for him," she stated. "Please, Simon. I need time."

He walked over and kissed her, his mouth moving gently on hers, promising passion. For an instant, she leaned into him but then she pushed away. "I'll be right back."

"Okay." He tapped his fingers on the box he'd set on the table. "I'll go put this in the car. No one will know it's there, and it'll be handy to take to Papadopoulos."

Simon carried the box outside, his thoughts on Leslie. When would she trust him, know that he wasn't like Jason? At least Jason wouldn't be back to haunt them again. The thought gave him a perverse satisfaction, followed by shame that he didn't feel deeper sorrow for a life ended too soon, by violence.

On the other hand, every indication pointed to Jason's being involved with some rather unsavory people. Like Harlan Gage, for instance.

Simon had called a friend in Athens to run a check on Gage. The man had a string of arrests, a couple of convictions for petty crime in England, but all along there were suspicions of connections to bigger, more organized illegal operations. Just no proof.

They might never find the answers, now that Jason was really dead. Papadopoulos would get the estate settled, Leslie would sell the house—there was no way he could see that she could afford to keep it—and she would leave.

Pain twisted inside him. No wonder he'd grown quickly bored with the other women he'd known. He'd been waiting for Leslie; their meeting had been fated. And he knew he'd never feel this way—confused, intrigued, challenged and happy—with any other woman.

He locked the back door, and waited for her in the front hall.

What if he told her he loved her?

At that revolutionary thought, his heart leaped. Before he could examine this idea, he heard footsteps coming down the stairs. His heart jumped again.

She was so beautiful, the elegant angles of her face softened by the dim golden light that suffused the house at sunset. Her hair floated loose on her shoulders, like that of a fairy princess in a child's storybook. He caught the fragrance of gardenias from her soap, and he wanted to carry her back upstairs and love her until they both were sated. Until she would promise to stay forever.

Stunned by the intensity of his emotions, he took refuge in levity. "You clean up nice, Leslie." He offered his arm, and she tucked her hand into his elbow. "Shall we go?"

"We need to talk to Eugenia," Leslie said. "About Allegra."

"We'll stop there before I go home to change."

SIMON WAS SILENT during most of their dinner at the taverna. Leslie, her mind filled with the conversation she'd had with Eugenia, hardly noticed. But when the waiter brought their after-dinner coffee, she shook herself back to the present. "We have to talk."

He smiled faintly, enigmatically. "Yes. There has to be a connection between all the things that have been happening. We have to find it."

"Eugenia was out when Jason was shot," Leslie said. "So she didn't see anything."

"What about Allegra?"

"She's not sure, says she may have been a long-ago guest at the house. Could have been calling herself Allie or something." She leaned forward. "Actually, she suggested we ask Cecil about her."

"Good idea." Simon nodded. "I've been wanting to talk to him myself. That path, and a few other things."

Leslie's brow furrowed. "She also mentioned Eva, Jason's first wife." She gave a short, humorless laugh. "She implied there might have been something between Eva and Cecil. Isn't that too fantastic?"

Simon didn't laugh. "Maybe it's not."

Leslie shrugged. "Anyway, I also asked about the repaired coal chute. Eugenia thinks it was done last February."

Last February, when numerous visitors had come to Jason's house at all hours of the night. Well, it could wait until morning. He'd rather tackle it in daylight.

THEY HAD barely entered the kitchen and locked the back door when the lights went out. Lightning stitched across the sky, followed by a low roll of thunder. Simon looked up. "Could be a storm. I thought I saw it rising over the sea."

He juggled the flashlight he held. "Wait here. I'll check the fuses."

"Be careful."

"Aren't I always?" He lifted her palm and placed a kiss in it, giving her a wink heavy with innuendo. Little lightning bursts went off inside her, as if the storm had invaded her body.

He was back in a moment. "The breaker's on, so it must be a generalized power failure."

Leslie stood by the window, looking out toward the street. The stillness of her body seemed unnatural, and he hurried to her side. "Leslie, what is it?"

Then he saw what held her attention. Street lamps glowed faintly through the trees. He went into the dining room. Yes, lights were still on all over the village.

"Simon, what did Cecil do before he retired?" Leslie had her arms wrapped protectively around her waist.

"Cecil?" He frowned. "I think he was an engineer. Yes, that's it, an electrical engineer."

# Chapter Twelve

Leslie gasped in horror. "You mean Cecil is the one behind all this?"

Simon frowned skeptically. "I hate to think that. He's a bit eccentric, but essentially harmless. He's lived here for years without a hint of trouble."

"Still, Eugenia doesn't like him, and she seems a pretty good judge of character." Leslie bit her lip. "His eyes are strange, as if they've forgotten how to laugh. Eyes are important in figuring out what goes on in a person's head."

"That may be." Simon's frown deepened. "But I think motivation is more important, if we're considering suspects. Harlan Gage, for instance. He wants something from the house, has been snooping around several times that we know of—and how many times that we don't?"

Simon shoved his hands into his pockets and hunched his shoulders. In the dim, intermittent light from the lightning flashes, his face looked troubled. A heavy click from the pantry had him spinning his head around. "Is there another flashlight?"

"Yes, on the pantry shelf, next to the fuse box."

He strode into the pantry. Leslie heard something fall and roll away, and a muffled curse from Simon. Then the light came on, a long beam causing her shadow to loom over her, dark and grotesque. The beam veered away from her, and she saw him concentrating it on the fuse box.

A moment later, the house lights came on.

Simon came out, dropping the flashlight on the kitchen table. "That's weird. When I looked before, I'm sure the main breaker was in the On position, yet the lights were off. It must have been shifted to the Off position."

"Is it possible to rig the lights so someone outside the house could turn them on and off whenever they wanted? Or give me a shock, like the light switch did the first evening?"

"These days, anything's possible," Simon said. "But let's not be too hasty to blame Cecil. I think Gage lied about this being his first visit. I wouldn't be surprised if Gage was in and out of this house quite often when Jason was living here."

"You mean you've seen him before?"

"No, I haven't. Gage first arrived in the village publicly a few days before you came. However—" He paused significantly. "However, Gage could have been here dozens of times without any of the villagers seeing him, if he came in a car and drove straight here. This house is pretty isolated. You don't have to drive through the village if you come from Kérkira. Even on the bus, you could be let off in any number of places rather than the square. The drivers are quite agreeable about that."

"But if Gage had a key, why knock on the door when he wanted to come into the house?"

"To throw off suspicion? To make sure no one could pin anything on him?" He raked his fingers through his hair, clearly uncomfortable.

"What is it?" Leslie asked, alarmed.

"Leslie, I don't want you to take this wrong, but I've done some checking on our Mr. Gage. He could have rigged the lights. He's had quite a bit of electronic experience, most notably with house alarms and how to bypass them."

A cold fist clenched in Leslie's stomach. "What are you, some kind of cop? Not that I would hold it against you, but you might have told me. I don't like the feeling that you've been lying to me."

He briefly squeezed his eyes shut. "Leslie, I haven't been lying to you, but it's time you knew that I've been looking for Jason ever since he supposedly died in the sailboarding accident. There was something going on here that a division of the national police wanted investigated—suspected smuggling. One of my cousins works in that department, and last winter he asked to keep an eye on Jason."

"Does Jimmy know this?" Leslie asked, keeping her voice steady. If she didn't think, she wouldn't have to face the reality that she had fallen for another man who had hidden things from her. And this time she wasn't sure she would recover. This time her heart was fully involved.

"No. I'm not doing this in an official capacity."

"Why are you doing it at all?"

"I told you, to help out my cousin. There wasn't enough evidence to appoint a special investigator—like many government agencies, they're chronically short-handed."

"So you volunteered."

"You might say that. I was here, and I also have this conviction that I don't want my town to become a haven for criminals or a place where illegal activity can go on without anyone noticing."

"Jason wasn't a criminal." Leslie's voice rose in indignation. But at the same time, her shoulders slumped. How did she know? "I suppose you're going to tell me Gage is a known felon," she said in a resigned tone.

Simon rubbed the bridge of his nose. "I'm afraid so. That's why I insisted on staying in the house with you. In case he decided to break in one night. I wouldn't have put it past him. After all, you'd been warned to leave."

"By Gage?" she asked through stiff lips. Her body functions seemed to have gone on hold, and her chest hurt when she breathed. "Was last night part of your job, too?" she blurted out over the pain flooding through her.

Simon grasped her by the shoulders. "Leslie," he said tightly, "last night had nothing to do with Jason, my cousin, or any job. Last night was just us, you and me, making love."

"Why should I believe you?"

"Because it's true. Leslie—" No, he couldn't tell her. She'd never believe him. In fact, it would seem as if he'd made it up on the spot, to keep her from kicking him out.

He hauled in a deep breath. "I don't know if Gage is the one who warned you to leave. He's a crack shot, though. He could have killed Jason, but then, I suspect Cecil also owns a rifle. He used to hunt in his younger days. And Eugenia, oddly enough, also knows how to shoot. Her late husband belonged to a rifle club and taught her."

Leslie's eyes widened in disbelief. "That nice, gentle lady? Come on, Simon, give me a break."

"It's true."

"And what about you? Maybe we can add you to our list of suspects?"

Simon shook his head. "I'm afraid the last time I fired a gun was fifteen years ago, when I did my military duty.

And I never got to be a good shot. Besides, I was in the kitchen with you when Jason was killed.''

"You could have an accomplice," she said, but she knew she was reaching, trying to hurt him as he had wounded her.

"I don't. And I haven't been telling you to leave, have I?"

"That first evening, you weren't exactly welcoming."

"So sue me. Leslie, what's this all about? I promised I wouldn't hurt you.''

She sank down on a chair, her knees suddenly trembling. "You could have been lying. You knew more about Jason than you let on, and you didn't tell me.''

He pulled out the adjacent chair and sat down, clasping his hands between his knees. "Leslie, there was nothing to tell. No proof, no evidence. I did wonder at first if you might have been involved in his business, but I quickly realized you couldn't have been.''

"Thanks," she said sardonically. "I think.''

Simon exhaled wearily. "Why don't you go to bed, Leslie? I'll be up as soon as I have a word with the officer outside.''

She flung her head up. "You don't have to stay. No one's going to break in here while he's out there.''

"What about the basement?''

"We don't even know if that's how they're getting in.''

"Even so." Getting to his feet, Simon took his chair into the pantry and braced it under the doorknob. Since it opened outward, that would hold it against all but the most determined assault. And as added insurance, he balanced a half-dozen empty jars on the chair's woven cane seat. If anyone broke in, they would make a hell of a racket.

He came back into the kitchen, dusting off his hands. Leslie regarded him without the least bit of softening in her eyes. His heart plummeted. So he'd really done it.

But he didn't see any other way he could have handled it, and sooner or later she would have discovered his secret. Tomorrow he would have to see Jimmy, give him the records of his observations of the house since Christmas. One way or another, Leslie would have found out.

"I'm not like Jason, you know," he said quietly. "Good night, Leslie."

SHE WAS LYING IN BED, the sheet primly tucked under her arms, when he came into her room. Her expression was not welcoming. "What do you want, Simon? I'm sure you figured it out—the party's over."

His jaw hardened. "It's not over, Leslie. It's only beginning."

He deliberately stripped down to his underwear, his eyes never leaving hers. He snapped off the light, walked around the bed and got in under the sheet. Leslie scooted over until she was practically hanging over the edge of her side of the bed. He didn't try to touch her.

Sleep was going to be a long time coming.

LESLIE STARED at the dark ceiling. At intervals, lightning strafed the room with a blue luminance, but it lacked fire, as if the storm had given up. Thunder rumbled in the distance, sounding like a faraway train.

"Just for the record—" Simon's voice washed over her with a touch that was at once soothing and irritating, like a washcloth when someone had sunburn "—I'm sorry."

"Are you?" she asked, determined not to give in. "A little late, isn't it?"

He shifted violently, the bed rocking beneath them. "What did you expect me to do? I didn't know if I could trust you. But I know I do now. You should be satisfied."

Satisfied? She almost laughed. Last night she'd been satisfied, loved into a delicious lassitude such as she'd never experienced. But today, harsh reality and the knowledge that it was all an illusion had slapped her in the face.

Suddenly she didn't want to argue anymore. She didn't want to deal with it. "Go to sleep," she said tiredly. "Or, better yet, go into the guest room. We'd both be more comfortable."

He said nothing after that, but she could tell from his breathing, soft but a little too fast, that he was as wide-awake as she.

What was she angry about? she asked herself, ruthlessly analytical. Wasn't it because she couldn't stomach the thought of another man hiding part of his life from her so soon after finding out the truth about Jason? Part of the truth. The rest they might never find, she reminded herself bleakly.

*I didn't know if I could trust you.* Simon's words echoed in her brain. Her anger began to subside, shame taking its place. If she was brutally honest with herself, she knew her anger hadn't been with Simon. It had been with herself, a knee-jerk reaction to what Jason had done to her.

How else could Simon have handled it? Blabbed all his secrets to her at their first meeting? Including telling her Jason might be a criminal, as well as devious and dishonest? That would have endeared him to her.

He was right. Better that she'd found out about Jason through her own investigations. It was her own fault, anyway. No one had sent for her. Her own curiosity and impulsiveness in coming to Corfu had gotten her into this.

And she would have to work her own way out of it.

"I'm sorry, too," she said in a small voice. To her surprise, tears clogged her throat and made the words quaver. "You were right and I was wrong. I overreacted."

By this time, the tears were leaking out from under her tightly closed lashes, and running down into her ears. She clamped her lips together, stifling a sob.

The next thing she knew, he had his arms around her, holding her, keeping her safe, as he'd tried to do all along. If only she'd let herself admit it. Her face pressed into the curve of his neck, she cried in earnest, unable to help herself. It was as if all the crying she'd suppressed in the past year burst forth, as if a dam had broken.

Through it all, Simon held her, sliding his hand up and down her back. His fingers tangled in her hair, and he gently smoothed it, whispering something she didn't understand.

The sobs diminished to ragged hiccups. Leslie stirred restlessly against him, tasting the salty tears on her lips and on his skin. Embarrassment heated her face. "Simon, I'm sorry. I've made you wet."

He laughed quietly. "Don't worry, I'll dry."

He laid his palm on her cheek, cool and faintly rough. With a little murmur, she lifted her hands and locked them around his neck. His muscles clenched, and she could feel his heartbeat speed up until it thudded against her chest. Strong. Solid. His quick-drawn breath, and the hardness of his body, told her he was aroused, instantly responding to the feel of her against him.

His mouth came down to cover hers, and she thought of nothing more except the softness of his lips and the wonder of loving him.

SIMON was already out of bed when Leslie woke the next morning. She quickly showered, dressed and went downstairs, where he was making pancakes.

Any awkwardness she might have felt from last night disappeared as he greeted her with a matter-of-fact, rather absentminded kiss. In fact, she felt a little piqued that he could so easily take her for granted.

But then he turned away from the stove after flipping the pancakes on the griddle, and gave her a wink and a grin full of promise that sent heat surging through her body. Nothing was resolved between them—she had no idea what he might be thinking in terms of the future—but the feeling that they were partners again was enough for now.

Only partners? said a sly little voice in her mind.

Okay, lovers, she admitted, in a physical sense. As for her emotions—well, she still shied away from examining those too closely.

When they'd finished eating, Simon stacked the dishes in the sink. "Now we're going to check out that coal chute." He picked up the flashlight he'd left on the table.

Luckily, the bin had been swept clean years ago and contained only the usual dust and spiderwebs. Simon shone the flashlight around the area, which was about three yards across. The floor consisted of wooden planks, laid in squares. "Could be old pallets," Simon muttered. "Bricks are delivered on skids like that."

He bent and pulled at one section after another. They were tight, nailed to each other, or to a frame underneath. Then, in the far corner, the pallet came up in his hand. Not just up, but attached to a hinge, too. He gave a long whistle.

Leslie leaned over his shoulder to have a look. Underneath the pallet was the outline of a trapdoor. Simon took hold of the ring embedded in the heavy oak. It lifted readily.

Beneath them gaped a deep hole. "No way down," Leslie said, disappointed.

Simon settled back on his heels. "Or up. What we need is a ladder. I saw one in the garage. Do you want to stay here while I get it?"

The basement lights flickered, as if in warning. Leslie stiffened her spine, taking the flashlight from his hand. "I'll wait here, but hurry."

He was back in ten minutes that seemed an eternity, but nothing disturbed the quiet of the cellar.

The hole beneath the coal chute turned out to be only about ten feet deep, judging from how much of the ladder protruded above it. "Not a bad climb, then," Simon remarked.

He went down first, and Leslie, nervous about spiders and mice or, heaven forbid, rats, waited until he gave her the all clear. She heard him say something else, and then she saw the passage below, lit by electric lights. "You mean there's power down there?" she called, her voice bouncing from the wooden walls.

"Come on down."

She climbed down the ladder and looked around. The passage was narrow, apparently blasted out of solid rock. Mostly solid rock. At intervals the walls were shored up with wooden planks. The light bulbs hanging from the ceiling were dusty, and gave off only a dim light. There was no sign of any ladder other than the one they'd used.

Prudently keeping the flashlight in his hand, Simon led the way along the passage. Leslie inhaled the pungent scent of earth and dampness. Occasionally the hand she ran along the wall beside her encountered a trickle of water, miniature waterfalls that had given birth to a dull lichen in the cracks in the rock.

"It's not a natural cave," Simon said. "You can see the serrations in the rocks from blasting. My guess is this was probably built before the house, possibly as an entrance to the original wine cellar."

"Do you think anyone's been using it?" Leslie asked.

Simon shrugged. "Hard to say. I guess we'll know when we reach the end."

They reached the end sooner than they expected. The tunnel took a right-angle turn and they came into a slightly wider area, blocked by a solid oak door. Its hinges were tarnished brass and its lock an old-fashioned one that would require a much larger key than any they'd seen in the house. And its design was such that it would be impossible to open without a key.

"Well, that's that," Leslie said, unable to hide her disappointment. Every route they took seemed to lead to a dead end.

The light bulb above this area had burned out long ago, leaving the corners in darkness. Simon played the flashlight beam around, and let out a whistle. "Maybe not," he said. "Take a look at that. Don't they look familiar?"

Leslie bent down and glanced at the blank labels. "They certainly look like the crates we found in the wine cellar. But how did they get down here?"

"Either they were lowered down the chute, or they were removed from the house and came in from beyond that door. And with all that's happened, I'm willing to bet that they don't contain bottles of wine." He took Leslie's arm and led her back along the passage. "If I had a hammer, I could open one, but I think it's wiser to get Jimmy in to take a look at them. My cousin gave me quite a lecture about disturbing evidence."

Reaching the bottom of the ladder, he sniffed the air, frowning. "Do you smell anything?"

Leslie's nostrils flared as she inhaled. "Only damp earth, and that chemical smell from the crates. Why?"

"For a moment, I thought I smelled gas, either sewer or propane." He shrugged. "It's probably nothing."

"GUNS!" Leslie exclaimed as Jimmy pried the lid from one of the crates.

"That's why Gage was so interested in the wine cellar," Simon said thoughtfully. "But someone moved the crates."

"Did he think we were going to let him haul them out of the house, just like that?" Leslie said incredulously.

"Maybe not at first, but after he brought a letter from Jason, wouldn't that have been authority enough?" Simon walked over and checked the brass lock on the door beyond them. "At least before I told you about his record."

Jimmy stood up from his examination of the crates. "I'm going to post a guard here around the clock. We'll see if someone comes to pick up the crates. I don't think they could have gotten them down the shaft, so they had to have come through that door. On the black market these weapons are worth a small fortune."

Leslie gnawed worriedly on her bottom lip. "Do you think Jason was involved with this?" The thought chilled her. How little she had known about the man she'd married.

Jimmy shrugged. "We may never know now, unless we catch the person who picks these up, and he talks."

He rattled off a series of instructions to the officer at his side before turning back to Leslie. "He'll be staying here,

Leslie. That should ease your mind. You'll be safe in the house.''

He grinned and winked at Simon. "Simon can go back to his work. That is, if he wants to.''

Leslie's face grew hot. "I'm sorry, Simon. I didn't even think, but I've kept you from your work for several days now."

"Don't worry about it, Leslie." Simon sounded distracted. "I'd like to get to the bottom of this. Jimmy, I take it there wasn't a key on Jason's body that would have fitted that lock."

Jimmy shook his head. He reached into his pocket and pulled out a ring with four or five keys on it. "I almost forgot. Leslie, you can take them. That's all we found in his pockets, other than a wallet, which should be released to you in a couple of days. One of these keys opens the basement door, and another the wine cellar. I tried them when I came in. So far, we haven't found what locks match the others."

"Some of the storage rooms in the basement, I'd say," Leslie suggested. "We changed the locks on the outside doors."

Jimmy nodded. "Maybe Jason got locked out after you changed them, and he was trying to get in when he was shot."

"That still doesn't give a motive for the shooting," Simon said.

"These guns may," Jimmy said grimly. "If he knew where they were, and someone else wanted them. I think it's time we had a talk with Mr. Gage."

"Isn't he at the inn?" Simon asked.

"Not this morning, he wasn't, although he hadn't officially checked out." He heaved a gusty sigh. "That doesn't mean he didn't walk, though. I would need a reasonable suspicion about lawbreaking before I could check his room." He spread his hands, grinning wryly. "So we just do what cops get good at. We wait. And if the waiting doesn't produce results, we'll get a warrant and force that door in the tunnel."

"Why a warrant?" Leslie asked. "Even if I can't give permission, I'm sure Mr. Papadopoulos will."

"Until I'm sure this is actually on your property, I don't want to tamper with anything that may become evidence," Jimmy said. "We've come quite a way along this passage. We might have crossed your property line. We could be below Cecil's garden."

"Speaking of Cecil," Simon put in, "you don't mind if we have a word with him, do you, Jimmy?"

"You didn't get hold of him yesterday?" Jimmy said.

"No, he didn't answer the phone, so I assumed he was out."

"I need to talk to him, too," Jimmy said. "But it will have to wait. I'm expecting the forensics expert, who's coming to check out the garden, at any moment. I've got the British police contacting some of the people who were here when Melanie disappeared, but so far there's no reason to suspect any of them. It's a slow business, as usual. By the way, don't mention the guns to Cecil, will you?"

"Of course not," Simon assured him. "We just want to know if he saw Jason in the last couple of months. Clear that part up."

Jimmy's eyes softened in sympathy as he looked at Leslie, making her feel rather a fraud. "That's fine. I can understand that you want to put this behind you as quickly as possible, Leslie. You must be anxious to get back to Canada."

Was she? She glanced at Simon, but he was talking with the other policeman and didn't notice. Would he care when she left? She tried to tell herself it wasn't important, but the thought of leaving created a hollow ache in her chest. "I have time to settle things," she said to Jimmy.

"IT'S NOT GOING TO WORK," Leslie said, her temper rising. Along the winding driveway, birds sang in the dense foliage. Just another gorgeous summer day, if she forced herself to forget about murder, gunrunning and the body she'd found in the attic. And now Simon was being difficult. "He's not going to give us the guided tour of the studio, no matter what you say."

"He showed me the studio once before," Simon said. "No reason why he shouldn't again."

"Except that the other day he nearly had a heart attack when he saw me in there. I tell you, Simon, he's hiding something."

"Then why didn't you tell Jimmy?"

"Tell him what? That I think Cecil's strange and that he's given to irrational rages? He'd laugh at me. You told me yourself that everyone considers Cecil harmless."

"I don't think he would lock you in the attic and set the house on fire," Simon said. "You told me he wants to paint you. I presume he means while you're still alive."

"I should hope so," Leslie said somberly. "Anyway, why don't we try it my way? You go up to the door. He'll invite you in. You keep him busy until I see if there's a way into the studio from outside. If there is, fine. I'll have a quick look and get out, and knock on the door as if I've just arrived."

Simon's black brows drew together in a scowl. "I don't like it. It's too risky."

"Risky?" she blurted out, exasperated. "How can it be? I won't get caught. And if I don't find a way in, I'll knock on the door and we'll figure out a way to get invited to look at his paintings.'' She brightened as inspiration struck her. "I know— you can offer to buy one of his pictures. What artist doesn't want to sell something?''

"Cecil may be the first," Simon said gloomily. "Okay, go ahead. I'll cover for you, but don't make any noise."

"Okay." She let out a breath of relief, although her heart was hammering against her ribs. It was surprising that he didn't hear it.

"SIMON, my boy, how nice of you to drop by." Leslie heard Cecil's effusive greeting over the barking of the little dog. Lucky Scruffy wasn't out. She wouldn't be prowling the perimeter of the house long if he was.

At least Cecil sounded in a good mood. And not like a man who had anything to hide, she realized in chagrin. But then, he probably didn't know the police had been at her house again.

Blackberry vines had crept almost up to the walls of the house at the studio side. As she had noticed before, several pairs of French doors gave access to what had once been a terrace but now was merely an area of old paving stones with weeds growing lustily in the cracks.

She pushed through the shrubbery, muttering imprecations as the overgrown blackberry vines tugged at her clothes. Despite the jeans and long-sleeved shirt she had worn, the thorns hooked painfully in her skin. To add to her discomfort, with the sun almost straight overhead, the air was still and hot. Sweat rolled down her face and between her breasts.

She tried the rusted handle of the French door, letting out a silent cry of triumph when it yielded. Good, she wouldn't have to crawl deeper into the nearly impenetrable thicket.

Wincing as the rubber soles of her sneakers squeaked on the hardwood floor, she slid into the room. The light was dim, the shutters down over the windows opposite her. Little dots of light covered the floor in a geometric pattern.

Glancing at the closed door leading to the rest of the house, she tiptoed across the room. The hot, close air smothered her, reminding her of the day she'd been locked in the attic. Her footsteps faltered. She forced herself to go on, her movements slow and laborious, as if she were walking underwater.

Renewed sweat broke out on her skin, and she wiped her palms on her denim-covered thighs.

This was crazy. If Cecil came in, or if Scruffy sensed her presence . . .

As if the thought had conjured him up, a sharp bark sliced through the thick heat. Leslie nearly jumped out of her skin. Her hand against her throat, she waited. No clawing of dog nails against the closed door. No angry Cecil bursting in.

Willing her heart to resume its normal place and pace, she methodically circled the room. She knew which picture she wanted to look at, but it wasn't where she'd seen it the other day.

After ten minutes, she was ready to give up, but then she saw a cloth covering a frame that lay under a pile of turpentine-soaked paint rags. Leslie dropped the pungent rags on the floor, covering her nose barely in time to stifle an explosive sneeze. She paused a moment, lightheaded. If suppressing a sneeze didn't kill her, Cecil surely would, if he caught her in here.

She pulled the paint-stained drape to one side, revealing a stretcher with a canvas tacked to it. Elation filled her. It was the right size.

Carefully turning it over, she looked at the painting. Yes, there she was, a blond woman in a colorful garden filled with make-believe flowers and convoluted shrubs. She shivered. The other day she hadn't had time to look closely, but now the hands extended in entreaty seemed sinister, as if the woman were pleading for deliverance from a prison.

Frowning in concentration, she examined every inch of the painting. It wasn't signed, which was odd. She'd noticed that Cecil signed all his works in the bottom left-hand corner with flourishing initials, and dated them, as well.

Clenching her teeth in frustration, she was about to put the picture down when she saw what looked like scratches in a contrasting color at the top right-hand corner, almost off the edge of the canvas, where it was nailed to the stretcher.

A date? No, it was a word. Squinting, she held it up so that light from the window fell on it.

Ice condensed in her veins, and she had to clutch the table with one hand to keep from falling down.

The word she read was *Allegra*.

# Chapter Thirteen

What was keeping Leslie? Simon sat listening to Cecil's cheerful chatter and drinking iced tea until he was ready to spit nails. How long could it take to find out she couldn't get into the studio? Or, alternately, to look at one painting and beat it out of there?

He'd seen Scruffy sniff at the bottom of the closed door a couple of times. In fact, Cecil had noticed, too, but he'd laughed and said he sometimes hid dog biscuits in the studio. He'd snapped his fingers and the dog had jumped up into his lap, where it sat now, tongue lolling, dark eyes fixed on Simon as if he were sizing him up for dinner.

A knock sounded on the door. Scruffy yapped shrilly. Simon jumped to his feet as if a spring had poked him. "What's wrong, my boy?" Cecil asked, shushing the dog. "You seem a wee bit tense."

Simon swallowed to calm himself. "I'm expecting Leslie. Mind if I get the door? That must be her now."

Cecil got to his feet, tucking Scruffy under his arm. "Let's see, shall we?" He opened the door. "Leslie, how kind of you to drop by. I was just saying to Simon, you don't visit often enough."

"Sorry I'm late." Leslie sounded breathless. Despite the light tan she'd acquired, her face was as pale as cream.

Something had disturbed her, Simon thought, which meant that she must have gotten into the studio. He took her hand; it shook in his, trembling like a frightened bird.

"Come in, Leslie," Cecil said. "It's very warm today. No use baking in the hot sun. I've got iced tea made."

Simon held her back, whispering. "What did you find?"

She shook her head as Cecil looked at them with a knowing smile. "Come along," the old man said.

In the living room, Simon and Leslie sat down on the sofa. Balancing Scruffy on one arm, Cecil poured Leslie a glass of iced tea from the pitcher on the tray. He leaned close to hand it to her.

Leslie jerked her head back as he touched her hair. "A tiny spider," Cecil said slyly. He held up the creature, crushed between his thumb and forefinger. "Did you come through the garden path?"

"No, I must have brushed against a shrub at the corner of the house. There's a policeman in my garden."

"Oh, yes, I'd forgotten. Please allow me to offer my condolences. Such a terrible thing. Even in Platania we're not safe anymore."

Leslie shifted in her seat, sipping her tea as Cecil crossed over to his chair and sat down. Simon was gratified to note that her color had returned. Her hands appeared steadier, although the ice cubes clinked when she lifted the glass. She set it down, tugging at her sleeve, but not before Simon saw livid scratches marring the smooth skin of her forearm.

"Did you see Jason during the last two months, Cecil?"

Simon almost groaned. Did she have to blurt it out like that?

Cecil stared at her, his mouth working. Then he blinked and averted his gaze. "No, of course not."

He was lying; Simon knew it as well as he knew his own name. Which brought up an interesting possibility. Someone had to have been helping Jason during the time he was hiding, providing food, doing laundry, whatever. Could that someone have been Cecil?

But first, the business they'd come for.

"I'm thinking of redecorating part of my house," Simon said casually. "You wouldn't have any paintings ready for sale, would you, Cecil?"

Cecil looked at him, his small eyes narrowed. "I might," he said slowly. "Do you want to have a look? Come along. You, too, Leslie." He walked briskly to the studio door and unlocked it, throwing it wide.

Behind his back, Simon took Leslie's arm, slipping up her sleeve to look at the scratches. "Are you all right?" he whispered.

"Fine." Her voice was brittle.

Putting Scruffy on the floor, Cecil raised the shutters that had been down, flooding the room with sunlight. Cecil walked over to his cloth-draped easel, which in her rush Leslie hadn't examined earlier. Pulling off the cloth, he turned it into the light from the window he'd just uncovered. "You see, I've started your portrait."

Leslie closed her eyes, afraid to look. She felt Simon's hand on her shoulders, and she drew strength from his touch. Looking at the painting, she almost laughed. What had she expected, some bizarre caricature? Instead, she found patches of color, a nebulous, undefined blob where her face would be.

Cecil touched her hair again. "I'd like you to pose for me. Your hair, it's giving me trouble. I can't picture it when you're not here. It changes color, depending on the light. It's so pretty, like a waterfall in moonlight.''

"Like Allegra's?" she asked, stepping away from the two men and hugging her arms around her waist.

Anger—or was it fear?—leaped into Cecil's eyes. Leslie held his gaze, although inside she quaked at her own daring. "That painting that was in here the other day, it was Allegra, wasn't it? Was that what you didn't want me to see?"

Cecil's lips were white. His Adam's apple bobbed in his throat. "What do you know about Allegra?" he asked in a strangled tone.

"I know that someone seems to think I'm her," Leslie said. "He or she is sending me flowers and gifts. The latest is an antique necklace. Was it you, Cecil?"

"Antique necklace? No, I wouldn't know anything about an antique necklace. Why would I? I've never been married. I've no use for women's jewelry."

"Perhaps not." Leslie didn't dare look at Simon, sure he must be gesturing for her to stop. "So who was Allegra? No one has heard of her, but she must have been here sometime. She's the woman in the picture, isn't she?"

Cecil drew his shoulders back and tipped up his chin. "And what if she is?" he said icily. "In fact, I painted Allegra many years ago, as a gift for her fiancé. She stayed here one summer, but she left suddenly and forgot to take it. When I wrote to her, my letter came back, unopened."

"Did she stay at the house?"

"Yes. It was used as a bed-and-breakfast inn at the time."

Simon spoke for the first time. "Why doesn't anyone remember her?"

"She kept to herself. She called herself Allie, saying Allegra was too old-fashioned, but I found it charming."

"Did Jason know Allegra?" Leslie asked.

Cecil shook his head. "No, I don't think so. His parents were dead, and he hadn't come to the house for years. I believe he was living in Athens then. It must have been about the time he married Eva."

"Were you there when Eva died?" Simon asked.

"Where?" Cecil blinked at them. His gaze darted around the room, landing on Scruffy, who was rooting in the pile of rags that Leslie had forgotten to pick up. With startling agility, he bent and scooped the dog into his arms. "Bad dog. Mustn't do that."

"In Athens, when Jason's wife had her accident," Simon persisted. "Were you there?"

Cecil eyed him suspiciously. "I was out with Jason that evening. We found her when we returned to the house. Actually, Jason found her."

Cecil's gaze swung to Leslie. "He killed her, you know."

Leslie gaped at him. "If you were with him, how could he have? Unless you helped?"

"Of course I didn't help," Cecil said scornfully. "Eva was a lovely girl. We were all fond of her. No, I figured it out later. We stopped at a taverna two blocks from the house, for a late dinner. Jason said he was going to the kiosk on the corner, to make a phone call. He went to the house, killed her and came back."

"Did you tell the police this?" Simon asked.

"No. Jason was my friend. Friends stick together. We were together for the evening. No one asked me if Jason left at any time. After all, Eva deserved it. She was seeing another man."

"Was she?" Simon said coldly. "Wouldn't divorce have been less messy? I understand Jason came close to being charged with murder."

"If they divorced, Jason wouldn't have gotten her money. No, the only way he could inherit was if she died." He sighed. "Poor Eva. If only she'd kept her mouth shut. We could have been happy."

Leslie stared at him in horror. "You can't be saying you're the man Eva was seeing?"

"Why not?" he asked, cool as fresh snow. "They were both my friends."

Leslie grabbed Simon's arm, suddenly afraid she would throw up on Cecil's polished hardwood floor. "Simon, let's go. It's too hot in here."

"Please come again," Cecil said, following them to the door, the perfect host.

"YOU DON'T BELIEVE HIM, do you?" Simon said. "It's too crazy. I had someone check the police records. There truly was no evidence to indicate anything but an accident in Eva's drowning. And her housekeeper was there until ten minutes before the men came home. Wouldn't she have noticed if Jason had been in and out earlier?"

"I'd like to believe that," Leslie said, pressing a hand against her stomach, where Cecil's strong iced tea rolled around miserably. "But I don't know what's the truth anymore."

Jimmy met them by the back door of the house. He shook his head in response to Simon's inquiring look. "Nothing. Just dead leaves and trampled grass. Not even a cigarette butt."

"What will you do now?" Leslie asked.

"Wait, I guess. That's all we can do. If someone comes after those crates, or even snoops around the house, we'll haul them in for questioning."

He headed toward his Land Rover. "There will be two men on duty here at night, one in the basement and one outside." He shrugged. "It'll leave me shorthanded, but it can't be helped. Tomorrow I have extra people coming in from Kérkira."

"Anything we can do?" Simon asked.

"Keep your eyes peeled. If you see anything at all suspicious, call me." Halfway into the car, he paused. "How did you make out with old Cecil?"

A dozen thoughts spun in Leslie's head. Before she could sort them out, Simon answered. "Nothing very useful, I'm afraid. Allegra once stayed in the house—that's where the name came from."

"Any chance that Cecil might be Leslie's secret admirer?"

"Offhand, I'd say unlikely."

Leslie cut in. "I don't know, Simon. His obsession with my hair is pretty strange. Allegra was blond, too." She frowned as another thought hit her. "And Melanie."

"Forensics report said there were traces of feathers in her throat. She was likely smothered with a pillow," Jimmy explained.

Leslie shuddered.

"It doesn't look as if she suffered," he added. "She was probably unconscious from dehydration at the time. She wouldn't have felt a thing. And then her killer put her in the trunk and boarded up the space."

"But who?" Simon said. "Even if what Cecil said about Jason killing Eva is true, I can't see him killing his own daughter."

"He didn't," Jimmy said. "I had a phone call a little while ago. Jason was on his friends' yacht the night Melanie supposedly died. When they got back to the house in the morning, she was gone and her robe was on the beach. Jason's in the clear."

"What about Eva?" Leslie asked. "Was she having an affair with Cecil?"

"Could be," Jimmy said. "It would explain his falling-out with Jason. They were friends before. After Eva's death, they no longer spoke." He stepped up into the Land Rover. "Jason was away a lot when they stayed here during the summers, and Cecil was the nearest neighbor. Who knows what she did in her spare time?"

LESLIE WOKE ABRUPTLY, pushing aside the sheet that had covered her. Her clothes were stacked neatly on a chair. Heat flooded her body as she remembered how she and Simon had practically fallen on each other after lunch, so eager to make love that they'd left clothes scattered from one end of the house to the other.

She'd never done anything like that before, making love in the bright light of afternoon. Simon had awakened a capacity for passion she'd never dreamed lived within her.

For a moment, she closed her eyes as pain clenched her heart. How could she leave when the time came?

And she would have to leave. The house might have given her a reason to stay, but the huge mortgage made it impossible to keep it. Once the debts were paid, there would be nothing left.

No, she couldn't stay.

What if Simon asked her to? taunted a little voice in her head. Tempting, but the situation would be complicated. And so far, Simon had uttered no words of commitment, no sign that he saw this as anything but a brief summer romance.

To her, it was much more. But could she trust that the happiness she'd found with Simon would last forever? Was she in love with him or only with the delicious sensuality she felt in his arms?

Shaking off her unproductive musings, she got up and went into the bathroom. A note was stuck on the mirror.

Back in an hour.

S

She smiled at the big, flourishing initial, so evocative of his self-confidence. A self-confidence she wished she had.

Locking the bathroom door, she took a quick shower. The shivery feeling she got when she remembered the black-gloved hand hadn't entirely left her. Who had it been—Jason? Or some other person who wanted her out of the house?

She was safe now, wasn't she?

In the kitchen, she paused. An elusive memory nagged at her, something that had drifted through her mind just as she awakened.

Outside in the garden, the mynah whistled. Leslie looked out the window. He had escaped again and now sat in the crook of the large tree where she'd found his treasures. Below the tree, the gray cat eyed him, then lifted his paw and began to wash his face.

She snapped her fingers. Keys. That was what she'd been dreaming of. The first keys the mynah had brought her had never been tried. Now where had she put them?

She pulled out the cutlery drawer. Silverware lay in neat compartments, nothing out of place. The junk drawer. Every house had a junk drawer. Opening the next drawer, she rummaged through an assortment of old electricity and phone bills, finally dangling the keys in triumph.

One of them had to open the small room behind the armoire.

The basement door stood open and the lights were blazing, if one could use such a term for forty-watt bulbs. She walked down the stairs and over to the coal bin. The ladder stood in place.

Leaning over the edge, she called down. "Hello, is anyone there?"

After a moment, the policeman appeared below her. "Can I get you anything to eat or drink?" Leslie asked.

"Perhaps a little later," he said in careful English.

"Well, I want to check something out in the wine cellar. If Simon comes in, tell him where I am, would you, please?"

The young man frowned worriedly. "Shouldn't you wait for Simon to go with you into the wine cellar?"

"I'll be fine," she assured him.

"Well, okay." He still looked doubtful.


LESLIE MUTTERED in annoyance. The armoire was locked. What did that mean? Had Simon found a key and locked it during one of his security checks on the house? Or had their basement prowler come back? She'd thought that problem had disappeared with Jason's death, but was it possible someone else also had access to the house?

Maybe Simon was wrong about the door leading to a bomb shelter. Maybe it led to another passage into the house.

She spun around, the hair on her arms prickling. Was that a sound behind her, on the other side of the wine rack? She stifled a rueful laugh. Probably a mouse.

She turned back to the armoire. If none of the available keys fit, she would get a screwdriver or a hammer and break the lock.

"My, my, what have we here? A nosy little pigeon."

Leslie turned so quickly she bumped her head and saw stars. Harlan Gage stood in the aisle between the racks, a rifle in his hands. The wooden butt rested against his hip, the barrel pointed almost negligently at her stomach. The way he held the gun showed easy familiarity with it.

"Is that what you used to kill Jason?" she said through frozen lips.

Surprised flashed in his eyes. "Me? You think I killed Jason?" He gestured an abrupt negative with his free hand. "Don't try to lay that on me. It's true, Jason got cold feet. He didn't want to go through with the deal. But I didn't kill him. Someone else must have, and I have my suspicions, but they'll never prove it, so there's no use throwing accusations around. The people we're dealing with have some nasty tricks they love to try on those who betray them. Jason's number came up."

"So you suspect someone you did business with killed him." Leslie filed away the information, some of her fear subsiding. At least she wasn't dealing with a killer. Not yet.

Gage glanced nervously around. "I'm not saying anything more. I'm going to deliver the guns. I don't want to end up like him."

"Did you forge the letter you showed me?"

He shrugged, the gun barrel dropping slightly. "I didn't have to. I reminded Jason how easy it is for someone to die in a hot attic, or a burning house. He wrote it quite willingly. Oddly enough, he did care about you. He nearly had a heart attack when he heard you were living in the house."

Leslie's mind began to work again, her fear replaced by a cold fatalism. If she could keep him talking, the policeman below would wonder why she hadn't come back. Or Simon would return. After all, his note had said an hour. She didn't know how long he'd been gone when she found it; he could be back at any time. "Do you know where the guns are?"

"Yes, I made that fool Cecil tell me about an hour ago. I got the keys and I made him show me the passage into the house."

"Through the armoire?" she asked, gesturing toward the massive cabinet.

"Armoire? No, Jason tricked me there. The passage is where that blasted cop is standing right now." He lifted the rifle, prodding her in the ribs. "I need those guns. My contact is picking them up on the beach tonight. You're going to help me."

"Like hell she will."

Leslie gulped in relief at the sound of Simon's voice, a relief mixed with renewed terror. He wasn't likely armed, nor would he have taken time to call the policeman up to help. Her only hope rested on the chance that the cop would become worried enough to investigate before it was too late.

She couldn't see Simon, but she guessed he was in the next aisle over. "Those crates aren't going anywhere," Simon said. "I'd suggest you drop your gun, Mr. Gage."

Gage hadn't turned, hadn't removed his hard gaze from Leslie. He poked the gun barrel into her stomach. Leslie gasped and doubled over in pain, involuntary tears spurting from her eyes. "Come any closer, Korvallis, and she gets it. I've got nothing to lose."

Leslie slowly straightened, rubbing her stomach with one hand and using the other to clear her eyes.

A bottle slipped out of the rack and smashed at Gage's feet. Leslie was gratified to see him start. Even hardened criminals had some nerves left.

"Move toward the door, Leslie. He won't shoot you in here. The walls are thick, but a shot would bring the cop running. And he needs you to trade for the guns. You're no good to him dead."

She could only pray that was true, but Simon's confident words gave her courage. Pretending she was still weak from pain, Leslie took a step away from Gage, holding on to the wine rack beside her.

Another bottle fell. Pungent brandy fumes rose around them.

"Run, Leslie. I'll take care of him."

Two bottles at once shattered on the floor, the wine spraying Leslie's legs. Gage, looking rattled, swung the gun to the left, toward Simon's voice. Leslie took a deep breath and lunged away from Gage, down the narrow passage toward the open door.

In her haste, she forgot to allow for the wet wooden floor and her rubber-soled sneakers. She stumbled, slipped and almost fell. Gage slammed into her. He yanked her arm around, bending it viciously up her back. She cried out at the agony that shot through her shoulder.

"Leslie, are you all right? I'll kill the bastard."

"Simon, get the police!" she gasped, biting back another cry as Gage's grip tightened cruelly. She twisted her body, hoping to get him off-balance. Not a chance, she realized. His strength was far superior to hers.

"Move, bitch!" Gage snarled, prodding her with the rifle barrel.

Leslie's head whirled, and she staggered as he forced her to walk ahead of him. Dizziness fogged her brain, either from pain or from the brandy fumes. She sensed rather than heard Simon keeping pace with them in the adjacent aisle. Dimly she hung on to the thought that he was nearby.

Why didn't Simon get the officer in the passage? Or was he reckless enough to try jumping Gage himself? With a sinking heart, she knew that was just what he would do.

He would have to be quick and clever to take Gage by surprise.

Gage must have anticipated such a move. They reached the last row, and Gage whipped her around the end of the rack, pushing her into Simon's path. Simon nearly beaned her with the wine bottle he held poised to strike Gage.

The two men glared at each other, their hatred palpable. Simon's fist was clenched so tightly around the bottle that she feared he would crush it.

"Drop it," Gage said. "I don't really care which one of you is my ticket out of here."

Simon obligingly dropped the bottle. It shattered on the floor, sending jagged chunks of green glass skittering under the racks. The yeasty aroma mingled with the alcohol smell of the brandy.

It was a standoff. Leslie forced herself not to struggle. *Simon, run,* she silently pleaded. Why didn't he go when he had the chance?

"I can't leave you," he said distinctly.

Startled, Leslie gaped at him, momentarily forgetting the pain in her twisted arm. Had she spoken the words aloud without noticing, or had he read her mind?

The question fled as the lights went out, plunging them into dense blackness.

Everything seemed to happen at once. Gage's hands loosened on Leslie's wrist. A heavy body struck her, and she fell to the floor, her hands skidding on the wet wood. Curses rang through the room.

Realizing she couldn't help Simon in the dark, Leslie flung herself away from the two men rolling amid the bottle shards. She groped in her pocket for the small flashlight she'd carried down. Gone. It must have fallen during her struggle with Gage.

She ran her hands over the floor, searching for it. A sharp piece of glass sliced into her palm. She clasped the other hand over the wound, shuddering as blood dripped between her fingers.

The meaty thump of a fist striking solid muscle, accompanied by a long groan, made her flinch. Simon or Gage? She couldn't tell, nor could she see.

The fight ended, just like that, the silence broken only by rapid, noisy breathing. Holding her breath, unable to move, Leslie waited.

And exhaled in relief when she heard Simon's voice. "Leslie, quick, run up to the fuse box and turn on the lights. I've got him."

Adrenaline lent her speed and she flew up the stairs. The main breaker was in the Off position. She flipped it back into place, and saw the light over the stairs blink on.

"OKAY, here's the plan," Jimmy said a while later as she sat at the kitchen table, a rough diagram of the area around the house in front of him.

Simon glared at a much-subdued Gage, who sported strip bandages on various parts of his hands and face. Simon had a couple across his cheek, attesting to the inadvisability of rolling around on broken wine bottles. Except for the lingering ache in the muscles of her arm and shoulder and a bandage across her cut palm, Leslie felt ready to take on the next battle.

"The passage comes out in Cecil's storage shed, which he swears he never uses. He says he had no idea the tunnel was even there."

"Do you believe that?" Simon asked.

Jimmy shrugged. "It hardly matters. I suggested Cecil go down to the village for dinner. I wouldn't want him to be hurt while we stake out the beach."

"Cecil knew Jason was alive long ago," Gage said sullenly.

"We'll talk to him about it," Jimmy said. "Now, Mr. Gage, since you've decided to save your skin by cooperating with us, here's your chance."

By midnight, it was all over. Gage signaled his contact, who drove a jet boat close to the shore. The crates, filled with rocks as insurance against something going wrong, were loaded onto the boat. As soon as the boat made its wide loop out to sea, toward the yacht anchored offshore, coast guard spotlights trapped it like a spider in a web.

Another coast guard vessel trained a light on the yacht's deck. Through the binoculars Simon had lent her, Leslie could see Wheeler, his mouth moving as he argued with the officers boarding his boat.

Jimmy was justifiably proud of the night's work. And pleased to have Gage and Wheeler in custody. Especially Wheeler, who was wanted in several countries for various offenses including gunrunning and drug smuggling.

LESLIE FROWNED as she got ready for bed. "Allegra. We still don't know who Allegra is. Or who sent me the gifts and flowers. Did Cecil think I was her, or did Jason know she was a former tenant of the house and use her name to try to drive me away so he could complete the business with the guns?"

"Maybe we'll never know," Simon said, lying on the bed, taking a quiet pleasure in watching Leslie brush her hair. "Unless Cecil decides to give us more details."

"If we can believe anything he says. Do you think he helped Jason?"

Simon stacked his hands behind his head. "Probably. Gage is still adamant in denying he knew Jason was alive until a couple of days ago. And I'm inclined to believe him. Otherwise, those crates would have been picked up long ago."

He glanced at her dresser. "By the way, where did you put that necklace? I'd like another look at it. In all the excitement, I'd almost forgotten about it."

Leslie laid down the brush and pulled out a drawer, rummaging under the clothes in it. "I'm sure I put it in here," she muttered. Her movements became frantic. She threw lacy underwear onto the floor, finally pulling out the drawer until Simon could see its bottom.

He sat up, all languidness vanishing. "Are you sure that's the right drawer? Maybe it was one of the others?"

She pulled each one out. "They're all empty."

Simon swung his feet to the floor. "That does it. Either our prowler's been back, or one of the cops going through the house today took it. And that's highly unlikely."

The color drained from Leslie's face. Simon drew her toward him, into the cradle of his thighs where he sat on the edge of the bed. "Don't worry about it, Leslie. Not tonight. Remember the notes and the roses? They disappeared, as well. Your admirer doesn't seem to want you to keep anything."

"All the doors are locked, aren't they?"

He nodded, his thumbs tracing a delicate pattern along her throat. "Windows, too. I stuck a chair under the basement door handle. We're safe."

Leslie gnawed at her lower lip. "I guess," she said uncertainly.

"No one can get in," Simon said forcefully. "I promise you. Now come to bed. It's time we got some sleep."

"Sleep?" she asked, mischief coming into her eyes. She pressed closer. "I think at least one part of you isn't ready for sleep."

Simon grinned. "I'm waiting patiently."

Leslie made an impudent face at him and stepped back. Unzipping her jeans, she dropped them on a chair. They made a loud clunk as they landed. Her mouth fell open. "The keys. I forgot about the keys."

"What keys?" Simon sat up.

"The first keys the mynah brought. I wanted to try them in the bomb shelter lock. That's why I was in the wine cellar."

"And Gage interrupted."

"No, the armoire was locked. I couldn't open it. Gage came just as I was going to get a screwdriver."

Simon settled back against the pillows, his bare skin gleaming in the soft lamplight. "It can wait until morning, can't it?" he said unenthusiastically.

She pulled the jeans back on, briskly zipping them. "No, it can't. It'll keep me awake all night, wondering. But you don't have to come. The entrance to the tunnel is nailed shut. I'll be okay."

He pushed himself to the edge of the bed, standing up. Her mouth went dry as she stared at the hard, lean lines of his body. Putting out a tentative hand, she touched the warm, resilient skin. She tenderly traced the minor cuts from broken glass and the almost healed laceration from when he had hurled himself through the window to rescue her from the attic.

"You could have been hurt, you know," she said huskily. "Why didn't you leave me with Gage? What good would it have done if we'd both been killed?"

"I couldn't leave you with him," Simon said simply. "I couldn't take the chance." He broke off, his eyes falling closed. Stepping forward, he pulled her against him and just held her for a long moment. Then he let out a shuddering breath and released her, his lips curving as he dropped a kiss on her forehead. "On account," he said. "You'll get the rest as soon as we wreck your blasted armoire and satisfy that cat's curiosity."

SIMON SNIFFED the damp basement air as they passed the furnace room. "I'm still thinking I smell gas."

"How can you tell? It reeks in here of brandy and wine. What about the drain in there? Is it sewer gas?"

He exhaled. "Possibly. The water table's low at this time of year. Sometimes that causes it."

"Is it dangerous?"

"Only in large quantities. The smell isn't very strong."

Although the glass had been swept up by one of Jimmy's officers, the wooden floor was still damp in places. Simon dispatched the armoire lock by twisting a screwdriver in the keyhole until it released. The inner panel opened easily, revealing the solid wooden door, with its modern lock. "Let me have those keys."

Silently, Leslie handed them over, tensely holding the flashlight while he tried one after another until she heard a sharp click. "That's the one. Leslie, give me the flashlight, please, although if it's a room, it's probably wired."

"Let me see, too." She crept forward, placing her hand on his shoulder, the skin cool beneath her fingers.

He pushed the door open. Not unexpectedly, the hinges moved silently, obviously well oiled. A musty smell, reminiscent of herbs or dried flowers, greeted them.

Simon flipped the light switch next to the door. Nothing happened. He played the flashlight beam around the room, revealing shelves loaded with canned goods and bottled water. In the far corner stood a cot, half-hidden under a rumpled pile of blankets. A dusty light bulb hung suspended from the low ceiling.

All senses alert, he circled the room, examining the food supplies, a shelf of books, a small gas hot plate with no bottle of gas attached. "This doesn't look like a bomb shelter. It looks more like a prison cell." He pulled aside a curtain on the wall directly opposite where they'd entered.

"Another entrance?" Leslie asked.

"Actually, it's a bathroom, toilet and sink." He turned the flashlight toward the wall, leaving Leslie in almost total darkness. "Wait a minute, I think it is a door." She heard a muffled thump. "Looks like it's bolted from the other side. I'm going to get the hammer and see if I can remove one of the boards."

Leslie stood beside the cot, blinking in the flashlight beam as he emerged from the alcove. The musty smell seemed stronger. Probably from the pile of old woolen blankets.

She pulled at one to straighten it. At that instant, the light passed across the bed.

Blond hair spilling over a cobwebbed pillow. A naked skull grinned toothily at her.

Leslie's breath froze in her throat. Like a doll losing its stuffing, she sank to the floor in a dead faint.

# Chapter Fourteen

Bitter nausea rose in Simon's throat as he looked down at the skeleton on the cot. For a moment, he felt light-headed and feared he would join Leslie on the floor. He took a deep breath, nearly gagging as he swallowed several times to control the churning in his stomach.

He knelt beside Leslie, groping for her wrist. Her pulse was a little fast, but strong. He shone the light on her face. Her eyelids fluttered. She was about to come out of it. "Leslie," he said softly. "Wake up. We've got to get out of here."

Her mouth moved, but no sound emerged. She opened her eyes, lids heavy and languid. She half smiled. "Simon," she said.

Then the horror returned. She struggled against his gentle hold, her eyes frantic. "Jimmy. Did you call Jimmy?"

"Not yet," he said, as calmly as he could. "I didn't want to leave you."

She closed her eyes, and a shudder racked her body. "What's been going on in this house?" she whispered.

"I don't know," Simon said grimly, feeling sick. "But we're going to find out." He pulled her up, keeping one arm around her waist. "Can you stand?"

Leslie swayed, then found her balance. "I think so."

He led her to the door. "Just wait here for a second. I want to have another look at that body."

She nodded shakily and stepped through the armoire, standing with her arms hugging her waist. Simon went back to the cot, bracing himself for what he would see.

He let the blankets that were piled untidily on the cot slide to the floor. Underneath them, a single blanket and a sheet covered the skeleton, as if someone had tucked her lovingly into bed, ghoulish as that thought was. He lifted the folded blanket. She was dressed in a prim cotton nightgown buttoned to the neck. Faded rose petals and crumbling lavender flowers lay scattered around her on the bottom sheet. That accounted for the herb smell they'd noticed; a body this long dead had little or no odor.

He pulled up the blanket again and was about to turn away when the light reflected off a shiny object. A low whistle escaped his lips. Half-hidden in the lace collar of the nightgown, he saw the necklace that Leslie had received.

He played the flashlight beam on the bookshelves above the cot. The flat jeweler's box lay there, along with a tiny vase that held an almost fresh rosebud. Red, like the roses that kept appearing upstairs.

Crouching down, he looked under the cot. Dust bunnies swirled away from the slightest movement. "I might have expected it," he muttered as he used his handkerchief to pull out an old-fashioned suitcase. It had once been expensive; the leather was still supple. A gold monogram adorned the side of it: *ALC*.

*A* for Allegra?

Still holding his handkerchief, being careful not to smudge any prints that might be on the handle, he unsnapped the locks. They opened readily, revealing an assortment of dresses, skirts, bathing suits and underwear. Thoughtfully, he closed the case and pushed it back under the bed.

"It's completely bizarre," he said to Leslie as he took her arm. "I've never seen anything like it."

"Is that Allegra, by any chance?"

"I suspect it is. The initials on the suitcase are *ALC*. What's really odd, though, is that someone must be visiting her regularly."

"Yes, but who?" Leslie said faintly.

"Good question. Is it possible it was Jason?"

Another shudder ran through her. "What about Cecil? After all, he has the painting of her."

"That's true. And there's Gage to consider. He wanted to look in the armoire." Simon frowned. "No, it can't be him. Gage was only in his thirties. I'd say, from the clothes in the suitcase and the condition of the body, she's been dead for at least twenty-five years, possibly longer."

They reached the top of the stairs. Simon felt Leslie trembling as he led her across to a chair. Under the bright kitchen light, her face looked as pale as cheese. "Are you all right?" he asked, wondering if she was going to faint again.

"If I could have a glass of water, please."

She made a visible attempt to pull herself together as she raised the ice water to her mouth. The glass clicked against her teeth as it shook. Holding it with two hands, she managed to drink most of it. She wiped her mouth with the back of her hand. "Thanks." She took a deep breath, grimacing as if she hurt inside. "It's the same as Melanie, isn't it? A hidden body, not likely to be found unless the house was searched from top to bottom."

Simon tapped his fingers on the table. "Not quite the same as Melanie. She was just left in the trunk. This is more like a shrine."

"And I'm supposed to be next," Leslie said dismally. She jumped up from the chair. "I'm getting out of here," she said, her eyes glancing wildly around the room. "I'm not staying in this house a minute longer."

Simon gently pushed her back into the chair, kneading her shoulders. His own hands were unsteady, and his stomach lurched uncomfortably. He imagined he could still smell the sweet scent of death and flowers. He dragged in several breaths, steadying his stomach.

Going over to the door, he opened it, letting a fresh breeze scent carry in the scent of growing plants.

Two bodies, now. Three, counting Jason's, but that didn't fit the pattern, and they already knew who had killed him—the greedy Mr. Wheeler.

Two bodies, both women, both blond, both hidden. The evidence pointed to a single killer—a killer who also stalked Leslie.

He glanced out of the open door. Dawn was creeping across the clear sky. A soft gray light filled the kitchen, promising another gorgeous summer day. Had it been a lovely day like this when the woman downstairs died?

Obsession. Love gone wrong.

"Do you remember a movie that's on late-night television sometimes?" he said musingly. "*The Collector*. It was about a man who locked a woman up and kept her, imagining he was in love. I wonder if this was the same thing."

Leslie looked at him, her eyes large and frightened in her white face. "He wanted to collect me, as well."

Simon's heart twisted painfully. In two strides, he reached her, and then he lifted her from the chair, and folded her into his arms. "I'm not going to let him. He'll have to go through me to get to you." He set her back on the chair. "Wait here while I call Jimmy."

He came back from the living room within minutes. "Is he coming?" Leslie asked.

"I didn't get him." Simon pushed his hand through his hair. "The phone's dead." He took her hand and pulled her up. "We'll try another phone. But first I'm taking you home."

"I'm sorry, Simon, but I can't let you do that."

The voice that spun them both around was soft, almost regretful. Cecil stood in the pantry doorway, his face unshaven, his clothes rumpled, as if he'd slept in them. Scruffy's furry face peered out at them from the crook of Cecil's elbow. Leslie, exhausted from a night without sleep and from the traumatic events that had kept her up, had a sense that this wasn't really happening. At any moment she'd wake up and find herself in her bed.

Hysterical laughter bubbled up in her throat. The old man and the dog—for the first time she noticed the similarity between them. They would have looked ludicrous, except for the gun in Cecil's other hand.

The gun he was pointing straight at them.

"I can't let you take her away, Simon. She's mine."

"I belong to myself," Leslie said, setting her jaw. "No one else."

"And I won't let you have her," Simon said, placing himself in front of her. "Not like the others. You fixed the phone, didn't you? And the lights."

Cecil's hand wavered, and momentary confusion clouded his eyes. "Phone?" He nodded, his eyes clearing. "Yes, I fixed the lights and the phone. You won't need them now. It was simple. I rigged a timer, to give the appearance that someone was at home when Jason was away on business. It worked with or without the fuse box. It also discouraged people like Mr. Gage from snooping around."

Simon's mouth dropped open. "You knew about the guns."

Cecil nodded. "Very inconvenient when you came, Leslie. Jason and I had to move them out of the wine cellar. It wasn't easy getting them into the tunnel."

"There are two tunnels, aren't there?" Simon said. "The other one is behind the room with the body, isn't it?"

"Yes, but you can't use it," Cecil said smugly. "Only I know how to control it, and I don't need a key. Jason never knew about it."

"But you were hiding Jason," Leslie said, a mélange of emotions seething beneath the determinedly neutral tone of her voice. "Did you help him fake the accident with the sailboard?"

A shadow crossed Cecil's face, and his fingers tightened on the gun. Leslie felt the tension in Simon's body as he braced himself to defend her. She gently moved the hand he held in front of her and stepped ahead, to stand at his side. Returning his questioning look with a faint smile, she laced her fingers through his. "We're in this together," she whispered.

"Well, Cecil?" she said, more loudly.

Without taking his eyes from them, he put Scruffy on the floor, where the dog sat, growling in his throat. Cecil admonished him and took a firmer grip on the gun. "Yes, we staged the accident. I picked him up with the boat the shepherd saw. We had to do it. The last gun deal was going wrong, and Jason had received serious death threats. And Gage made everything even more precarious. He was an old business rival of Jason's."

"Goes to show you shouldn't do business with criminals," Simon said.

Cecil's eyes glittered and he lifted the gun. "Please, Simon, I don't want to hurt you."

"Put the gun down and no one will be hurt."

Cecil appeared not to hear. His eyes swung to Leslie, his expression wistful. "You should have loved me, Allegra. You should have loved me. I can't let you leave."

He'd gone completely over the edge, Leslie realized, her fear turning to pity. The old man looked fragile and unhappy. And possibly insane. But that could work in their favor, if they played it right. He thought she was Allegra. If she could play on his memory, they might have a chance of getting out of this alive.

"I did love you," Leslie said, taking a gamble.

"No, you didn't, Allegra," he said sadly. "You wanted to go away. I had to keep you safe. But you just lay there, not eating, not talking. But I took care of you. For thirty years, I took care of you."

Abruptly he reached out and grabbed Leslie's hand, keeping his gun trained on Simon, who was forced to let go of her. "Your hair is so pretty," Cecil said, stroking his hand down its glossy length. "Just like hers."

Back in the present, then, Leslie realized, steeling herself to stand still under his touch. She was almost convinced that he wouldn't shoot them. Especially if she could keep him talking. Sooner or later Jimmy would try to call, and when he discovered the phone was out of order, he would come in person.

If she could keep Cecil occupied until then . . .

She heard a raucous laugh from the garden, through the open door, and hope rose in her. Baby was out again. Which meant Eugenia might be here at any moment, looking for him. All they needed was a small distraction, and they could grab Cecil's gun.

Cecil glanced at the open door. "That stupid bird of Eugenia's. He kept interfering, stealing keys. It inconvenienced us a great deal. For a while we couldn't get the guns from the wine cellar, until the bird left the keys here and we got them back. Nice of you to leave the stuff he brought on the kitchen table, Leslie." He frowned. "There was one key ring we never found, though."

"The ones we used to get into Allegra's room," Leslie said.

Cecil nodded. "Luckily, I didn't need it."

"When exactly was Allegra staying here?" Simon asked.

"One summer, thirty years ago." Cecil's face grew soft and dreamy. "The summer I was having my house built. We each rented a room in this house. She spent all her time with me. But September came, and she was going to leave. Dear Allegra, why didn't you love me as I loved you?"

"She would have come back," Leslie said in a soothing tone. "She would have."

"What about Melanie?" Simon asked, edging closer to Leslie again.

Cecil roughly cleared his throat. "Melanie," he said in a contemptuous voice. "She kept coming to Platania. Her hair was so pretty, shining like gold in the sun. I sent her flowers and gifts. She thought they were from Simon. After Simon left that night, I told her she didn't need him. I told her I would love her. She laughed and called me an old man." His gaze shifted from Leslie to Simon. "You were wise, Simon. She was a witch. She had to be eliminated. She couldn't love anyone except herself."

Leslie pressed her hand against her stomach, her throat closing. "You locked her up in the attic."

"I didn't hurt her. I gave her something to make her sleep. But I knew I couldn't keep her, with Jason so often in the house. I used a pillow. I killed her softly."

"As you would have killed me," Leslie said. "It was you, wasn't it? And you tried to drown me in the bath, and you shot at me the first night."

"I only wanted to scare you, to get you away from the house." Cecil shook his head. "I wouldn't kill you. You said you love me." He turned to Simon. "I didn't mean to make trouble for you, Simon. I asked Jason not to bother you, but he wouldn't listen. He said to let you take the blame when he thought Melanie drowned."

"Thanks," Simon said sardonically. "But why did he want to make trouble for me?"

"He said it was your fault, Simon, when the hotel company pulled out of the agreement to buy the house. And he put Melanie up to accusing you of harassing her. He wanted to ruin your reputation, and, if possible, your business, to get revenge."

"How?" Simon frowned. That would have been after his father's death. He'd gone back to London for a couple of months. The real estate development firm in which he'd been a partner had called him back to complete several projects he'd worked on earlier. Now that he thought of it, one of their big projects at the time had been in Greece. "Wait a minute—what was the name of that hotel company?"

"Sunshine Resorts," Cecil said.

Simon nodded. "Now I get it. The new location on the mainland—the company I worked for arranged the sale and the financing. I wasn't even involved in that deal, but Jason probably didn't know that, and held me responsible for his losses. And I suppose all those trumped-up accusations about Melanie were also part of it.'' A bitter smile curved his lips. "I guess justice has been served after all, although it's too late for my father. And too bad Jason had to die for it in the end. I would have been happy just to see him in jail for fraud or gun smuggling."

"Why did you come, Leslie?" Cecil said plaintively. "Why did you spoil it? If we had completed the deal with the guns, Jason could have gotten out of the trouble he was in. Instead, Wheeler killed him." He dragged in a raspy breath. "When I saw you, I thought you were Allegra, but Jason told me you were his wife."

A tear crept down Cecil's face, to disperse in the bristly stubble on his chin. He let go his hold on Leslie's arm, and she was able to put a little distance between them.

"Every time I saw you," he said, "I thought you'd come back to haunt me. I couldn't stand it. And Jason was going crazy, jumping at every shadow. It was all falling apart."

"You tried to scare me away," Leslie said. "And when that didn't work, you fixed my brakes."

"Your brakes?" Cecil said indignantly. "I never touched your brakes."

"Then who did, Cecil?" Simon asked. "You left flowers, and a note that was practically an admission of guilt."

Cecil's narrow shoulders slumped, and he swayed on his feet. Simon took a deep breath, and Leslie knew he was tensing himself for attack. She turned her head and caught his eye. Wait, she silently told him.

"Gage. Gage did it," Cecil said. "Gage taunted us about it, said our stupid amateur schemes to scare Leslie away weren't working, so he would try a sure thing."

"Well, it didn't work," Simon said bluntly. "Your funeral flowers were premature."

"They were for Allegra," Cecil said. A dry sob shook his bony frame. "It was all for Allegra. I couldn't let you find her resting place."

"You were afraid I'd find the bodies, weren't you?" Leslie said.

"Yes!" Cecil wailed. "I couldn't let them take her away from me!"

Outside, the mynah shrieked again, making Leslie start. He was closer, she thought. Any minute now, he would probably fly in the door.

Unnoticed by Cecil, Simon had again moved right next to her. "Get ready to duck," he murmured, his breath fanning her ear. "Whatever happens, remember this—I love you."

"What?" Leslie gasped, her heart thudding.

A flurry of feathers whipped past their heads. Cecil screamed and jerked his head violently to one side, his arms coming up to protect his face. The gun clattered to the floor. He stared at his empty hands for an instant, then dropped to his knees, frantically scrabbling for it.

Scruffy barked hysterically as the gray cat leaped into the room, hissing as if he were demented. He swiped one paw across Scruffy's nose, sending the little dog yelping into the corner. He skidded to a stop in front of Cecil. Cecil sneezed explosively. The cat, in a complete panic, sank needle-sharp teeth into Cecil's ankle.

Leslie scooped up the gun, realized it was useless in her hands, and tossed it to Simon, who neatly caught it.

"Baby!" Eugenia's peremptory tone echoed across the room. "Come here at once."

She stopped just inside the kitchen door, her mouth dropping comically open as she took in the sight of them. The mynah perched on top of a kitchen cabinet and let out a series of earsplitting shrieks. The gray cat, his front paws clawing the bottom of the cabinet, hissed at the bird. And in the corner, Scruffy yapped like a dog gone crazy.

A door slammed, cutting through the din. Leslie spun around. Cecil was gone, down the basement stairs.

"Quick—the breaker!" Simon snapped.

She jerked open the pantry door and threw up the switch. The basement stairs at her feet vanished into darkness. She listened. Not a sound came from the basement.

In the kitchen, too, silence had mercifully been restored. Eugenia held Baby between her cupped palms. She murmured to him and the bird chortled softly, rubbing his yellow beak along her cheek.

Simon, the gun dangling from his hand, cradled the cat in the other arm. The creature's fur once more lay in velour-soft order, and he purred blissfully, all thoughts of eating Baby temporarily subdued.

"He can't get away," Simon said. "Without power, he won't be able to operate that door."

"Unless he left it open," Leslie said.

Simon gave the gun a distasteful glance and laid it on the table. "Eugenia, will you give Jimmy a call? Our phone's dead. Tell him to send someone to Cecil's house, as well, in case he goes back there. But my feeling is he won't leave Allegra."

Eugenia looked from one to the other, her expression baffled. "Would you mind telling me what this is all about?"

Simon gave a strangled laugh. "Later, Eugenia. Right now, we need Jimmy."

"Okay." She shrugged her broad shoulders and hurried away, long skirt swaying around her ample hips.

"No wonder Cecil could come and go as he pleased in the house and we never saw him," Leslie said. "It didn't make any difference when I changed the locks. He had his own door.''

''Probably rigged with a device like a remote garage door opener, but it won't work without electricity,'' Simon said. ''You know, I think I'll buy Baby a bag of bananas as a reward. If he hadn't kept stealing keys, we might never have noticed anything going on. Or thrown Cecil and his dubious associates into a tailspin.''

Leslie paced across the floor. Her knees shook with exhaustion, and her hair felt as if Baby had nested in it. And Simon—what had he said?

She didn't want to think about it, and yet the three words kept ringing in her head. *I love you.*

What was she going to do? One thing she knew for sure, he had a lot more courage than she did, where emotions were concerned.

''Relax, Leslie,'' Simon said quietly. ''You're just wearing yourself out. What's Cecil going to do? We've got his gun.''

''What if he has another?''

Simon's mouth tightened into a grim line. ''If it'll make you feel better, I'll close the basement door and brace a chair against it.''

A dull thud from the basement made them both jump. The cat growled and launched himself out of Simon's arms. He streaked through the door and disappeared into the bushes.

''What was that?'' Leslie gasped as her heart leaped into her throat.

''I'm going to find out.'' Simon picked up the gun and headed for the basement door.

''Wait, Simon,'' Leslie said, closing her fist around his arm. ''That might be what he wants.''

"I'll just go to the top of the stairs and see if he's coming up."

Leslie tiptoed behind him. Together they peered down into the darkness. They heard nothing, although a flickering light was dimly visible.

"Could be a candle," Simon said. "I saw some down there. Or maybe just the sunlight coming into the basement windows."

Leslie turned, and came up against his hard chest. Simon clasped her shoulders to steady her, and fire ran down her body at his touch. Awareness shimmered between them like heat lightning.

Leslie licked her dry lips, her mind in turmoil. "Simon—"

"Yes, Leslie?" His chocolate-colored eyes gazed at her, soft and confident and faintly amused.

"Simon, what you said—"

"Simon, are you here?" The voice cut between them with the force of an icy shower.

Reprieved. She wasn't sure whether it was chagrin or relief that made her light-headed. The moment she sensed might be the most critical of her life was postponed. Maybe if she had more time, she could sort out her feelings.

"Jimmy." Leslie turned and greeted him with an enthusiasm that must have startled him.

"Eugenia told me some garbled story on the phone, about Cecil with a gun. Is that the gun?"

"Yes." Simon reversed the gun and handed it to Jimmy.

"I've got a man watching Cecil's house." Jimmy efficiently inspected the gun, then let out a short laugh. "This isn't even loaded."

"You mean we went through all that for nothing?" Leslie burst out.

A heavy boom shook the floor under their feet. They all froze where they stood. "Not an earthquake," Jimmy said. "The light bulb isn't moving."

Another bang, sharper and higher, made Leslie clap her hands over her ears. Jimmy and Simon ran for the basement stairs. They paused at the top. Leslie followed, stopping abruptly when she smelled smoke, a pungent, acrid smoke that stung her nostrils and made tears spring into her eyes.

"Gas. There *is* a gas leak." Simon took a deep breath. "Cecil!" he called down the stairs, holding his handkerchief over his nose as a black, oily cloud billowed up from the basement.

Leslie could hear an ominous crackling. A chill enveloped her, despite the heat she felt under her feet. The place was on fire. The explosions were the wine and brandy bottles bursting, which would add more fuel to the flames.

"Cecil," Simon yelled again. "Can you hear me?"

He started down the stairs, but Jimmy grabbed his arm. "You can't go down there."

"The electricity!" Leslie cried, before her voice was choked off by a cough. "If it's on, he can get out through Allegra's room!"

Reaching for the breaker at her side, she turned it on. Lights flared briefly, then snuffed out with little pops as the bulbs exploded in the heat.

"Cecil." Simon's voice cracked.

Jimmy took his arm. "Simon, it's no use. He can't hear you."

Mad laughter echoed up the stairs, scraping across Leslie's already lacerated nerves. Her blood chilled as she heard the words, probably the last words Cecil would ever

utter. "They can't take you away, Allegra. We'll be together forever. Forever."

The shrill voice died away as another explosion rocked
the house on its foundations. Leslie staggered and would
have fallen, but Simon grabbed her just in time.

"We can't help him," Jimmy said. "And we'd better
get out of here. That sounded like a gas explosion, and
there'll be more. This place is done for."

HOURS LATER, Leslie and Simon stood gazing at the ruined house. Blackened timbers formed a roof open to the
red-streaked sunset sky, the heavy tiles having collapsed
into the hole that was all that remained of the basement.
A couple of stone chimneys stood like obelisks, the only
other survivors of the fire.

"Well," Jimmy said, coming up to join them as all but
one of the fire trucks rumbled away. "At least the insurance will cover the debts."

Leslie glanced at him in surprise. "How did you
know?"

"Papadopoulos has been cooperating with us. Jason
was suspected of a number of serious crimes. When he
supposedly died in the sailboard accident, we asked the
lawyer to inform us of anything he found in his papers
that might lead us to his associates, much bigger fish in an
organization that has branches everywhere. At least
Gage's and Wheeler's arrests have helped us, and will
probably lead to more arrests. Good thing you managed
to keep that box of papers from the attic safe. There might
be something in there."

"I hope so," said Simon fervently. "And poor Cecil
was mixed up in it, too."

"Only marginally, from what Gage says. And only in
this deal because he helped Jason. He was more con-

cerned about a new owner desecrating the shrine of his beloved Allegra.''

"At least he's at peace now," Simon said soberly. "And who knows? Perhaps he and Allegra are together at last.''

"What will become of his work and his house?" Leslie asked.

Jimmy shrugged. "I don't know. There may be some distant relatives. I guess we'll have to get Papadopoulos to work on that next.''

"Come, Leslie," Simon said. "Let's go home.''

As he drove the little Renault through the village, Simon glanced at Leslie. What was she thinking? Was she planning her return to Canada? He wouldn't blame her if she did. Her introduction to Corfu hadn't been exactly a pleasant vacation.

His heart ached when he thought of her leaving. But what right did he have to expect her to stay? She hadn't reacted to his rash declaration, except for that weighted moment in the pantry, when he had seen the question on her face but had been unable to read the emotion behind it.

"I'm sorry, Leslie," he said.

Her elbow resting on the open car-window ledge, she lifted her head from its resting place against her hand. "Sorry? Sorry for what?" The words were slurred; she looked unutterably weary.

"Never mind," he said. "Later.''

Soft gray dusk filled his room. He stripped her down to her underwear and tucked her into his bed. She sighed, and fell asleep.

He slowly removed his own clothes and lay down beside her, breathing in the vanilla fragrance of her skin. Her hair had a smoky tang to it, and again he felt a chill. He could have lost her to Cecil's madness.

Laying his arm across her body, he tucked her closer, tempering the fierceness with which he wanted to hold her.

Later, he told himself. He would have time later.

Leslie woke when a lemon-colored sunbeam slid across her face. Morning? It couldn't be. She pushed her hair out of her face, grimacing at the feel of it. A warm, naked leg lay over hers.

Smiling, she turned, slowly, so as not to awaken him. His eyes were closed, those incredibly long lashes softening the angles of his cheeks. His face was dark with two days' beard growth. He looked younger in sleep, his lips parted as he snored gently.

"Simon, I love you," she whispered, her heart clenching with a fierce tenderness. It was as if the long, deep sleep had wiped away all her doubts, all her fears. "I love you."

"Do you?" Simon asked, in a voice husky with sleep. He opened his eyes, and stretched as lazily as a cat.

Leslie's smile slipped, and momentary panic fluttered in her chest. She pulled back, inching toward the edge of the bed.

His arm snaked out to bring her against him. She landed on his chest with a little oof. "Simon, you were sleeping."

He smiled at her, his eyes as warm as melted chocolate. "I wake up when a woman says she loves me. It's never happened before."

She playfully cuffed his shoulder, her embarrassment fleeing. "I bet."

"No, it hasn't, except for my mother, and that isn't the same." He nuzzled her hair, then traced his lips down her cheek and over her mouth, covering it in a deep, hot kiss. "So now that you love me and I love you, what are we going to do about it?"

Leslie tucked her face into the hollow of his shoulder. "I'm not good at relationships, you know. I married Jason for all the wrong reasons."

"Then you can marry me for the right reasons. Is it so hard to trust yourself?"

"Yes," she blurted out.

He ran his finger down her straight nose, then gently outlined her lips. "Don't sweat it, Leslie. Isn't that what you say in Canada?"

She laughed; she couldn't help it. "Yes, that's what we say."

"Then I'll teach you to trust yourself. We've got the rest of our lives to work on it."

She sighed. "There's still so much that's unsettled. My job, for instance. How are we going to work that? I suppose, since you can't move your orchards, I'll have to live here."

"Kérkira has branches of several major banks," Simon said. "You should be able to get a transfer, or a whole new job."

"I suppose." She smiled suddenly. Yes, hadn't she come here expecting to find adventure? Not that she wanted her life to be as hectic as the past week had been.

Her smile slipped. "There's more," she said soberly. "Funerals for Melanie and Jason and Cecil. The will. The insurance. I just know I'm going to be a lot of trouble for you."

"We'll work it out," Simon said with that irrepressible confidence that had attracted her from the beginning. "Together."

He moved so that she lay beneath him, savoring the feel of his hot skin against her, the difference between them, male and female. He began to kiss her, and all thoughts of trouble drifted away.

The adventure was just beginning.

## HARLEQUIN®

# I N T R I G U E®

Into a world where danger lurks around
every corner, and there's a fine line between trust
and betrayal, comes a tall, dark and handsome man.

Intuition draws you to him...but instinct keeps you
away. Is he really one of those...

Don't miss even one of the twelve sexy but secretive
men, coming to you one per month in 1995.

In November, look for:
#345 LETHAL LOVER
by Laura Gordon

Take a walk on the wild side...with our
"DANGEROUS MEN"!

DM-10

# OFFICIAL RULES
## PRIZE SURPRISE SWEEPSTAKES 3448
### NO PURCHASE OR OBLIGATION NECESSARY

Three Harlequin Reader Service 1995 shipments will contain respectively, coupons for entry into three different prize drawings, one for a Panasonic 31" wide-screen TV, another for a 5-piece Wedgwood china service for eight and the third for a Sharp ViewCam camcorder. To enter any drawing using an Entry Coupon, simply complete and mail according to directions.

There is no obligation to continue using the Reader Service to enter and be eligible for any prize drawing. You may also enter any drawing by hand printing the words "Prize Surprise," your name and address on a 3"x5" card and the name of the prize you wish that entry to be considered for (i.e., Panasonic wide-screen TV, Wedgwood china or Sharp ViewCam). Send your 3"x5" entries via first-class mail (limit: one per envelope) to: Prize Surprise Sweepstakes 3448, c/o the prize you wish that entry to be considered for, P.O. Box 1315, Buffalo, NY 14269-1315, USA or P.O. Box 610, Fort Erie, Ontario L2A 5X3, Canada.

To be eligible for the Panasonic wide-screen TV, entries must be received by 6/30/95; for the Wedgwood china, 8/30/95; and for the Sharp ViewCam, 10/30/95.

Winners will be determined in random drawings conducted under the supervision of D.L. Blair, Inc., an independent judging organization whose decisions are final, from among all eligible entries received for that drawing. Approximate prize values are as follows: Panasonic wide-screen TV ($1,800); Wedgwood china ($840) and Sharp ViewCam ($2,000). Sweepstakes open to residents of the U.S. (except Puerto Rico) and Canada, 18 years of age or older. Employees and immediate family members of Harlequin Enterprises, Ltd., D.L. Blair, Inc., their affiliates, subsidiaries and all other agencies, entities and persons connected with the use, marketing or conduct of this sweepstakes are not eligible. Odds of winning a prize are dependent upon the number of eligible entries received for that drawing. Prize drawing and winner notification for each drawing will occur no later than 15 days after deadline for entry eligibility for that drawing. Limit: one prize to an individual, family or organization. All applicable laws and regulations apply. Sweepstakes offer void wherever prohibited by law. Any litigation within the province of Quebec respecting the conduct and awarding of the prizes in this sweepstakes must be submitted to the Regies des loteries et Courses du Quebec. In order to win a prize, residents of Canada will be required to correctly answer a time-limited arithmetical skill-testing question. Value of prizes are in U.S. currency.

Winners will be obligated to sign and return an Affidavit of Eligibility within 30 days of notification. In the event of noncompliance within this time period, prize may not be awarded. If any prize or prize notification is returned as undeliverable, that prize will not be awarded. By acceptance of a prize, winner consents to use of his/her name, photograph or other likeness for purposes of advertising, trade and promotion on behalf of Harlequin Enterprises, Ltd., without further compensation, unless prohibited by law.

For the names of prizewinners (available after 12/31/95), send a self-addressed, stamped envelope to: Prize Surprise Sweepstakes 3448 Winners, P.O. Box 4200, Blair, NE 68009.

RPZ KAL